WHEN the FAKE SNOW FALLS

HEATHER GARVIN

Copyright © 2024 by Heather Garvin

All rights reserved.

No part of this book may be reproduced in any form or by any electronic or mechanical means, including information storage and retrieval systems, without written permission from the author, except for the use of brief quotations in a book review.

Ebook ASIN: B0CW1GCWXG

Paperback ISBN: 979-8-9885299-3-4

Cover Illustration: Laia Tinaut

Editor: Kristina Haahr

This is a work of fiction. Names, characters, businesses, events, and incidents are the product of the author's imagination.

author's note

When the Fake Snow Falls contains on page intimate scenes and is intended for mature audiences only.

To all the girls, both naughty and nice, here's the perfect book boyfriend to bring you some spice

one

HOW ANYONE SURVIVES the day without a 2:00 p.m. pick me up, I have no idea. I tuck a strand of hair behind my ear as I stare at the menu boards above. The wood paneled walls and black iron décor hardly make the coffee shop feel cozy or in the holiday spirit, but they've tried with the hanging ornaments, strung garland, and a Christmas tree in the back corner. Southern Roast is the best place to get coffee in town—once you realize it is, in fact, a coffee shop and not a restaurant that serves half pound racks of ribs with sides of cornbread.

My lightweight cardigan slips, leaving my shoulder bare and the strap of my tank exposed. It's still 85 degrees, but I refuse to let Florida win. If it's December, I should be able to wear a sweater, damn it. It might be made of the thinnest possible fabric, and I can only wear it while I'm somewhere with air conditioning, but I'm wearing it. I pull up the soft material and wrap it tighter around myself.

"One coffee, black." The voice of the man in front of me pulls me from my thoughts. His voice is deep and smooth, with just enough gravel to pique my interest. I can only see the back of him. Dark hair and a suit are all I get, but you can tell a lot about a person by their coffee order. Black coffee either means he likes the control of being able to add cream and sugar himself, or he's the no-nonsense type who needs straight fuel.

His chestnut brown hair is styled in a way that might fool some women into thinking he wakes up that way, but I know better. I can smell the Johnny B. styling gel on him. His business attire is pristine. Not a wrinkle on his navy pants or a scuff on his brown leather shoes. He cares about appearances—either that, or he has a wife who cares about it.

I casually crane my neck to the left and scan his hand resting on the counter.

No ring.

He looks over his shoulder at me, and only then do I realize I never stopped craning. Staggering a step, a whoosh of air leaves my lungs. "Sorry. I was just—I was . . ." Heat flares in my cheeks, and I point past him. "Danishes."

He smiles, and it's a disarming smile my mother would *love*. Seriously, doesn't this man have any obvious flaws? At this point I would have been relieved to see a chipped tooth.

He steps aside. "Don't let me be the one to deprive you of baked goods."

His voice has a commanding undertone that makes me wonder what else he doesn't want to deprive me of. "You're fine," I say with a raise of my hand—half trying to wave, half hiding my face behind it.

He lets out a low laugh before stepping aside anyway as he pays. I guess to give me a better view of the . . . Danish I was staring at.

The barista hands him his cup, and he scribbles on his receipt and leaves it behind before walking off to add cream and sugar to his coffee. I guess it's the control for him.

"Peppermint Mocha, please."

The girl behind the counter nods, and I stare down at the sliver of white paper.

Number?

The temperature of the blood in my body rises to a simmer. I snatch the paper and stare down at it. In my twenty-seven years of life, I have never seen such a perfect specimen of man, and now he wants my number?

My eyes dart to where he mixes his coffee with his back turned like he doesn't have a care in the world. Before he can turn around, I quickly jot down my number and slide the receipt back where he left it. I'm constantly handing my number out to potential clients. What's one more person?

As he walks toward me again, it takes all my self-restraint not to stare at him.

In one fluid movement, he slides the receipt off the counter and raises his cup. "Ladies," he says with a nod before ducking out of the shop. I watch through the glass storefront as he tucks the small white paper into his pocket and takes a sip of his coffee.

My lips twist as I try to fight my smile, and I don't tear my eyes from him until he's out of sight.

"One peppermint mocha for Candace," the barista says with a grin as she hands me the cup.

"Thanks." I return the smile and head out of the shop feeling lighter. My eyes can't help but wander in the direction he went, but he's long gone by now. Did he really ask for my number? Or was it a thirty second fever dream?

My phone chimes, and my breathing halts. That was fast. Maybe he's one of those people who are highly efficient. It's only when I see it's a group text with my parents that my lungs open again.

MOM:

Candy Cane! I've got something special we can do this Christmas.

My parents never fail to go big on Christmas. Their house

in north Florida is always decorated top to bottom. Even their yard out front ends up looking like Santa's workshop.

A message from my dad shortly follows. It's a link for some type of wellness cruise. I step aside on the sidewalk to get a better look. The thumbnail for the site shows everyone wearing all white and the tagline reads: *Nothing Frees Your Spirit like the Open Sea.*

> MOM:
> So much for easing her in.
>
> DAD:
> She won't come. Might as well just send it to her.
>
> Although we'd love to have you!
>
> MOM:
> What do you think???

I think they've both lost their minds. It's been a slow descent, but every year they get a little more *mind, body, and soul,* and I get a little more *I have bills to pay and don't have time for this shit.*

> CANDACE:
> You guys do know this isn't your average cruise, right?

They know. It's probably why they're so excited, but I have to ask. My parents are the type to unknowingly join a cult, and I do feel some small semblance of responsibility to protect them from themselves.

> MOM:
> It's better! You follow a detox program catered to you by their experts.

DAD:

It's supposed to be very healing.

I'm about to ask if they're sitting on the couch together, but I already know that's the case. They're both retired. Both enjoying their life as empty nesters with one overly independent daughter they can't seem to match up or marry off no matter how hard they try.

As if on cue, another message comes in from my mother.

MOM:

You might even meet someone!

I roll my eyes and start walking again as I type my response. As much as I don't want to go on this cruise, the thought of not seeing them for the holidays already has my Christmas spirit waning. Part of me is tempted to ask if they can go on the cruise any other week of the year, but if I know my parents, they wouldn't have chosen these dates lightly. It's probably a limited sale they don't want to pass up, and as much as I want to spend time with them on land, I'd hate for them to miss out.

CANDACE:

I think it all looks great, but I already have clients booked that week. You two have fun! We'll celebrate together in the New Year.

There's a longer pause this time, and I know they're discussing how to respond. They're probably talking about how guilty they'll feel, but also how I have my own life here in Sanford. It will be fine because they know I won't be alone. That will make them feel better, and they'll still go on the cruise like they should.

> **MOM:**
> Are you sure?

> **CANDACE:**
> Very sure.

> **DAD:**
> You won't be sad on Christmas?

I let out a huff of laughter before typing my response.

> **CANDACE:**
> Not even a little.

I glance up to take inventory of my surroundings. Most people working in the area have already taken their lunch break, but there are still a few stragglers crossing the cobblestone street as I head to the salon.

Beauty Mark Salon & Styling Bar sits nestled between a chic boutique on one side and one of those wine and craft places on the other. I love seeing people make an entire afternoon out of this tiny strip of sidewalk.

My hand slips from the cool metal handle when another text comes in.

> **MOM:**
> It's booked! Wish you were coming with us Candy Cane!

> **CANDACE:**
> Me too. Love you both.

Four messages come in back-to-back showing gifs of bears drawing hearts and emojis blowing kisses.

The bell dings over my head as I pull open the door, and our assistant greets me before looking up. "Welcome to Beauty

Mark!" Amanda calls out over the chatter of other stylists and their clients.

"It's just me." I smile at her and head to my station. Just like the coffee shop, the salon manager has started spreading the holiday cheer. Mistletoe hangs sporadically from the ceiling, holly and garland drape the front desk and frame the doorways, and there's even a Charlie Brown style Christmas tree tucked in the corner.

Amanda beams when she sees that it's me. "Oh! Hey, Candace. Your three o'clock called and said she might get here a few minutes before her appointment. She was wondering if you could take her early."

I take a sip of my drink and nod. "Of course." I should have known better than to duck out because I know exactly which client she's referring to. Giving Amanda a look she knows all too well, I say, "I swear Nicolette just likes to keep people on their toes."

She lets out a snort. "Probably."

My eyes fall to the sad excuse for a lunch I packed this morning: half a leftover salad and a yogurt. Neither of which I can eat quickly and gracefully if my client is about to walk through the door. My eyes wander to the coffee I just set down at my station. *You, my friend, have been upgraded to lunch.*

Neatly hanging my cardigan on the wall hook, I reach for my black apron and slip it over my head. I tie the strings behind my back as I eye myself in the mirror. My shoulder length dark hair is styled and waved. I added a little purple on the ends last week, and I'm happy with how well the color has held. It's rare that I have down time at the salon, but when I do, it usually means a new color gets put in my hair. I've had blonde, blue, pink, red, and now purple—most of which I've let Amanda do so she can practice. She's a few years younger than me, but we hit it off from day one.

Securing the bow behind my back, I give myself one last

look before I plaster on my customer service smile and act like I didn't just skip lunch. Without my cardigan, the inked lines of roses and lilies trailing from my right shoulder are on full display. I have a few smaller tattoos scattered about, but the half sleeve is the most noticeable. Everything else is from when I was a teenager and still wanted the option of hiding them if I needed to.

My phone buzzes in my back pocket, and I wonder what great detail my parents forgot to include about their trip. But the notification isn't from my parents. It's from an unknown number.

> UNKNOWN NUMBER:
> I know you're probably working, but I had to say thank you. Getting your number made this shitty Tuesday feel like a Friday.

My heart stutters. With all the talk of my parents' holiday plans, I had almost forgotten about the guy at the coffee shop. The reminder has me buzzing with energy, and my Tuesday suddenly feels a lot more like a Friday, too.

two

IT'S A SIMPLE TEXT, but it's charming. He's flirting. It's subtle, but just the thought of the man I saw this morning flirting with me has my nerves jacked.

There was something different about him, but I can't put my finger on it. I have no idea what made me gawk to the point of toppling over. I went out with a pretty hot guy last week, so it's not like I've never seen a man dripping with sex appeal.

> UNKNOWN NUMBER:
>
> And by Friday, I mean Christmas. You somehow made it feel like Christmas.

I almost laugh. Two texts in a row? He has to be bold or desperate. Either way, I find it refreshing. Putting yourself out there always feels like a standoff. You can't show you care too much because you might scare them away, but if you don't seem like you care at all, they think you're not interested. The whole back and forth is exhausting.

> CANDACE:
> If it means that much to you, next time I'll bring the fake snow.

My phone pings before I even have a chance to set it down.

> UNKNOWN NUMBER:
> Not fake snow.

His response has me lifting a brow, but I can't argue with him. Florida is always trying to be something it's not by using things like fake snow. There's nothing like looking into a storefront window and seeing the edges of the glass sprayed with white while the sun bakes into your back.

> UNKNOWN NUMBER:
> I have a thing about useless products, and nothing is more useless than fake snow.

Two sets of back-to-back texts? Interesting, but he doesn't seem desperate. After laying eyes on him, I find it hard to believe he'd struggle for any woman's attention.

> CANDACE:
> Can I interest you in some lights for your palm tree instead?

The bell over the salon door chimes, and I look up to find my next client stalking toward me in a sleek pencil skirt and a white blouse that dips at the neckline. Even before getting her hair done, Nicolette never falls short of flawless. She's the type of woman who knows what she's doing when she pieces herself together each morning.

She's my most regular "regular." The woman hasn't missed an appointment since she started coming to me almost a year ago. She books a shampoo and blow dry every Tuesday and a full cut and color every six weeks. She might be a little needy, but she tips well. And since she started coming to see me, she's referred me to all her equally well-paying friends. They make up a good chunk of my clientele now.

Taking off her oversized sunglasses, she slips them into her Louis Vuitton bag. "Candace, you are a saint. An absolute saint!"

My phone vibrates once, then twice, and I know it's the guy from the coffee shop. Curiosity prickles in the back of my mind, but I force myself to put my phone in the cabinet and close the door as I give her a welcoming smile. "It's nothing, really. You know I'm here," I say in my best customer service voice. "I always have time for you." She smiles with relief as she takes a seat in my chair. Running my fingers through her blonde strands, I ask. "So, what are we doing today?"

"The usual wash and style. I have plans at six. That's why I wanted to come early."

It isn't even 2:30 p.m., and her hair never takes that long. That's Nicolette, though. She isn't thinking about how long her hair usually takes. She isn't even thinking about the person I have scheduled after her who will likely have *their* hair done before six. Time means nothing to her. It's her world, and we're all abiding by her agenda.

"Dinner with someone special?" I ask. Maybe she's nervous for a big date. Some people start getting ready hours ahead of time.

"Oh, not really," she answers with a wave of her hand. "Just a work thing."

"Ah," I say with a nod. "Well, we'll make sure you look great."

She flashes a cat-like smile. "You always do."

I put the cape around her, fasten the snap at the base of her neck, and give her my best smile. She starts to talk about her holiday plans, and I fall into my routine of reacting to her story at all the right moments with plenty of "oohs" and "aahs." It's an act, but it's one I play well. There are plenty of clients I can be genuine with, but then there are the clients like her. Women like Nicolette take a little more finesse—mostly because I'm determined to stay on her good side. I'll keep her happy if she'll keep inching me toward a higher tax bracket.

My fingers massage and lather the shampoo into her hair, and she closes her eyes. Without her endless chatter, I let myself relax a little, too. I think about the two unread messages waiting on my phone. It's not like we were having a serious conversation. His messages are probably equally insignificant to the one I sent him, but now that I have a break, they're all I can think about. When some people text, they don't know how to let their personality shine through. I didn't get that impression from him. Texting with him feels more like having a face-to-face conversation. I can imagine his tone and inflection, and that alone makes him more interesting than most of the guys I've dated this year.

"Have you?"

I blink. "Have I what?"

Nicolette gives me a funny look, and I know I'm caught. Heat flushes my cheeks, and I try to remember what she was just talking about. She holds my stare for a moment like she wants me to know she's displeased, and even though I am a confident adult for the most part, it shrinks me back into feeling like a scolded child.

"Have you ever been to Stowe for the holidays?" she asks, slowly like she needs to enunciate each word.

"Oh. Sorry, no I haven't. Is it nice?"

"*Gorgeous*! You must go. It will beat any ski resort you've stayed at. Make sure to book early. The good lodges always fill up fast."

I know for a fact, I wouldn't be able to afford the *good lodges* she's referring to, but I give her a tight-lipped smile and assure her I'll look into it. It always amazes me how out of touch people with money can be. Does she honestly believe I take the same type of trips she does with her expensive purse and designer sunglasses? What about me screams that I frequent ski resorts in Vermont? On second thought, maybe she's just being nice. It's always a little hard to tell with her.

"Well, I'm sure you'll have a great time. Going with a someone special or friends?" I ask casually.

She gives me another funny look, and I wonder which detail about her life I've forgotten now. Thankfully, it doesn't last more than a few seconds before she scoffs. "No. Men are not something you bring on vacation. Men are something you pick up along the way." She gives me a look that I'm sure I'm supposed to reciprocate or understand, but I just chuckle.

"That's certainly one way of doing things."

"Don't settle down." She shivers like she's shaking a bad memory. "I made that mistake four times too many."

"Wanted to keep your freedom?"

The way this woman chuffs a laugh makes my entire body tense. "I wanted to sleep with his brother." She lists on her fingers. "And his boss, and his friend, and the last one was just boring." She gives a careless wave of her hand as if cheating on multiple husbands is the same thing every woman goes through.

I keep my eyes fixed on her hair as I nod. As a hairdresser, I'm used to getting some interesting confessions, but I don't trust my face if I look her in the eye. Talk about shiny object syndrome. I feel sorry for any man who crosses paths with a woman like Nicolette.

three

AFTER FOILING an entire head of highlights and squeezing in a last-minute haircut, I'm done for the day. By the time I clean my station, I'm the last one in the salon. Even Amanda left a little over an hour ago. Sometimes it's nice being the last one here. The place is always chaotic with everyone's overlapping conversations and the constant sound of cabinets slamming and hair dryers blowing.

The smell of a million different chemicals and shampoos fills the air all day, but when it's just me, and my last client was a simple haircut, it feels like the dust has settled. Turning off the overhead lights, I welcome the soft glow of the Christmas lights outside. I throw my bag over my shoulder, lock up, and head toward my apartment a few blocks away. It's still warm, but there's a light breeze tonight. I hug my cardigan around myself, more out of comfort than a need for actual warmth, but at least the heat of the day has broken.

I open the text thread with the guy from the coffee shop. I haven't learned his name yet, but I know that's something I should ask soon. I read over his two messages from earlier.

> **UNKNOWN NUMBER:**
>
> Palm trees and Christmas lights go together like pineapple on pizza.
>
> Do people do it? Yes. Should they? Absolutely not.

Most of my afternoon was swamped, but I was able to send a quick text before my last cut of the day.

> **CANDACE:**
> What if I told you I love pineapple on pizza?

I sent that message over an hour ago. Maybe loving pineapple on pizza is a deal breaker. It would be ridiculous, but people these days will walk away for less. Going back to my messages, I tap on the thread with my roommate.

> **CANDACE:**
> I'll grab tacos if you pick up tequila?

His response comes in right away.

> **MILES:**
> Fuck yes.

I figured his answer would be along those lines. It's rare for Miles and me to disagree on much, let alone tacos and booze. Taking a slight detour, I head to our favorite place downtown.

Paco's Tacos hits me with the incredible scent of spices as soon as I open the door. My stomach grumbles, the smell of my favorite food serving as the perfect reminder that I haven't eaten since breakfast.

Loud chatter fills the small space, with the staff yelling orders back and forth from their tiny, open kitchen. This place is always packed, but the line usually moves quickly. My phone vibrates, and my heart drums as I check for any sign of the guy from the coffee shop.

He still hasn't sent me anything. All I have is a text from my mom, making sure Miles will be home for Christmas to keep me company.

I text her back as I step forward in line, reassuring her that Miles and I will have a great time celebrating in our apartment, and she shouldn't worry about abandoning us for her hippy friends. It might have been the wrong thing to say to a woman already riddled with guilt, but I only have to reassure her I was *definitely joking* twice.

My eyes scan the menu board above, and my stomach growls again. I know my eyes are bigger than my stomach right now, but I also have a hefty tip from Nicolette in my wallet. I'd usually need to put it toward my car payment, but she referred another one of her friends this week who took care of that, so I decide to order whatever I want as soon as it's my turn.

I somewhat regret my decision when the brown paper bag is heavier than I expected, and I'm a few blocks from home. I still have my car, but it doesn't get much use outside of visiting my parents—or when it rains.

Luckily, our apartment is on the first floor, so I don't have to scale multiple flights with my giant bag of tacos, but I've still broken a sweat by the time I make it through the lobby. Balancing the bag on my knee, I fumble with the key when a commotion sounds from above.

"There arose such a clatter," I say quietly to myself and wonder what the guy who lives there is up to now. We've never seen him, but I like to imagine him as an elderly man with a bushy white mustache. Our very own St. Nick, except his name is Lenny.

Another thud from overhead makes me look up as I open the front door. We asked a few neighbors about it when we first moved in, unsure if we should file a noise complaint, but they all referred to him fondly saying things like, "Oh, that's just Lenny. He's always building something."

So now, Miles and I try to embrace the spirit of Lenny with fondness, too. He's never loud late at night, so we really have nothing to complain about.

"Hey, Stink!" Miles says from somewhere in the kitchen as soon as I open the apartment door. It's his favorite term of endearment. I'm not even sure how it started, but he's always said it lovingly.

"Hey." I shut the door with my foot as I balance the heavy bag.

I find Miles's tall, lanky frame putting salt around the rim of two margarita glasses. He has his back to me, his many tattoos on display. From here, I can make out pieces of the koi fish on his back poking out from his tank and the octopus wrapped around his calf.

He looks over his shoulder, shaking his head at the weight of the bag in my arms. "Let me guess," he says as he turns back to making our drinks. "You didn't know what to get me, so you bought the whole damn restaurant."

Heaving our food onto the counter, I give him a dirty look behind his back. "You know I shouldn't be allowed in there unsupervised, and I skipped lunch."

"I saw you pack your lunch this morning," he says with a questioning look before he finishes pouring our drinks.

"Nicolette needed her hair done a half hour early."

"Of course she did." He turns to face me. His scruff matches his black hair, his dark features only accentuated by the neon green glasses he wears. "What's the damage?" He peeks into the brown paper bag on the counter before letting out a slow whistle. "*Two* sides of queso?" He hands over my margarita with a shake of his head.

Setting the drink down, I wave him off as I reach into the bag and pull out its contents. "Don't hate me for my love of melted cheese."

He grabs a taco and unwraps the neatly folded paper. "You

can have all the melted cheese you want as long as you pay your half of the rent."

I take a sip of my drink, remembering a time not so long ago when splurging on this much takeout *would* have meant struggling to pay rent. Hell, I hardly had time to stop for takeout between my last hair appointment of the day and starting my shift at the bar. Last year, my idea of splurging was upgrading to the name brand boxed mac and cheese for a quick dinner. I have to admit, as difficult as Nicolette and some of her friends can be, it feels like a breath of fresh air not having to work two jobs to make ends meet.

Last Christmas, I could hardly justify spending money on decorations. My eyes scan over our apartment. It's so cozy here now. It feels like a home—our home. Our apartment isn't the cheapest one we could have found, but Miles and I wanted to live downtown, and I promised him I'd find a way to make it work. I love living within walking distance from work, and even though Miles works from home, he's a big fan of the craft beer scene this city has to offer.

The space is small, but everything has been recently updated. While we were looking for apartments, our list of needs only had two items on it.

1. Must be in Downtown Sanford.
2. Must have plenty of natural light.

The second requirement was more for Miles than me. He's the one stuck working here all day, but I love how open our space feels thanks to a couple of big windows along the back wall and a screened patio with sliding glass doors. They're only partially blocked right now thanks to the too-fat Christmas tree taking up most of our living room. When Miles and I went to pick out a tree, we knew we couldn't get one too tall, but neither of us paid much attention to the lack of horizontal space our apartment had to offer. Now we can only get in and out of our sectional couch one way, and it blocks some of the TV.

I reach for a chicken taco. "Lenny seems to be hard at work."

He nods. "Yeah, I heard him earlier. I found out he built that elaborate display of ghosts in the lobby for Halloween. Maybe he's making a life-sized Santa's sleigh."

"We'll find out soon enough, I'm sure."

Miles grabs one of the to-go cups of queso and holds it out for me. "Dig in. We have a lot of cheese to go through."

I dip a chip. "Don't mind if I do."

Years ago, I figured I'd be settled down by now. If someone asked me where I saw myself in five years back then, I would have imagined a Tuesday night cooking dinner with my husband. If they had asked me a few years later, I'd imagine ordering takeout with my boyfriend. But now, I've accepted that the man I have the most intimate relationship with finds men as appealing as I do—maybe even more.

My phone buzzes on the counter next to me. A message from an unsaved number pops up, and I almost drop my taco to tilt the phone toward me. An unsaved number can only mean two things. It's either a potential client, or it's *him*.

> UNKNOWN NUMBER:
>
> Then I'd say you should let me take you out for some real food, so we can fix your broken palate.

I snort a laugh before I can stop myself, and Miles arches an eyebrow. "Why are you smiling at your phone like an idiot?"

"I sort of met someone today." My lips quirk happily as I stuff more food into my mouth.

He pauses. "You did?"

I swallow and can't fight the smug lift of my chin. "I did."

He narrows his eyes and leans forward. "Wait. Are you actually *excited?*"

My eyes widen playfully, sharing in his shock. "I am."

"Well, it's about fucking time. I'm sick of you talking about dating like it's a goddamn chore. Excited is how you're supposed to feel." He takes a sip of his drink and starts to dance in his seat. "Welcome to the club, Sis."

I laugh and continue eating. To be fair, I used to get excited about the prospect of a new date. But once you're lied to enough times, it starts to get old. I was even cheated on a few months ago, and we had only been dating for a couple of months when it happened. I don't understand the dishonesty. If you want to keep something casual, just say so.

"What's his name? I want to find him."

I open my mouth to explain that I don't actually know his name yet, but my smile fades when a second text comes in.

UNKNOWN NUMBER:

When do they let you hang up the apron and stop serving coffee?

Serving coffee? I don't serve coffee. I might wear an apron at work, but there's no coffee being served in the salon—especially not by me. He can't think I work at Southern Roast, can he? I mean, I was in line as a customer, just like him. Unless he didn't mean to ask me out at all. But he left his receipt for me. The only other person around was—*Oh . . .*

Shit. Shit. Shit.

The barista.

four

MILES CATCHES his breath from laughing. "So let me get this straight. You thought some guy wanted your number, but he was asking out the girl giving him coffee?"

I glare at him, and he only laughs harder.

"And now he thinks he's talking to said barista, but he's really just talking to you?"

I take a deliberate bite of my taco.

He cackles. "You hijacked their meet cute!"

"I did not," I say with a roll of my eyes.

He takes a sip of his margarita, but his smile never fades. "You're right. You flat out killed it. You're a love assassin."

I flick a chip at him. "Would you stop? I will tell this ridiculously good-looking man who makes me laugh that I am not the barista of his dreams."

Miles gives me a sideways glance. "Or you could try to make him fall in love with you and *then* tell him?"

I think about the possibility but shake my head. "Stop trying to make this messy."

He shrugs and goes back to eating. "I love a scandal. Sue me."

I frown at my phone and take another bite. Damn. How did I miss his note being meant for someone else? Had he been flirting with the barista while I was gawking at him? I *was* surprised by the gesture, but I figured he was just shooting his shot. Nothing wrong with that.

Oh, god. Maybe he's been going into that coffee shop and flirting with her for months. Maybe this was the day he finally built up enough courage to ask her out, and I ruined it. How am I supposed to rectify something like this?

"Candace."

My eyes snap up to find Miles staring at me. "You look like you need to reboot."

"I'm fine," I say too quickly. "I mean, I barely know the guy. I'm not heartbroken."

He takes another sip of his drink. "But?"

I hold his stare before letting out a sigh as I set my food down and finally relent. He knows me too well. "He just had this vibe. This . . . presence." I wave my hand aimlessly as I try to put my finger on it. How do I describe what made him stand out when I barely understand it myself? My eyes widen when I land on it. "He was like Ryan Gosling in *Crazy Stupid Love*."

Miles tilts his head as he recalls the movie. "Hot," he acknowledges. "Dressed well?"

I crack a smile. "Impeccable taste." I take a moment to figure out what I'm trying to convey, but all I can think to say is, "He just had this way about him . . . like he could steal the attention of an entire room like *that*." I snap my fingers. "And he looked like he'd be willing to do the *Dirty Dancing* lift."

"Weird. But it sounds like he made quite the impression, so why not see if he'd be interested in you instead?" He does a little shoulder shimmy. "Tell him what a freak you can be and change his mind."

I let out a breath of laughter. "Are you ever not thinking about sex?"

"Rarely," he says matter of fact. "And those few minutes are easily the worst part of my day."

I roll my eyes. "Tragic."

"I'm just saying, you could do it. There's no reason for him not to like you," he says, ignoring my point.

"He didn't mean to ask me out. I might not even be his type." I'm not going to ask this guy for any favors—especially not one that involves a date.

Miles gives me an expectant look.

"What?" I ask as I scoop another heap of queso onto a chip. That look always makes me uncomfortable. It's the look he gives when he's about to tear into me like Miranda Priestly and demand I change my clothes.

"Trust me, you're his type. Either that or *I'm* his type." He shrugs and shifts his attention back to his food. "Which, I mean, who could blame him?"

My lips twist, and I'm tempted to flick another chip at him. "Fine."

With glittering eyes, he nods toward my phone. "Well, what are you going to say?"

I groan, not even Paco's Tacos can bring me solace. "Nothing while you're watching." I flip my phone over on the kitchen counter, placing it face down. "I'll figure it out later."

"You do that."

I let out a breath. "He'll be disappointed."

He nods. "Maybe."

I shrug. "And that'll be it."

"I see."

I blink, waiting for more.

Miles takes another bite, ignoring my confusion. He looks around the apartment aimlessly before settling his eyes back on me. "Oh. Would you like to know what I think?"

I give him a heavy-lidded stare. "Do tell."

He takes a deep breath like he's preparing a monologue

now that I've consented to listening, and I'm suddenly rethinking my answer. "Look, babe. Did this guy mean to ask you out? No. But does that mean he wouldn't be interested in you? Fuck no." He gestures toward me. "Look at how cute you are! And you're never overly excited about the guys you meet —or even the guys you date lately. So, the fact that you're disappointed means this guy caught your interest." He looks me up and down before shrugging. "You might dress like a peasant, but I can help with that. You have a lot to offer."

A faint smile pulls at my lips. "Already eager to help?"

"I'll answer that after I meet him."

"Oh, you'd love him." I give him a reassuring nod.

"Mhm. I bet I would." Miles lets out a laugh and goes back to eating. I do the same, but I can't help thinking about what he said.

There's no point in being disappointed. There's a good chance I would have lost interest after talking to him for a few days. It's not like *that* hasn't happened before. He might be too needy or annoying, or he might collect plastic forks from restaurants like the guy I went on a date with two months ago. Hell, he might even lie about secretly having a wife and kids. I'll figure out his fatal flaw, but I won't have any answers until I suck it up and tell him I'm not the barista from Southern Roast.

five

THE SOFT GLOW of the lamp on my bedside table casts shadows on the white walls. Thankfully plain and minimalistic is in right now because my bedroom is pretty bare. The only thing I've bought is a standing wood frame mirror in the corner and a sage green throw blanket.

Miles is in the living room rewatching episodes of *Schitt's Creek*. Normally, I'd be out there with him, but I don't need him asking for real-time updates of the text exchange I'm about to have.

Taking a breath, I open the last messages from whoever this guy is. He wants to take me out and fix my broken palate. Except he doesn't want *me* to be a part of any of that. He wants the barista. I've tried remembering what she looks like, but I can't. I was apparently too distracted by the guy I unintentionally stole from her.

My thumbs hover over the screen. There's no good way to tell someone you're not the person they think you are. With a sigh, I type the first thing that comes to mind.

> **CANDACE:**
> I have good news and bad news. Which do you want first?

The three dots appear, and my eyes stay glued to the screen until his message comes in.

> **UNKNOWN NUMBER:**
> If you've been kidnapped and need to be rescued before our date, I have to warn you, among my many talents (and there are many) fighting isn't one of them.

I shake my head at the message with a tight-lipped smile. Who *is* this guy?

> **UNKNOWN NUMBER:**
> I quit karate at the age of eight, and as a result, I'm useless.

My smile widens as I respond.

> **CANDACE:**
> Don't worry, no karate needed.

I wait for him to answer, my heart thudding in my chest a little harder than it was before.

> **UNKNOWN NUMBER:**
> Sounds like we both dodged a bullet.
>
> Okay, give me the good news first.

My teeth sink into my bottom lip.

> **CANDACE:**
> You're sure?

UNKNOWN NUMBER:

Yes. I like to consider myself an optimist.

Letting out a sigh, I type.

CANDACE:

I really do love pineapple on pizza.

The three dots appear but then stop before reappearing again.

UNKNOWN NUMBER:

You've lost me. How exactly is this good news?

Your terrible taste in pizza is hardly something to celebrate.

The corners of my mouth twitch, and I playfully glare at my phone even though he can't see me.

CANDACE:

The bad news is that I'm not the barista, but there's a good chance she will have excellent taste in pizza for you.

I don't know why I'm so nervous. It's not like I intentionally catfished the guy. I'm sure he'll understand.

But it's still embarrassing.

He had no interest in me, and the fact that I wrote my number on his receipt makes it indisputable that I was interested in him. I can't back out and pretend I didn't mean to give him my number. I found him attractive, I texted him back, and I knew exactly who I was talking to the entire time.

He, on the other hand, never thought twice about the girl who stood behind him in line today.

I jump when my phone buzzes in my hands.

UNKNOWN NUMBER:
You're not?

Who are you?

I frown. They're easily the least playful messages he's sent so far. All flirtation gone, the butterflies in my stomach, dead.

Before I can respond, another message from him comes in.

UNKNOWN NUMBER:
Oh! Danishes?

I wonder if he still thinks I was looking at Danishes when I was clearly checking him out to the point of accidentally giving him my number when he didn't want it.

CANDACE:
Yeah.

When a response doesn't come, I send a follow up text out of panic.

CANDACE:
I'm sorry for getting in the way.

I smooth my hands over my hair and let out a breath. Well, at least it's done. Band-Aid officially ripped off.

UNKNOWN NUMBER:
You liked me?

I arch an eyebrow.

CANDACE:
To be fair, I don't know you.

UNKNOWN NUMBER:
Yeah, but you liked what you saw?

I blink at my phone screen, not sure how to answer. Part of

me wants to say . . . *obviously?* But before I can come up with a coherent thought, he texts me again.

> UNKNOWN NUMBER:
>
> Shit. That's not what I'm trying to say. I'm just surprised.

My eyebrows furrow.

> CANDACE:
>
> Should I be afraid to ask why?

> UNKNOWN NUMBER:
>
> I don't think so.

He starts typing, and I hug my knees to my chest as I stare down at my phone, waiting for his next message. As soon as it comes in, I snatch my phone and start reading.

> UNKNOWN NUMBER:
>
> You know how there are some people who look like they'd happily talk to someone they don't know?
>
> You didn't look like one of those people.

My lips purse. Is he saying I'm unapproachable? I'm almost tempted to ask him *why*.

> CANDACE:
>
> Fair enough. Now that you mention it, the barista was extremely welcoming, and I'm sure it had nothing to do with her being paid to smile.

> UNKNOWN NUMBER:
>
> Ha. Ha. That's not why I was going to ask her out.

> CANDACE:
> I'm sure you have an excellent reason.

I wonder what he likes about her. After seeing how he described me, I'm intrigued. Is she a daisy with a bubbly personality? I wish I paid more attention to what she looked like while I was there today.

> UNKNOWN NUMBER:
> I don't want to tell you.
>
> You'll judge me.

I let out a huff. I didn't even ask him to tell me, but now I definitely need to know.

> CANDACE:
> You owe me. I thought I was being hit on today.

There's a long pause before he starts typing, like he's trying to figure out what he needs to say, but the message that comes in is far from poetic.

> UNKNOWN NUMBER:
> I have a thing for blondes.

My tight lips burst with laughter, and I shake my head. He can't be serious. *That's* his reason? I suddenly don't feel so bad about ruining their meet cute after all. What kind of guy only goes for one hair color?

Another message pops up.

> UNKNOWN NUMBER:
> Are you judging me?

There's no reason to sugarcoat things, I type back my honest response.

> **CANDACE:**
> I am.

> **UNKNOWN NUMBER:**
> I thought so.
>
> Look, it's unintentional. Every woman I've dated has been blonde by circumstance, and now I've simply accepted my fate.

I roll my eyes even though he can't see me.

> **CANDACE:**
> Your fate of only dating blondes?

> **UNKNOWN NUMBER:**
> I don't only date blondes. I've just only ever had relationships with them. There's a key difference.

> **CANDACE:**
> Fine. You're only attracted to blondes. But hear me out.

> **UNKNOWN NUMBER:**
> Debatable, but I'm listening.

I snort a laugh.

> **CANDACE:**
> Maybe it's time to look at the fact that dating blondes is the one thing that has consistently never worked out for you.
>
> And I'm not saying that as a girl who gave you my number today. I'm saying that as a friend.

There's a pause before the next message comes in.

UNKNOWN NUMBER:

That is . . . an excellent point.

I probably shouldn't encourage this man's terrible theory on love, but with a sigh, I type out my next message. Miles will disapprove, but I don't want someone who doesn't want me. It's as simple as that. And a guy who only goes for blondes? It sounds like I may have actually dodged a bullet after all.

CANDACE:

But if you're really into blondes, just go back and ask her out again. I promise not to interfere this time. I'm sorry about that.

UNKNOWN NUMBER:

Don't apologize. This has become a much more interesting night than I anticipated.

It has for me, too. Maybe not in the way I was hoping, but I like talking to him. He has this candid way about him that makes him feel . . . genuine. It's refreshing. And now that the flirting aspect is gone, the conversation isn't riddled with pressure. Even if it's not what I wanted, there's something that can be said for that, too.

UNKNOWN NUMBER:

You really think I should go back?

Of course I don't think he should go back and ask out some gorgeous blonde who serves coffee, but who am I to judge?

CANDACE:

You might as well. See how things would have worked out today if all had gone according to plan, right?

UNKNOWN NUMBER:

Another valid point.

Setting my phone down on my bedside table, I consider going into the living room and joining Miles. It's getting late, though, and tomorrow is a full day. I'm booked solid without much of a break for lunch or my always appreciated afternoon coffee.

My phone buzzes on the bedside table, and my eyebrows pull together before flipping it over. I didn't think he'd text me again. I'm not the person he thought, and he's going to ask out the right person. Simple as that. But as I look down at the message, I can't help but feel a tiny flutter.

UNKNOWN NUMBER:

So, outside of this, how was your day?

six

WITH MY BAG slung over my shoulder, I look both ways before jogging across the street. Coffee Shop Guy kept me up a little later than I expected, but despite texting into the early hours of the morning, names never came up.

Talking to him made me feel like a teenager again, giddy with flutters of anticipation, but I can't be interested in a guy like him. A guy who only goes for blondes? Please. That's ridiculous. If anything, his lack of interest should have broken whatever rose-tinted glasses I wore yesterday. A guy can be a ten, but as soon as I find out he's not interested, he drops to a solid six. Miles has always called it my superpower—the ability to disregard a man I thought was the end all be all in a matter of seconds.

I pull open the door to the salon a mere five minutes before my first appointment. Amanda looks up from placing small cups of candy canes in everyone's station.

"Hey!" She grins before a flash of concern shows in her eyes and she glances at the clock on the wall. "Rough morning?"

I let out a breathless laugh as I set down my things and reach for my black apron on the wall hook. "Something like that."

She lifts an eyebrow. "Want to talk about it?"

At the same time, my phone vibrates in my back pocket. I reach for it and see that it's another message from Coffee Shop Guy.

> **COFFEE SHOP GUY:**
> Eggs on peanut butter toast?

"What?" I mutter to no one in particular before giving my attention back to Amanda. "Uh, maybe over wine."

She laughs. "I can't tonight, but I'd love to know what has you looking at your phone like that."

I crack a small smile as I type back my response.

> **CANDACE:**
> I'm sorry?

I'm still not sure what to make of this new friendship I have with an unnamed man. He plans on asking the girl at Southern Roast out again, so why is he still texting me? About peanut butter and eggs of all things.

> **COFFEE SHOP GUY:**
> You like pineapple on pizza, so I want to know what other disgusting things you find delicious.
>
> Vanilla ice cream and soy sauce?

My mouth quirks as I type my response.

> **CANDACE:**
> No, and fuck no.

The bell chimes overhead as he sends another text.

COFFEE SHOP GUY:

All right. No need to get violent.

I laugh and slip my phone into the drawer before greeting the short, elderly woman, her shoulders bent with age. She's been coming to see me since I was a student in cosmetology school, and I love when she asks for tips on how to set her rollers at night.

"Ms. Bradshaw," I say with a grin. "It's great to see you." Taking her bag from her, I help her into the chair and get situated. Shaking open the fresh cape, I drape it around her and ask, "So, what are we doing today?"

By the time I have a break for lunch, he's texted two more times. And the weirdest part? I'm not creeped out. I think every woman has had her phone blown up by some guy who couldn't take a hint, but whatever I have going on with this guy isn't like that. His messages don't give me the urge to change my number and file a restraining order. If anything, I enjoy them.

COFFEE SHOP GUY:

Orange juice and Oreos?

Please tell me it's not the orange juice and Oreos. I don't think I could take it.

I roll my eyes as I bite into my leftover tacos.

CANDACE:

Where are you finding these combinations? Pineapple on pizza isn't even weird compared to most of these.

In the few minutes it takes me to finish my lunch, he's already answered.

> **COFFEE SHOP GUY:**
>
> I hate to be the one to break it to you, but you saying it isn't weird doesn't make it any less weird.
>
> Where have you been all day? I thought I scared you away.

My heart does a tiny stutter, and I mentally scold myself for it.

> **CANDACE:**
>
> Don't you have a job? Or do you just wear suits in coffee shops to look important?

With the way he was dressed, he must have a job. Either that, or he was dressed to impress and is actively seeking employment. No one dresses in well-pressed business attire for the fun of it.

> **COFFEE SHOP GUY:**
>
> I have a job, thank you. But what I do in the confines of my office is my business.
>
> Plus, my boss loves me.

Okay, so he's not unemployed.

> **CANDACE:**
>
> Lucky you.

I bite my bottom lip and ask what I've been wondering all day.

> **CANDACE:**
>
> Did you go back to Southern Roast?

While he types his response, I stare at the screen with bated breath. I shouldn't. His answer won't change anything. I'd be an idiot to let this go further than it already has, but for some reason, I'm *dying* to know.

> **COFFEE SHOP GUY:**
> I did. Her name is Layla, and we had a nice chat.

A moment passes with nothing, like he's waiting to see what I'll say, but if I know anything about this guy, it's that there's another text coming my way. Sure enough, a moment later, my phone buzzes.

> **COFFEE SHOP GUY:**
> But she has a boyfriend, so I didn't get her number.

Is that the reason he's still texting me? Am I a runner-up in this situation? I bristle at the thought. I should cut ties. I know I should. But I like talking to him. There's something about him that still has me intrigued . . . even if it's just as friends.

I used to joke with Miles and say I don't need new friends. That if I date someone, and it doesn't work out, there is no, *we can still be friends*. But I've never dated this guy, so I guess that rule doesn't apply.

> **CANDACE:**
> Well, you can't win them all.

I wait for those three dots to reappear, but they don't. Even after I've thrown away my taco wrapper and cleaned up my station to prepare for the next client, there's still nothing.

I stare at my last text and wonder if I should have said more. Maybe he wants sympathy? Maybe he was more disappointed than I realized, and I brushed it off as no big deal. I've never been good at being overly sympathetic with people. Maybe he needed more, and I fell short.

I blink, snapping myself back to reality. Does it matter? Why would I care if this man I don't know needed me to rub his back and tell him there are plenty of fish in the sea? Shaking my head, I toss my phone into the drawer and vow not to open it until I'm done with work.

seven

AN OCCASIONAL CAR passing on the cobblestone street is the soundtrack to my walk home. I love my walks in the middle of the week. The heat breaks when the sun goes down, the streets are quiet, and the various displays of reindeer and Santa hats make it feel like home this time of year.

There's something about living downtown and seeing the city while it sleeps. I used to come here when I was younger. In college, Miles would drag me out to all the bars, and I'd dance and drink the night away like my life depended on it. I loved the vibrant nightlife of the city, but I think I prefer getting to know the shop owners and becoming a regular at a local pub more.

My phone vibrates from deep within my bag. Miles is probably calling to ask what I want to do for dinner tonight. I hope he doesn't want to go out. Today was long, and I'm ready for my couch and Chinese takeout that I can eat straight from the container.

When I finally fish my phone out of my bag, I blink down at the number calling.

It's not Miles.

It's *him*.

I stop, and with my heart hammering in my chest, I swipe to answer.

Slowly bringing my phone to my ear, like it might detonate at any moment, I say, "Hello?"

"What's your name?" His voice is smooth, deep, and low. It's the type of voice that has no business belonging to someone who's just your *friend*. There's no background noise, and I imagine him sitting in a fancy apartment somewhere with a whiskey on the rocks in his hand.

I blink. "What?"

He laughs, and even through the phone, the sound ricochets from one vertebra to another. "Your name?"

"Oh." I force my feet to move in the direction of home. "Candace. My name is Candace."

I can hear the smile in his voice as he says, "Nice to meet you, Candace."

"You, too." It takes me a moment to get my bearings and ask him the same. I hope his name is something ridiculous, like Barty or Edmund. "And yours?"

Another low chuckle. "Chase."

Chase. I try to picture him again and assign the name to the man I saw yesterday morning.

Fuck, it's hot.

I inhale a steadying breath. "Well, it's nice to meet you. Want to tell me why you're calling?"

"Do you want to get drinks with me?" He asks it like he's asking what my favorite color is. He's the epitome of casual, and it feels like it's taking everything inside me not to freeze up on the spot.

"No." The word comes out sharp on my tongue, and I wince. So much for not freezing up.

Chase finds my response funny, another laugh leaking through the phone. "No? Damn, Candace."

The way he says my name makes my knees weak, but I can't get drinks with him. I have a feeling I'm not the one he wants to get drinks with, and I have just enough pride to keep myself from being anyone's backup.

"I'm sorry. I just—Why are you asking me out for drinks?"

There's still a smile in his voice when he says, "Because I thought it would be fun?" The sound of him getting up and walking replaces some of the stillness on his end. "Look, I'm about to leave the office, and I figured I'd see if you were free. That's all."

"I'm not," I say too quickly.

"Yes, I gathered that." Even his clipped response has a hint of playfulness to it.

My eyes dart to the buildings around me, and panic spurs in my chest. What if he's in one of these? We both went to the same coffee shop, so he probably works around here. I'm literally surrounded by potential office buildings. What if he spills onto the street and crashes into me like the beginning of some terrible rom-com movie?

I swallow down the thought and pick up my pace. I'm only about a block from home. If I hurry, maybe I can round the corner before he even leaves the building.

"Candace, are you running from someone?"

"What?" I ask, wincing at how out of breath I sound.

Yes, you.

The words are on the tip of my tongue, but I clamp my lips shut to silence my breathing.

"You just sound . . . like you're in a hurry?"

I know I'm being ridiculous. Running from a man I'm on the phone with. Who happens to work in the same city. But even as I rationalize my fears, my steps quicken.

Because I don't trust myself around him.

I've always been level-headed. Never one to get swept off their feet. Never at risk of getting hurt. I've been through breakups, makeups—hell, one guy even proposed. I learned a lot from that one in particular. Now, I like to think I can spot red flags from a mile away, and Chase is a walking red flag. He might look good in a suit and have a voice that makes my insides turn all gooey, but he's affecting me way too much too soon for this to be a fair fight.

With my apartment in view, I lie through my teeth. "Yeah, sorry. In a bit of a hurry."

"Big plans tonight?"

"Yeah," I answer with a huff as I pull the door to the lobby open. "You could say that."

His end of the phone falls quiet again, like he stopped to listen to my chaos. "Well, I hope you have a great time." He lightens his tone as he adds, "I mean, you're passing up drinks with me, and I'm definitely a great time."

My laugh comes out sounding more like a scoff. "I'm sure you are."

"Are you doubting me?"

My cheeks flush even though he can't see me. I didn't scoff because I don't believe him. I scoffed because I *do*. But before I can say anything, he speaks again.

"Let me prove it to you. Get drinks with me. You pick the night."

My feet come to a screeching halt in front of my apartment door. "Why?" I've known this guy for less than two days, and he's already making my head spin.

"Because I like you," he says, like it's the easiest thing to admit. "And I think it would be fun."

Why am I so tempted by this? I'm not supposed to get butterflies from a guy like him. Haven't I learned anything from all the terrible guys I've gone on dates with this year? I should tell him no. I should hang up the phone and ignore all future calls and texts, because if he can get to me this much after two days, I should cut my losses and hit the road. My mouth opens, but no words come out.

"It's only drinks," he says with that dangerous hint of a smile still in his voice.

I roll my eyes to the ceiling, and my shoulders drop in defeat. "As friends." It's not a question. If I'm going to do anything with him, there needs to be clear boundaries.

"Of course," he agrees without hesitation. "Strictly friends having a great time together."

A breath of laughter slips out of me. "Okay. Well, I just got ho—here. I'll text you."

"I look forward to it."

We say our goodbyes and hang up, and I'm left staring down at my phone with a storm of emotions brewing in the pit of my stomach. After adding his name to the contact info, I fight the urge to text him right away. Because as much as I know I shouldn't, I'm looking forward to it, too.

eight

THE CLINK of my keys in the entryway dish spurs a, "Hey, Stink!"

"Hey!" Setting down my bag, I peek into the living room. Miles has a headset on, wearing nothing but neon pink boxer briefs and a tank top as he plays Fortnite. He's pulled his office chair out of his bedroom so he can sit closer to the TV, and between that, the coffee table, and the obnoxiously large Christmas tree, the apartment has never looked so small.

"Did you wear pants at any point today?"

He wiggles a little in his chair like he'd be shaking his ass if he were standing. "I did not."

"The luxuries of working from home," I answer wistfully.

He glances over his shoulder at me. "Well, I did have to listen to the workings of Lenny for hours on end, so it's a fair trade. How was your day?"

There's still no elaborate Christmas decoration in the lobby, so I wonder what the guy upstairs could be working on. Heading into the kitchen, I reach for the bottle of Chardonnay on the counter. "Kind of weird?"

Miles has one side of his headset slipped behind his ear. "How so?"

I pour my wine into a stemless glass. "That guy called me tonight."

He glances over his shoulder as he continues to play. "The guy from Southern Roast?"

I nod. "Chase. He wanted to get drinks."

Abandoning his match, he spins the chair around and rips the headset off. "Bitch, then why are you here?"

I give him a warning look. "He also asked out the barista again today, but she turned him down."

"So?"

I blink. "So, I don't want to be his shitty backup plan."

"Wow." Miles crosses his arms.

I frown, setting my glass on the counter. "Wow what?"

He raises an eyebrow. "You just never struck me as being this petty."

I balk at him. "*Petty?* I'm just trying to avoid getting involved with a fuckboy."

He rolls his eyes. "How do you even know he asked out the other girl, anyway?"

"He told me." I take another sip and try to hide how much I'm still stuck on being called *petty* of all things.

Miles lets out a snort of laughter. "So, if he's a fuckboy, he's bad at it."

I shrug. "Maybe?" I honestly don't know what type of guy Chase is. "Either that, or he's overly honest."

He gives me a dubious look. "Well, aren't we suddenly generous?"

I'm almost afraid to ask, but I say, "With what?"

Miles waves his hand aimlessly in the air. "All this *benefit of the doubt* we're giving."

I roll my eyes. "I turned him down, didn't I?"

"And what did he say?"

"What do you mean?"

Without breaking his unwavering stare, he says, "What did he say when you turned him down?"

Sucking in my lips, I shake my head. He knows me too well.

"Candace."

"Okay," I say, forcing out a breath. "I may have lied and said I was busy." I hold up a finger. "But I did tell him that when we reschedule, it's strictly as friends."

Miles sits up straight and does a slow clap. "Bravo. Way to lay down the hammer. Show that fuckboy what you're made of." When I don't give his snide remark the time of day, he grabs his phone and starts typing.

"What are you doing?"

Without looking at me, he says, "Finding him."

"Wait. Why?" My attempt to hide my panic is pointless.

"To see if he's a fuckboy or if he's just 'overly honest.'" He gives me a pointed stare on those last two words, and I stick my tongue out at him.

Miles will find him. I'm convinced Miles can find anyone. I once dated a guy who played intramural softball, and he found a guy on the opposing team without so much as his name just because he thought he was cute.

I'm more worried about what the consensus will be once he does find him.

Getting to his feet, Miles walks up to me. "Is this him?" He flips his phone around for me to see a smiling photo of Chase.

Chase Mitchell.

I gape at him. "How did you do that so fast?" Even knowing his capabilities, I'm always impressed by them.

Miles lets out a sigh like he was hoping this one would be more of a challenge. "He follows Southern Roast."

I tilt my head. "Huh, I don't even think I follow them, and they're my favorite coffee shop."

Miles scrolls. "He follows a lot of business pages, but I can't decide if that's a red flag."

I move closer to him so I can get a better look at the screen. "He doesn't look like a fuckboy based on his feed." It doesn't look like he posts often, but when he does, they're usually pictures of things—a coffee, food, a stunning beach landscape.

"He could just be good at hiding it." Miles taps on his tagged photos, and that's where we find a different version of Chase.

There are so many beautiful women.

"Fuckboy in hiding!" Miles cheers and he scrolls down, and down, and down, to show all the pictures of Chase smiling at the camera with stunning women at his side. Some photos have men and women in a group setting, but there are definitely more women in these than not.

My *overly honest* theory crumbles at my feet.

"When are you getting drinks with this hot man as just his friend?" Miles asks, still scrolling.

"We didn't get that far."

He nods to my phone on the counter. "Text him."

Now it's my turn to stare. "You just said I was being too generous by not turning him down!"

"I know, but I've reconsidered." He shrugs. "And you need to get laid."

I almost choke. "What are you talking about? I go on dates all the time."

"Yes, dates. But when's the last time you slept with someone?" He cocks a knowing eyebrow, and my eyes narrow.

"It hasn't been that long." I do the math on my fingers. "It's only been . . ." I frown. "Eight months?"

"*Eight?*" With a shake of his head, he says, "Damn, Candace. I thought you were going to say three—*maybe* four." He looks me up and down. "Eight months. Jesus Christ."

I let out a bewildered laugh. "Come on, that's not so bad!"

"What about that guy you went on a few dates with back in October? I thought you liked him."

"I did like him," I say simply. "Just not enough to sleep with him." Pointing at him, I add, "Which ended up being a good thing because he lied about taking care of his grandma. She was definitely the one taking care of him."

He points to my phone again. "Seriously, text him," he says before spinning around to go back to his game. It looks like the match has since ended.

With a groan, I make a dramatic show of reaching for my phone and pulling it toward me. "But whyyyy?"

"Because, even if it doesn't turn into anything, you need to go on a date with a guy you actually want to sleep with."

"Who says I want to sleep with him?"

Giving me a lazy sideways glance, Miles deadpans. "You're blushing."

Being called out only makes my cheeks flare more, but I aggressively flip my phone over. "Fine. I'll text him."

CANDACE:

> 8 tomorrow night. Stem and Leaf.

I'm surprised when a response quickly comes in.

CHASE:

> Sounds good, friend.

nine

TAKING A STEADYING BREATH, I stare up at the sign for Stem and Leaf. I'm stopped on the sidewalk a few feet before the entrance. The limestone wash on the brick exterior brings a stark contrast to the black trim around the glass paneled doors. Even the dark framing of the windows pop with the modern color scheme.

All day I've been a wreck. Five clients, a coffee break courtesy of Amanda, and a few oddly encouraging texts from Miles, have made the hours fly by. But even with the distractions, all I've been able to think about is Chase and our impending *friend* date.

After work, I ran home to freshen up and change. Miles wanted me to wear a little black dress I have in my closet for special occasions, but nothing about the plunging neckline on that dress makes me look like I'm anyone's friend. Instead, I opted for black leggings with a lightweight cream sweater and a pair of strappy sandals. There was mild protest from Miles. I'm pretty sure he muttered something about "couch potato chic" being all the rage, but I ignored him.

It's 8:03 p.m., and I know I should go in. I'm out of view

from the bar windows, so he won't be able to see me if he's already inside, but there's a possibility he isn't here yet. The last thing I need is for him to walk up and find me staring at the sign overhead like I might bolt at any second.

There's always a moment of uneasy jitters before a first date, but why is this date—that isn't even a date—making me more nervous than the others? It can't *all* have to do with how good he looked in a suit. I might not know much about Chase, but just the way he conducts himself over the phone had me feeling like a girl with a crush. I need to get a grip. Squaring my shoulders, I force my feet forward and walk inside.

He's here. There are probably twenty other people who are also here, but somehow my eyes land on him first. He's wearing a light blue button-down that almost looks white. The sleeves are rolled to expose his forearms, and paired with black slacks, he looks just as sleek and modern as the rest of this place.

He's staring down at his phone as he casually sits with his ankle resting on his knee. There's a slight crease between his brows as he types a mile a minute, and I give myself a little time to take in the sight of him.

He is one beautiful man. Even the dim lighting in the back corner of the bar casts a glow over him like it's his own personal spotlight. He keeps his dark hair styled perfectly, his clothes are immaculate, and if his forearms are any indicator of the muscle that lies beneath . . . God help me.

"You can sit anywhere you like," one of the servers says as she passes with a tray of wine glasses, and I blink, forcing my attention back to my surroundings.

"Thanks." I quickly head toward Chase, and he looks up like he's caught my movement out of the corner of his eye.

The crease of his brow smooths, and nothing could have prepared me for the genuine grin that spreads across his face. He gets to his feet and extends a hand for me to shake. "Candace. It's great to see you."

"You too," I say with a polite smile as I meet his outstretched hand. It's warm and strong, and the way his thumb grazes my skin could start a fire on a rainy day.

He doesn't let go right away. Instead, he turns my hand over and looks down at it before lifting an eyebrow. "Artist?"

Of course, he notices the random splotches of hair dye that always stain my skin. Pulling my hand out of his grip, I say, "Hairdresser."

Eyeing me with interest, he pulls out my chair before returning to his own. "Really?" He runs a hand through his hair, gripping it at the roots with a light shake. "I could use a haircut."

My eyes widen before I can stop them. "Do *not* cut your hair."

He pauses, and his eyebrows shoot up in a way that makes him look innocent—almost puppy-like. "You have an opinion about my hair?"

My lips twitch into a faint smile. "I have an opinion about everyone's hair." Pointing to his head, I add, "And I have at least ten clients who would kill for hair like yours."

He drops his hand, and his hair somehow looks better messed up. Without bothering to fix it, he says, "Well, I'll make sure to get my next haircut from you, so I guess I'll wait for you to tell me it's too long."

The way he says it is so *sure*—so certain we'll still know each other by the time he needs a haircut. My stomach drops, and I look around for our server as a way to change the subject. "Have you ordered yet?"

The corner of his mouth quirks. "No, I was waiting for you." He nods to the bar behind me, lined with black stools. "Our server is the one with the blonde ponytail, though."

Looking back at him, I say, "A blonde? Well, you certainly lucked out." The words are out before I can stop them, but his smile only grows.

"Tonight, I'm here with you."

I arch a brow. "Don't let me stand in your way of love."

Amusement flickers in his warm, mahogany eyes before he leans forward, resting those impressive forearms on the table. "Tell me, Candace. What's *your* type?"

"Chardonnay," I answer dismissively, my eyes searching for the blonde ponytail he pointed to moments ago.

When I look back at him, I find him watching me intently. The same playful expression on his chiseled face. "What's your type?" he asks again.

I tilt my head like I have to think about it before settling my eyes on him again. "Blonde."

He laughs and shakes his head.

"With tattoos," I say, eyeing his naked forearms. Meeting his dark stare again, I add, "And blue eyes." I arch an eyebrow to challenge his response, but our server walks up before he can say anything.

"Hey, have you two had a chance to think about what you might like?" she asks with a dazzling smile.

Chase doesn't even glance at her. He keeps his eyes on me, the same amused expression when he says, "She'll take a Chardonnay." He leans back in his chair, still appraising me with a smirk. "And I'll have a bourbon, neat."

"Sounds good. I'll have those right out for you," she says happily.

I look up at her and smile. "Thanks." He's still watching me with a slight lift to his lips when I bring my attention back to him. "What?" I ask.

"What made you decide to get drinks with me?"

My cheeks threaten to heat, but I tilt my head innocently before they have a chance to betray me. "Don't you remember? You quite literally promised me 'a great time.' Maybe I need that right now."

I'm walking a fine line between flirting and casual conversation, but nothing will happen between us. Chase has *fuckboy* written all over him, and regardless of what Miles says, I don't think I'd want something *that* casual with him. Because as attractive as he is, he also gives off this odd sense of transparency I find refreshing. It's too dangerous of a combination.

We get our drinks, and Chase holds up his glass for a toast. "To having a great time." Our drinks lightly clink. Pausing before bringing the glass to his lips, he says, "That's what friends are for, right?"

Everything about him is light, laid back, and open, but I can't help digging for some underlying meaning between those words. Slowly taking a sip of wine, I don't bother hiding how deeply I'm considering him with his well-pressed clothes and perfect hair. "I guess we'll find out."

ten

WE'VE BEEN HERE for over an hour, and I wipe a stray tear from the corner of my eye, trying to rein in my laughter.

Chase leans forward, his eyes wide and wild. "It's not funny! I boarded up her entire fucking house before that hurricane." He presses his pointer finger against the tabletop in quick jabs. "Ten. Windows. *Ten.* Do you know how much work it is to cover windows with plywood alone? Have you ever done such a thing?"

I take a breath so there's enough oxygen in my lungs for me to speak, but my voice still comes out high and squeaky with my futile attempt to hold back laughter. "But why would you do that after only one date?"

This isn't the first ridiculous story he's told, and everything hurts. My cheeks hurt from laughing, and my eyes burn from the makeup that is surely in them.

He gapes at me. "She asked!"

I take a sip from my third glass of Chardonnay and shake my head. "So? Why not pretend you were busy? If a hurricane was coming, you could have said you left the state to stay with family."

He shrugs, leaning back in his chair. "I liked her. But as soon as I was done, she told me she wanted to weather the storm alone. Both literally and figuratively."

I shake my head, but my lips still twist with amusement. "Unbelievable."

He takes a sip of his bourbon, not bothering to hide his tight-lipped smile. "I hope you're referring to her and not me."

"Oh, no. I'm definitely referring to you. After one date? What was so special about this girl?"

He opens his mouth but pauses before any words come out.

Pointing a finger at him, I say in a warning tone, "I swear to God, if you say she was blonde."

He says nothing but sucks in his lips like he might combust if he doesn't tell me how yellow this girl's fucking hair was. My head shakes in disapproval.

He grimaces. "On second thought, she was more of a caramel?"

I give him a heavy-lidded stare. "You're terrible, you know that? I hope you know how terrible you are."

He grins, his brown eyes sparkling with mischief. "I'm well aware." Leaning toward me, he adds, "What about you? Worst first date."

I know my worst first date by heart. It's the *first date* story I've told dozens of times. "Probably when a guy asked if I could pick him up and then when I got to his house, he said he wasn't feeling well and asked if I could make him soup."

Chase's eyes widen. "Damn. He was looking for a wife to replace his mother, wasn't he?"

I let myself take another sip before setting my glass down and nod. "You could say that."

"How did the date end?"

My eyebrows pinch. "What do you mean?"

"Well, did you stay and make the soup, or did you slam the door in his face?"

A humorless laugh leaves me. "Oh, I made the soup. Then I dated him for two years until he proposed."

Chase freezes mid sip before slowly setting his glass on the table. Sitting up straight to face me head on, he gives me an incredulous look. "You didn't."

I'm not proud of my relationship with Greg. It was at a time in my life when I was lost and trying to figure out who I was. As it turns out, I didn't find her until I was on my own.

He holds up both hands. "Wait, wait, wait. He proposed, and you turned him down?"

"Yup."

He blinks. "Don't most couples talk about getting married before it happens?"

I shrug. "He didn't."

He's looking at me like he's just unlocked some type of secret code, and it's a little unnerving. "Why did you say no?"

Now it's my turn to give him an incredulous look. "Because I didn't want to marry him."

He scrunches his nose playfully. "Were you nice about it? Did he take it hard?"

"Of course, I was nice," I say with a laugh. What happened between Greg and me was years ago. He's long since found a girl to marry him, and I'm pretty sure they have multiple children together.

He appraises me again with a smug look on his face.

"What?" I ask with another huff of laughter. "Don't look at me like that."

His smile warms. "You're different than I thought."

I raise an eyebrow as I bring the glass to my lips. "And how's that?"

Wiggling his fingers in my direction, he says, "Less prickly."

"Oh, don't be fooled." I give him a pointed stare. "I can be very prickly."

His smile stretches, and it's impossible to keep my own at

bay. Nothing feels small sitting across from this man. Everything about him is significant. Like just his presence somehow makes the wine sweeter, the music better, and the atmosphere more electric.

"Remind me not to get on your bad side." He holds my gaze, like he has full intentions of getting on that side just to see what it entails.

But that look.

He looks like he's delighted by the sheer fact I'm sitting across from him. Like nothing could make him happier than watching me sip wine. I thought I had encountered looks like this before, but now that I'm sitting here with Chase, I'm not sure. He looks like he has at least a thousand thoughts floating around in his head but reveals none of them. And I'm dying to know what they are.

"What about you?" I ask.

Something sparks in those brown eyes. "What about me?"

I gesture toward his overall physique. "This is all very put together." I eye him shamelessly. "Neat." A slow smile pulls at the corner of his mouth, so I keep going. "What's it hiding? Are you secretly a hoarder? Or is your car just filled with garbage?"

His deep laugh warms my chest more than the wine, but his only other response is a swift shake of his head as he looks down at his drink on the table. His thumb wipes away some of the condensation, and he simply says, "No."

"No to which?" I rest my chin on my hand as I stare at him, perfectly aware of the wine's effect on me. "I might be able to look past the car, but I need to know if I'm signing up to be friends with a hoarder."

His eyes flick upward to meet mine on the word "friends," and his stare unnervingly pins me in place. It only lasts a second before he lifts his head and casually says, "You could be friends with a hoarder. Just don't go to their house. But could you date a hoarder?" He tilts his head from side to side. "Probably not."

I swallow hard, but manage to choke out, "All I'm saying is that this . . ."—I gesture toward him again—"is very suspicious."

He grins. "Well, I give you full permission to scope out both my car and apartment any time you'd like."

I'm more tempted than I should be. I doubt Chase and I will become real friends. We'll probably stay light acquaintances that get together for drinks occasionally at best, but considering the effect he has, even that might be too much for me.

Or not enough?

I settle on him again with his kind eyes and soft looking lips. With his broad shoulders and muscular forearms. Nothing about this man says friendship. Everything about him says he could fuck me against his bedroom wall.

I mentally scold myself. For my own sanity, I need to find what it is that makes him less attractive. There's always something. When you first meet someone, they're full of potential. All the things they *could* be. But, of course, they're never really those things. There's always something that comes as a slight disappointment, like maybe he always talks about the future instead of enjoying the present. Maybe he goes on and on about weekends by the lake with all the in-laws and cousins, and every mention of your future hypothetical children feels like a death sentence.

Shaking off the memories, I blurt, "I don't want kids." The words come out in a panic, and I finish off the rest of my wine.

Pulling his head back, he blinks. "I don't like chocolate."

My words stutter, catching on my tongue. I needed him to say he *does* want kids. I needed that deal-breaker out in the open. His wanting kids would have been the perfect thing to friend-zone him. "Y—what?" I finally get out.

"Oh, is it my turn again?" He thinks, making a dramatic show of it. "I also don't like the Marvel movies."

I stare at him, a bewildered smile slowly spreading on my face. "You . . . that's not what I was trying to do," I say with a laugh.

He cocks an eyebrow and there's a playful glint in his eyes. "No? So, you just thought that I—as your friend—needed to know your stance on childbearing?"

My cheeks flush. "No." I shake my head, suddenly wishing I had stopped at two glasses instead of three. "I don't know."

"Look, Candace." He leans forward to level with me, and I catch a whiff of his intoxicating cologne, warm spices and teakwood flooding my senses. "I think it's great you don't want kids—fantastic even. But I think the more pressing issue here is how difficult it can be to find a good dessert without chocolate in it."

A faint smile pulls at my lips, but it feels like something inside me is cracking. I was hoping he'd argue with me. I was hoping his response would drive a wedge between us—something tangible I could use to separate myself from him. But instead, he somehow gave me the best response anyone has ever given me. "Oh, I think you have plenty of options," I say in a feeble attempt to recover.

"It can't have fruit either. All the desserts without chocolate always have fruit for some reason. What's the deal with that?"

Laughter bubbles in my chest, and the way he smiles in response makes me ache for something. For the rest of the night, I can't put my finger on what it is exactly, but I know it's something I've never had.

eleven

IN THE REFLECTION of the mirror, I make eye contact with my client, Michelle. My fingers run through her new cut and color, lightly giving her hair movement so she can see the added layers. We threw in a few lowlights too, since she was becoming "too blonde" as she put it.

I was tempted to tell her about the guy I recently met who would likely disagree but stopped myself. I don't usually tell my clients about my personal life—at least nothing I can't predict the outcome of, anyway. They know Miles is my roommate. They know I don't have any pets, but he's constantly talking about getting a cat. They know I used to bartend after I did hair all day, and they celebrated with me when I finally took the leap to go full time. They know the safe things—the *easy* things.

I make a point not to tell clients about the men I'm interested in, secret aspirations, or deep, dark secrets. And right now, Chase feels a little like all three.

After getting drinks, we walked around the city for a while. We got ice cream from a local creamery and ate as we strolled the streets, talking about everything and nothing. The conversation felt natural. It had none of the back-and-forth interview feel that usually comes with a first date.

Eventually, we ended up outside my apartment, even though his car was parked in front of the wine bar. Him walking me to my door was a sweet gesture, for a *friend*, but even as we stood there, saying goodnight, I was drawn to him. Thanks to the wine, I'm almost certain I watched his mouth as he said goodnight instead of looking him in the eye, and when he reached out a hand and said, "This was fun, Candace," it felt like someone had dumped a bucket of ice water over my head.

It *was* fun. It was the most fun I've had on a date in a long time—friends or not. Maybe that's why I keep replaying the night in my head. Going over his comments and motions. Analyzing times when he *could* have been flirting but wasn't.

He paid for my drinks, insisting I'd be able to do the same next time.

He walked me home.

He texted me as soon as he got home with a, "I can't tell you how much I needed that," text.

He has done all the things I'd want him to do if it were a real date. Even the past few days have been sprinkled with random texts to make me laugh, and I'm not sure how he does it. It feels like he knows me so well even though we met less than a week ago.

And through Miles's entire interrogation afterward, I couldn't stop smiling.

"It's perfect like always!" Michelle puts a hand on my arm, forcing me back to the present. "Please, don't ever leave. I don't think I could trust anyone else with my hair."

Giving her a warm smile, I reassure her. "I'm not going anywhere."

She grins and gets to her feet to dig out cash from her

purse. While she's counting, my phone vibrates in my back pocket. Somehow, I know it's Chase.

After saying goodbye to Michelle with a quick hug, I tuck the money into my apron and pull out my phone. Sure enough, Chase's name stares at me from the notification bar, and I have to bite back my smile.

CHASE:

Free today?

Two words. There are only two words, and somehow my entire mood has lifted.

CANDACE:

Saturdays at the salon are crazy busy. What's up?

CHASE:

Oh, right. Hairdresser. How are you holding up?

I look around at the state of my station. There's hair on the floor, dirty towels near the wash area, an empty shampoo bottle that needs to be thrown away, and tubes of Framesi color lying next to a dirty mixing bowl.

CANDACE:

I might need to squeeze in time to get some caffeine, but other than that, I'm holding.

CHASE:

Understandable.

I had to come into the office, so I'm downtown. I'll be there soon.

I stare at his message, trying to understand it. While we were out Thursday, I forgot to ask him what he does for work.

He's always dressed in a way that screams nine to five, so I didn't think he'd be one to work weekends.

As tempting as it is to text him back and ask him what he means, I don't have time to get into it with him. I set down my phone and start cleaning up. My next client will be here in fifteen minutes, and the place needs to be spotless before then.

After putting everything else away, I stand at the sink to clean out the small mixing bowl and color brush. The hot water used to sting my skin, but over the years I've gotten used to it.

"I wasn't sure what you liked, so I got a vanilla latte. Vanilla is always a safe choice."

I look over my shoulder to find Chase standing with a coffee in each hand. His hair is more relaxed, and he's wearing faded wash jeans with a gray T-shirt. It takes a minute for me to speak. How does he look so good in business attire *and* like this?

"Hey," I say before turning off the water and wiping my hands on my apron. "How do you know where I work?"

"I went with iced because I figured blow-dryers are hot." He hands me the cup. "Hope that's okay."

I stare at him.

"Oh, and the other night when we were walking, you proudly pointed over here and said, 'That's where I work.'" He gives me an amused look. "You don't remember?"

Now that he mentions it, I can vaguely recall. "Well, thank you." I lift the coffee to my lips and take a sip. "You can't go wrong with something like a vanilla latte."

He smiles an easy, beautiful smile as he leans against the side of my cabinet. Past him, Amanda has her wide eyes locked on me and mouths, "Client?"

I give her a subtle shake of my head as I take another sip, but it doesn't go unnoticed. Chase looks over his shoulder at

Amanda, who resumes sweeping hair off the floor like it's her life's mission.

When he brings his attention back to me, he has an eyebrow cocked. "A friend of yours?"

I glare at him playfully. "Yes. A very blonde, very off-limits friend of mine." He can have all the blondes in the world, just not that one. Not yet anyway. If I ever get to a point where having him near me doesn't thicken the air, then so be it.

His warm eyes shimmer at my response, the playful mischief inside him waking at the sound of my threat. "Why?"

Well, I certainly can't tell him the air thickening reason. With a shrug, I say, "She's too young for you."

"You don't know how old I am."

He's right—annoyingly right. I tilt my head like I haven't been scrutinizing his every detail since he walked in here. When we got drinks on Thursday, he was clean shaven. Now the smooth skin has a perfect layer of stubble. It's just enough to make me think he might even be a little older than me, but I'm not sure. Some men are just blessed with great facial hair.

"You're trying to figure it out, aren't you?" he asks.

I straighten. "It doesn't matter."

Another lift of his brow, that familiar look of amusement flashing across his features. "I'm too old for her, but it doesn't matter how old I am?" When I don't answer right away, he tilts his head. "You're young. How old are you?"

"Do you always go around asking women how old they are?"

"I ask my friends lots of things."

The way he's looking at me makes me forget my age for a moment. "Um, twenty-seven."

He puts a relaxed hand to his chest. "Twenty-eight. See, that wasn't so bad. We've learned a lot about each other today." He raises his drink as a sort of salute and takes a sip.

I let out a breath of laughter. "All we learned is our ages."

His lips are still at his cup when he smiles at my response, and it feels like my hands could melt all the ice in my coffee. "Not true." Lowering his drink, he says, "I also learned that your friend over there is off-limits, and that you felt the need to make sure I knew that."

"There's the blonde thing to consider."

He looks down at his drink, a subtle smirk forming. "Ah, yes. How dare I have a type?" He nods, agreeing with whatever I'm not saying. "They should lock me up."

My lips twist, and when his dark eyes lift to meet mine, his smirk only grows.

The bell chimes as my next client walks through the door. She's the daughter of another client—a bit of a moody teenager, but she usually has no fear when it comes to her hair, so that can be fun.

"She's here for me," I say to Chase as I set down my drink. "Thanks again for the coffee."

"Of course. Can't have you falling asleep at the chair." He gives a slight nod. "Have a good day, Candace."

I give him a brief smile. "You too," I say quickly before turning my attention to the girl getting settled in my chair. "Hey! How are you?"

She answers something generic, like "fine" or "good," but I don't catch it. I'm too busy replaying my last interaction with Chase. Even without the caffeine, I think I'd be buzzing from his presence alone.

twelve

THANKS TO MY SURPRISE COFFEE, I'm still full of energy after working later than expected. Amanda was there late too and asked if I wanted to grab a drink. There's a sit-down restaurant down the street from the salon that has a full bar, so sometimes we come here for wine and appetizers after a long day. Today, Amanda ordered an elaborate Christmas-themed drink with a cinnamon stick poking out of the glass. She hums along to the instrumental rendition of "Let It Snow" playing fully in the holiday spirit, but I keep forgetting it's December. I don't know what's with me this year. I guess most years I get daily calls while my parents transform their house into a winter wonderland, and last year, the bar I worked at had us wear Christmas themed socks and shirts during the month of December. Maybe this is the year for creating new traditions.

Amanda quickly sets down her drink like she's just remembered something. "I had no idea you were seeing someone!"

"I'm not seeing anyone."

"But that guy! Who was he? The one who brought you coffee."

I'm barely able to stifle a groan. He's the last thing I want to talk about. Amanda knows a little about my past dating life, but I don't think I'm close enough with her to divulge my ridiculous crush on a man who never meant to ask me out in the first place.

"Oh, he's just a friend." It's the truth. It is one hundred percent the truth, but it feels like the biggest lie I've ever told. As much as I want to only see Chase as a friend, there's something about him that makes my entire body hum happily. It's more than genuinely enjoying being around a friend. I think it may even be more than wanting to sleep with him, too. I don't know a lot about him, but I can see him pulling me into the dangerous territory where those two things merge.

She raises her eyebrows, not believing me. "I wish all my friends looked like that."

I laugh. "You also thought Miles was hot when you first saw him."

"Miles *is* hot." Her eyes widen. "Oh, *that's* why he's your friend." She shakes her head. "Damn. I swear they get all the good ones."

I can't fight my smile. "No, Chase isn't gay. He's just . . ." I shrug. "A friend."

"I think we should change that."

"Sure, I'll get right on it," I say, but the only thing we need to change is what we're talking about. "When are you free for me to show you how I layer foils for balayage?"

"I do still want you to do that," she answers with a sharp nod of her head. "But don't change the subject. Seriously, Candace, when is the last time a guy brought you coffee?"

After Greg, all my flings were just that—a few overly optimistic weeks or months that always either fizzled out or ended with him not being the man I thought he was.

And that doesn't even count the last year. For the past

twelve months, I haven't had anything that remotely resembled a relationship. Even the thought of the title feels foreign.

"Yes, Chase brought me coffee. Which is great, but it doesn't mean anything." I hold up my phone for her to see. "We barely talk."

She points. "It looks like someone texted you."

I turn the screen toward me, and sure enough, a notification from Chase is front and center.

"Is it him?" Amanda asks, and based on the smile in her voice, she already knows the answer.

Opening the message, I read.

> CHASE:
> I need to ask for a favor.
>
> It's a big favor, and I'm hoping you'll say yes, but also no pressure.

My heart rate rises at the thought of him needing anything from me. It looks like he sent it only three minutes ago. His ears must have been ringing.

> CANDACE:
> I'm not cutting your hair.

It's the only thing I can think he might need from me.

> CHASE:
> Not that.
>
> Although I do have full intentions of you being the one to cut my hair next.

"What does it say?" Amanda prompts. I almost forgot she was sitting across from me.

"Sorry," I say as I glance between her and my phone. "He's asking for a favor."

She wiggles her eyebrows suggestively. "Ooh. What type of favor?"

My phone lights up on the table and both our eyes jump to the screen.

As I reach for it, I say, "I guess we're about to find out."

> **CHASE:**
>
> Will you be my date for my company's Christmas party?
>
> I know, I know. As friends, but no one else there has to know that.

"He wants me to . . ." I frown at the messages, not sure if I should even open this door. I look up at Amanda and she's clinging to my every word. It's too late to backtrack now. "He wants me to go to his company Christmas party with him . . . as his fake date."

"Yes." She nods eagerly.

A burst of laughter leaves my lips. "You think I should actually agree to that?"

Somehow, her eyes widen even more. "You have to!" She relaxes a little as she goes on to say, "Listen. I don't know this guy, but he's hot." She points to me. "You're hot." She circles her finger in the direction of my phone. "And a fake date situation between two hot people is hot as hell."

"Right." I glance down at the screen before looking back at her, silently asking if it's rude of me to answer.

She waves her hand encouragingly. "Tell him yes."

But I don't tell him yes. Instead, I send a text to clarify for good measure.

> **CANDACE:**
>
> You want me to fake date you at your company Christmas party?

His response comes in right away.

CHASE:

Well, when you put it that way . . .

Yes.

I let out a laugh, but I don't answer him again.

Amanda leans over the table to catch a glimpse of my text. "Did you say yes?"

I shake my head as I set my phone down on the table again. "No, I'll answer him when I'm home and figure out what's going on."

"You're going to that party. Don't torture the man by making him wait for an answer." She holds her glass to her lips. "Do I need to chug this so you can go home and accept the invitation, or do you want to just text him here?" Amanda has never been shy when it comes to her opinion.

"You're stuck on this, aren't you?"

She nods. "I am. I saw him today, and that's reason enough. But I saw you today, too. You like him."

"I barely know him."

"But you like him."

I hold her stare, determined to prove her wrong but also not sure how much it's worth it. What's the point of lying to her?

"I might like him," I finally relent. Holding up a finger, I add, "But he's made it very clear I'm not his type. This won't turn into anything."

"But it could."

"But it won't."

She nods to my phone. "Text him."

A wave of uncertainty washes over me as I slowly reach for my phone again. Glancing at his last message, I pause before typing one-word.

> CANDACE:
> Okay.

My phone buzzes on the table, but this time, it's not a text—or even a double text. He's calling me. I'm sure all the blood has drained from my face, considering how much Amanda finds this funny.

"You can answer it!" she says with a laugh.

I shake my head. "No way. I'm here with you."

She rolls her eyes, but I reject the call before sending him a quick message.

> CANDACE:
> Out. I'll call you on my walk home.

I put my phone down on the table again, determined not to look at it until I leave. When I look up at Amanda, she takes another sip with that same, smug look on her face.

"Do I even want to know what you're thinking?" I ask, suddenly feeling more tired than I have all night.

She shrugs innocently. "I've just never seen you like this. Usually, you get mildly annoyed when guys call you. You'll wonder out loud 'Why can't he just text me?' I've never seen you so . . ." She gestures toward me with a circling hand. "Flustered."

"I am not flustered." Even as the words leave my lips, I feel the need to wipe my brow.

"No, definitely not," she says with a giggle.

"Can you tell me what's new with you? Please?" I don't think I've ever felt like more of a spectacle.

She nods, finally giving in. To my surprise, she doesn't bring up Chase or his company Christmas party for the rest of the night. Instead, we laugh, talk hair, and vent about some of the other stylists who never pick up after themselves. Everything starts to settle into our usual night out with drinks, and by the time we're ready to leave, my breathing comes easier, and my cheeks hurt from laughing.

"Have a great weekend!" She waves as she heads left toward her car, and I go right toward my apartment. "And keep me updated!"

She doesn't have to say the last part is a reference to Chase. I wave goodbye with a slight shake of my head. It isn't until she turns around that I'm brave enough to look at my phone again. I can only imagine the chain of messages he sent after I ignored his call.

I stare at my phone screen. There's nothing. Not a single notification from him. I told him I was out, and that I'd call him after, so why am I so disappointed by the sight?

thirteen

I SWIPE my phone open and press the call button next to his name.

He answers on the second ring. "Hey, Candace." He sounds calm, and confident, and genuinely happy to hear from me.

"Hey. I'm sorry I couldn't take your call earlier."

"Don't be sorry. Did you have fun?"

"I did." My words come out a little slow because even though the entire night was fun, I think him asking me to this Christmas party was the most exciting part.

"Well, I hope it wasn't a date. If it was, he should be the one walking you home right now, not me."

A chuckle leaves my lips. "No. Not a date. And I'm not sure this counts as you walking me home."

"Oh, it totally counts. We don't live in some fairytale city, Candace. Someone should make sure you get home."

"And you're that person?"

"I seem to be. It's not a role I remember signing up for, but it's one I'm happy to take." There's a pause before he adds, "Seriously. If you ever need anything, call me. It doesn't matter if it's past midnight or that I've just downed three fingers of bourbon . . . twice."

I pull my phone away from my ear to check the time. It's not just past midnight, it's almost one. It feels like Amanda and I only went out for a short time together, but then again, we did end up closing the salon just after 9:30 tonight.

"Shit. I'm sorry. I had no idea how late it was."

"Candace, stop apologizing. Did you hear me? Call me. Always call me."

"Yes, but you were apparently drunk when you said that."

He laughs on the other end, and it brings a smile to my lips. "Not drunk. I just couldn't sleep. I thought the bourbon might help."

"And did it?"

"Not even a little."

"Why can't you sleep?"

Chase sighs. "Work, stress . . . more work, more stress."

I've reached the front of my apartment and head inside. "What do you do?"

"Advertising. And my boss . . . Well, she's a piece of work sometimes."

"I thought you said your boss loves you?" I try to keep my voice steady as I walk through the lobby.

A humorless laugh travels over the phone. "Oh, she does. Maybe a little too much. That's actually why I need your help for the Christmas party."

"Okay?" I say, not sure where this is going.

"Look, I love my job. I'm up for a promotion, so I never say no to anything the company asks. I put in the extra hours and all that, but my boss . . . She's very nice, but . . ." There's a pause.

"Chase, just say whatever you're trying to say." I fiddle with the keys in my lock, and wonder if Miles is home, or if he'll come home at all tonight. He mentioned going on a date.

"Last year at the Christmas party, she got drunk and cornered me under the mistletoe." The words come out in a rush, and I stop what I'm doing, my ears catching up, processing on a delay. After a pause, he goes on to say, "Avoiding her for the rest of the party was exhausting, and I don't want to do it again. I thought if I brought a date this year, she'd get the message."

"You'd rather bring a fake date than just tell her you're not interested?" I've started moving again, and when I head into my apartment, it's empty. I turn on a table lamp and lie back on the couch.

He groans. "I have told her, Candace. You don't understand."

Something in his voice makes me take him more seriously. "Have you filed anything with HR?"

"No, I don't want to. I mean—I *want* to, but not until I get my promotion. Who knows, by then she won't be my boss anymore, so it will probably stop. Right now, I think she just feels like she has this power over me or something. I've told her it will never happen. It's all harmless for the most part, but she's relentless."

I frown. I had no idea he was dealing with so much stress related to his job. "Well, I'm happy to help in any way I can."

"Thanks. We can talk about it more later." His words muffle like he's running a hand over his face. "Did you make it home?"

"I did. Thanks for walking me."

His laugh sounds tired. "Anytime. I mean it."

My eyebrows furrow as I stare at my ceiling and run a hand through my hair. He seems like he cares—really cares.

Before I can ask, he says, "Hey, I should probably call it a night. The bourbon is kicking in, and I'm either going to fall asleep on the phone with you or start saying ridiculous shit I'll have to explain in the morning. I'd rather not put you through either."

I could argue that I'd be happy with either of those things happening, but instead, I smile even though he can't see me and say, "Goodnight, Chase."

"Goodnight, Candace."

I don't want to hang up, but I force myself to hit the red button first. Letting out a long breath, I imagine what going to this party with him means. Will he touch me? Kiss me? Will I be able to walk away from it all unscathed? The answers are most likely yes, yes, and . . . no.

fourteen

SUNDAYS ARE MY SATURDAYS. Nothing beats when the streets are vibrant and full of life. Miles and I usually get brunch, but even though I slept until almost 10:00 a.m. and have already cleaned most of the apartment, he still isn't back.

The quiet buzz of what sounds like a small electric saw comes from upstairs, and I wonder what Lenny is up to as I pull out my phone and text Miles.

CANDACE:

Just checking in.

It's not the first time he's been out all night, but it's rare. He must really like this guy. If he didn't, he would have been back last night, or he would have snuck out early this morning. He doesn't answer until after I've taken a shower and dried my hair. I'm standing in the bathroom, waiting for my curling iron to heat when he sends his text.

MILES:

Wait until I tell you about this man.

He can have my babies.

I snort a laugh as I type my response.

> CANDACE:
> Hear about him? I want to meet him after a statement like that.

This time, he immediately answers.

> MILES:
> All in time. I'll be home later.

Lifting the hot iron, I grab a small piece of hair and smooth the iron over the strands before expertly twisting my wrist to form a curl. As much as I love styling other people's hair, I don't get the same enjoyment out of doing mine. It feels like work, and the last thing I want to do on my day off is work. Luckily, it isn't too long, and it's easy enough to style. Otherwise, I'm not sure I'd have the patience.

The only thing missing from my Sunday morning is a freshly brewed latte. Throwing on a pair of jeans with a black loose-fit shirt tucked in to the front, I grab my sunglasses and head out the door. I still wouldn't say Florida *feels like winter*, but today offers a welcome break in the heat. It's the type of weather that lets you sit outside at a restaurant without being the thing that's cooking, and around here, that's all we can hope for.

There is a Christmas parade happening in the cobblestone streets. People crowd the edge of the sidewalk, leaving little room for anyone trying to go about their daily lives. As I weave through families and groups of friends, my lips lift at the sight. There's something so wholesome about seeing everyone get together to watch dancing elves as "Rockin' Around the Christmas Tree" plays from a nearby candy cane float. The sight reminds me of the candy cane forest my parents usually put somewhere in their front yard, and I hope they're enjoying the break this year.

But even with all the music and dancing elves, it's someone else that catches my attention as I approach Southern Roast. At this point, I'd recognize his figure anywhere, but the sight of Chase still has my stomach free floating.

He stands in front of the shop like he's debating going inside. His hand wipes across his mouth, and even though his face isn't pressed up against the glass, it's clear he's trying to get a look inside.

His hair is more relaxed, like it was yesterday, and I have to fight the urge to run my fingers through the thick, brunette locks. The stubble on his face is a little more noticeable, too. He must not shave on weekends. He's the type of guy who would look *great* with a beard, but I think I'd miss seeing his face if he grew one. His T-shirt should have a relaxed fit, but it's a little tighter around his muscular arms and shoulders. The way the fabric stretches over his chest and back allows my mind to wonder what he might look like underneath.

Slipping my sunglasses on top of my head, I say, "Not here for the parade?"

He looks over at me and laughs before rubbing the back of his neck. Looking over his shoulder at the dance number happening behind him, he shakes his head. "I'm busted, aren't I?"

Amusement pulls at my lips. "Looking for a certain barista?"

"Avoiding maybe?" He winces. "You're here to save me, aren't you?"

His words wrap me in warmth, but I try to shake it off by reaching for the door. When I pull it open and glance inside, there's no sight of blonde hair anywhere. Looking back at him, I say, "The coast is clear, you big baby."

Bouncing on his toes, he follows after me with a little more pep in his step. As he reaches for the door, holding it open, he asks, "So, what are you doing here? Meeting someone?"

I shake my head while my eyes scan the menu boards above. "Nope. I was planning on grabbing something to go."

Keeping his eyes on the boards above, he shrugs next to me. "Or we could stay."

Not bothering to hide my surprise, I ask, "No plans?"

He shakes his head. "None I'd choose over this."

I blink, unsure how to respond to that.

When I don't say anything, he pulls his eyes away from the menus to look at me. "Well, that and we should probably discuss our agreement."

He says it so casually, but those words echo in the back of my mind.

Our agreement.

The one where I'm supposed to pretend I'm this irresistible man's girlfriend all while adamantly trying to resist him.

Yeah. We should probably discuss that.

With a sharp inhale, I nod. "Yeah. Okay. We can do that."

Once we make our way to the front, I order a gingerbread latte and Chase steps forward, to say, "Coffee's on me," before ordering his black.

"No way," I say, gently turning to look up at him. "You said I could get the next one, remember?"

He has his card already out and doesn't even hesitate to hand it to the barista. "I meant the next time I drink bourbon."

My eyes narrow, but there's no point fighting him on it. The barista takes his card, swipes it, and hands it back in a matter of seconds. And when he touches the small of my back to guide me toward a table, I've forgotten how to speak, anyway.

He touches me so effortlessly, like he has no idea the effect it has. How could a man like him not *know* what he does to women? How could this man not know what he does to *me?* His touch might as well stop time. Everything slows. The only thing that doesn't is my rapidly beating heart.

On second thought, based on the number of women in his tagged photos, he probably does know. He probably does these things for that very reason.

The weekend brings more people here than usual, but most of them take their drinks outside to watch the parade. We grab a small table near the large glass window on the side of the shop where we can enjoy the festivities from afar while we talk. There's a fake Christmas tree in the back corner, clearly worn out by years of use. Its pine needles have thinned, revealing the black plastic trunk beneath, and I stare at it.

Chase follows my gaze. "Why are you looking at that tree like you have a personal vendetta against it."

I glance at him before looking back at the tree. "It's kind of disappointing, isn't it?"

He looks over his shoulder again, this time taking a longer look at the tiny, fake tree with shiny decorations that are disproportionately too big. Facing me, he grins. "I think it's inspiring."

I let out a laugh and bring my cup to my mouth. "You would."

He mirrors my movement with his own cup. "It's like the little tree that could."

"You know," I say as I sit up straight and abandon all thoughts of the tree. "Just once, I think it would be nice to go somewhere that actually feels like Christmas for the holidays."

There's a teasing glint in his eye. "Do we need to go buy fake snow? Because as useless as it is, we can go buy fake snow."

"No," I say with a laugh. "I want to go somewhere with *real* things that feel like Christmas. I've lived in Florida all my life. I just want Christmas to feel the way it looks in the movies for once."

"You know what I think?" He puts a hand on his chest. "As

someone who has experienced countless snowy winters and now a few hot ones." He looks at me like that fact alone is some magical credential that will justify whatever he's about to say next.

"Go on." I give him a wave of my hand.

He takes a sip of his coffee, looking smug but somehow still beautiful. "I think Christmas is what you make it. If it's not feeling like Christmas to you, maybe you should stop being such a Scrooge."

My eyes widen. "I am not!"

He nods solemnly. "I think you are." Brightening, he adds, "Don't worry, though. You're coming to my company's holiday party, and nothing puts you in the spirit like overpriced champagne and tiny desserts."

I tilt my head with a teasing lift to my lips. "Overpriced? No open bar?"

Chase nods, swallowing his sip. "Oh, it will be. I just imagine the champagne being overpriced for them." He gives a shrug. "Corporate America."

Mention of the party has an immediate effect on me, my heart rate beginning its inevitable climb. "Right." Determined to look more casual than I feel, I ask, "Where do you work, anyway? I just keep imagining Christmas episodes from *The Office*, and I'm not sure I'm on the right track."

He chuckles, and it's such a lovely sound. "Not quite like that. The party we're going to will be . . . bigger."

I eye him cautiously. "How big?"

"Big."

". . . As in?"

He smiles. "Look, I work for a successful advertising firm. Pitches, clients, terrible bosses. If you've seen *Mad Men*, kind of like that, but fast forward however many years and make it all digital."

I may be able to put on a front for a single client, but

pitching my ideas to a room of people? No thanks. "That sounds . . . stressful."

"It is," he says appreciatively, like I'm the first person to understand what he's been saying for years. He gets more comfortable as he leans back and rests his ankle on the opposite knee. "Anyway, thank you for agreeing to this."

I take a small sip. "I'm not sure what I'm fully agreeing to, but you're welcome."

His lips quirk. "That's why it's great we ran into each other. We can iron out the details."

Like how much he'll have to touch me? And if we'll kiss? And how many times? "Sounds good. When is it?"

"December 20th. It's a Friday, after work."

"Perfect. And how should I dress?"

"Very . . . nice."

I lift an eyebrow. "Fancy?"

He winces. "A bit. If you want to buy a dress for it, I'll cover the cost."

I shake my head. "No. I'm sure I have something. My roommate can help with that."

I try to think of a question outside of the ones that are screaming in my head about whether his mouth will be on mine at any point. He's only ever touched my hand or my lower back—briefly—and it was enough to send my nerves into a frenzy. The thought of kissing him, even if it's fake—even if it means absolutely nothing—has me equal parts excited and terrified. Excited because . . . well, look at him. And terrified because if he's already affecting me this much, it's going to be hard to stand my ground. My eyes have wandered to his lips again, and when my eyes flick up to meet his, he's watching me intently.

I clear my throat and sit up straight. "Do I need to bring anything?"

A trace of a smile. "Just your wonderful company."

"Right," I say with a nod. "My company . . ." But it's not just the pleasure of my company. If that were the case, we'd be going as friends.

There's a slight crease between his brows, like he's trying to read me. He leans forward to level with me, his coffee resting between his hands. "We don't have to do anything you don't want to."

I suppress a scoff. I'm not worried about the things I don't want to do. I'm worried about the things I will want to do but shouldn't. "But?"

A breath of laughter leaves him as he glances down at his cup before locking those mahogany eyes back on me. "But I've known these people for years. They know me."

I know exactly what he's implying, so I simply say, "And they won't believe it unless . . .?"

He studies me. His eyes jumping between mine. His lips press together slightly, and he looks more serious this way, like he's trying to solve a puzzle. "Can I kiss you?"

Air gets stuck in my throat. Does he mean now? In the middle of this bustling coffee shop with all these people and dancing elves outside? My heart races, and my eyes dart to our surroundings, but I swallow hard and nod. "Okay."

But he doesn't make a move to kiss me. He doesn't move at all. Those dark eyes just fall to my mouth, and he agrees, "Okay."

"Anything else?" I cross my legs and take another sip, desperate to look like I didn't think he was about to kiss me at this very moment.

His gaze shoots up to meet mine. "Maybe we should have a safe word."

I nearly choke on my coffee. "A *safe word?* What exactly are you planning on doing to me?"

Those beautiful brown eyes widen. "Nothing like what you're probably thinking," he says quickly. He runs a hand through his hair, and I love the way it always sticks up after he does. "I just want to make sure you're comfortable. We should pick a word, and if either of us uses it, we'll know we've crossed a line."

I raise an eyebrow. "Either of us?"

"Well, yeah." He tilts his head playfully. "Most of my girlfriends have touched me in one way or another."

"Right." My cheeks warm. Why am I so affected by this? Of course, I'll have to play the part. Agreeing to this doesn't just mean being touched and kissed by Chase, it means I'll have to be the one doing those things, too. I blink the thoughts away. "Sure. A safe word is a good idea."

He drums his fingers on the tabletop as he thinks. "What about 'fake snow?'"

I laugh. "Will there be fake snow at the party? Because if so, there's a good chance I'll talk about it."

"God, I hope not," he says with a grimace. "I'd like to think my company can do better, but you never know."

His response only makes me laugh harder. "You know, as tacky as it is, there's something beautiful about fake snow."

He gives me a sideways glance, his eyes untrusting.

"Think about it," I say with a smile. "It makes the impossible feel possible. There has to be some type of metaphorical beauty in something like that."

"Fake snow is an embarrassment to real snow everywhere, but I like to see you getting into the Florida Christmas spirit." His hand rests on mine, and you'd think he just licked my ear with the way my body reacts.

With a tight-lipped smile, I pull my hand from his and bring my cup to my lips. "I love how passionate you are about this."

"More people should be." He waves the topic away. "Okay, so not a great safe word."

"What about Jack Frost?"

He cocks an eyebrow. "The guy who makes it snow?"

"Yeah. I mean, it's not like he'll be the talk of the party, and I don't see why we'd have a reason to bring him up outside of it."

He mulls it over. "I like it."

"Glad you approve," I say with a hint of sarcasm.

Chase smiles, but his attention locks on something behind me. A rush of sound from the holiday parade outside floods the shop as someone opens the door to enter. Looking over my shoulder, I scan the room. It still looks as busy as it did when we got here. There's a small line of people waiting to order their holiday themed drinks. But then I see her. I see her long, blonde hair and bright smile as she walks in to start her shift.

I might not have noticed her when we were in here the other day, but based on the way Chase's eyes track her every movement, it's definitely her. It's the girl he wanted to ask out in the first place.

Well, Merry Christmas to me.

fifteen

THE SHIFT in his demeanor is subtle, but I see it. Gone is the confident, easy-going man who sat across from me moments ago, now to be replaced by a guy who looks like he doesn't want to be noticed.

Something so small—so quick—but so painfully loud. I know the girl has a boyfriend, but he clearly doesn't want her to see him here with me.

"Do you want to leave?" I ask.

He blinks. "Because of her?"

I nod.

That flawless, easy smile of his returns, but there's a trace of apprehension in his eyes. "I can take being rejected, Candace." He sits up straight, his playfulness returning. "Some might say I even thrive on it."

Holding his stare, a smile gradually warms my features. "You would."

He grins like I've complimented him.

"But we can still leave if you want to."

Without taking the time to think about his response, Chase shakes his head. "No. We still need to talk about this party."

My eyebrows furrow. "What else is there to talk about?"

"I think we should practice."

My mouth goes dry, and I take another sip. "Practice what exactly?"

"Being around each other in a way that's . . ." He wipes a hand over his mouth as he tries to find the right words.

"Convincing?"

"Convincing," he says with a nod, his voice rough.

"Makes sense." He can call it practice, but I'll call it desensitizing. This will be good. This will help me get over this stupid infatuation I have.

God, I hope he's a terrible kisser.

Chase doesn't have a view of the counter, but I do. The blonde barista can't take her eyes off him. She even mutters something to her coworker while her eyes stay locked on Chase. "Don't look, but I'm pretty sure they're talking about you."

He freezes mid-sip. "And what makes you think that?"

Raising my eyebrows, I take a deep breath. "Well, she keeps looking at you."

Slowly setting down his cup, he says, "Uh-huh."

"And talking to her coworker."

"Okay."

"And talking to her coworker while she's looking at you."

His lips press into a thin line, but it only lasts a moment before he shrugs it off. "Well, she's the one with the boyfriend. Not my problem." He smirks. "She's probably just surprised to see I've moved on so quickly."

I scoff. "Right."

He considers me before leaning forward and taking my hand in his. His thumb traces the backs of my knuckles, and the contact sends a rush through me. His touch is slow and gentle, but deliberate. Every graze of his fingertips against my skin feels like a strategic move in whatever game of chess he's playing. My entire body freezes at his touch, but I'm the opposite of cold. Liquid heat warms my core, and I desperately try to slow my shallow breaths as I hold his gaze.

"I have moved on. You're incredible, you know that?" He turns my hand over and traces one of the lines of my palm. Keeping his eyes trained on our hands, his fingers trace up my forearm and my entire body tingles. "Beautiful." His eyes flick up to meet mine with a devilish glint. "How's that for practice?"

The air finally leaves my lungs in a sudden rush.

Right. Practice.

I'm pretty sure my neck has turned a deep shade of pink, so I rest my chin in my free hand with my elbow propped on the table to hide it. "Is that how you talk to all your girlfriends?"

His lips twitch, and he looks down, his hand still tracing the exposed skin at my wrist. "No."

I might not have as much experience as Miles thinks I should when it comes to men, but it's not like a man has never touched me. Even so, of all the men who have ever run their fingers along my skin, none have cast a spell as strong as Chase.

"No?" I manage to get out.

He sits up straight, releasing me from his grasp. Even after I pull my hand back, my skin still tingles at the memory of his touch.

"That's the filtered version. If you and I were really together, there'd be no holding back."

Heart pounding, I tilt my head. "Try me."

"No," he says with a shake of his head and a breath of laughter.

I can't believe he doesn't think I can handle it. "Chase." His name is sharp on my tongue, and the way he snaps to attention, his lips parted, is enough to knock the air from my lungs. I've never said his name before, and by the way he's looking at me, I think he's having the same realization. The air in the room is charged, so I try my best to soften it by saying, "You're being dumb."

A slow smile tugs at his lips. "No, Candace." He says my name pointedly, a spark of mischief behind his eyes. "There are only two words I hope to never hear from you." He holds a finger for each. "Jack and Frost. And if I start saying filthy shit, you'll say both."

I roll my eyes.

"You and I are friends. You deserve respect."

I have never wanted to be disrespected more in my life.

My eyes slide to the barista again. "Is that why she keeps staring at you? Because you said unspeakable things to her while she has a boyfriend?"

He brushes off my comment with a wave of his hand. "Please. She and I didn't get that far. All I did was ask for her number, and she didn't give it to me. Maybe I'd rather spend my time with you, anyway." Chase finishes the last of his coffee before settling his eyes back on me. "Still up for this?"

"Please," I say in the same condescending tone. "You don't scare me." It's a lie. It's probably the biggest lie I've ever told, but the way he grins in response makes the whole thing worth it.

sixteen

MUSIC HITS my ears before I've reached the door to our apartment and fished out my keys. Coming home to Miles in *this* good of a mood is one of my favorite things. Before I even open the door, I know there is an eighty-five percent chance he's dancing somewhere in the apartment—possibly in his underwear.

The music pours into the hallway as I slip inside, and he doesn't hear me set my stuff down. I'm not complaining. From here, I have a great view of him with one leg hitched on the kitchen barstool while he twerks and raps along with Nicki Minaj.

Crossing my arms, I take a moment to fully appreciate the scene in front of me. He isn't in his underwear today, but his shorts are short enough to be mistaken for some, and his tank top has pictures of crabs all over it.

I love this man.

Heading into the kitchen, I make sure to walk around so he can see me. His eyes lock on mine, and his performance only escalates. Popping myself up on the kitchen counter a few feet away, I let my feet dangle and shake my head with a bemused smile.

He reaches for the speaker and turns down the music. "Thank you. Thank you," he says with a slight bow. When his eyes lock on me again, he says, "Where have you been?"

My smile comes out more like a grimace. "I might have a lot to tell you." Reaching out my leg, I tap him with my foot. "But I want to hear about your date first."

"Oh, I'm going to marry this man." I raise my eyebrows, and he shrugs. "Either that or I'll stalk him. The point is, if this man ever gets married, I. Will. Be. There."

"You know I'll help either way," I say with a grin. "When do I get to meet him?"

He leans his head from side to side as he thinks about it. "I don't know."

My eyebrows furrow. Miles has gone on a lot of dates, and he has never once brought up weddings. "Won't you see him again?"

"Oh, definitely." He gives me a reassuring nod. "He's just new to being out, so it might take him longer before he's comfortable coming over here and meeting anyone as my . . . anything."

"That's fair."

He bites his thumbnail. "It is. I'm just excited and want to scream it from the rooftops." He turns around to open the fridge and pulls out a High Noon. "I mean, I've been out since I knew the Pink Power Ranger didn't do it for me, so it's a little hard to wrap my head around, but I get it."

"Give him time," I say with a laugh. "He'll come around, and when he does, I'll be very excited to meet him. What makes this guy so different, anyway?"

"He just feels like a breath of fresh air. You'll love him." He takes a sip of his drink. "So, what's all this stuff you have to tell me? Does it have anything to do with coffee guy's penis?"

"Somewhat." His face lights up, and I point a finger at him. "Don't get too excited." Hopping down from the kitchen counter, I open the fridge and grab my own drink while I catch him up to speed on all things Chase, fake dating, and Christmas parties.

"And he said it's fancy?" he asks once we've moved to the living room and relaxed on the couch.

"Yeah, so I might need your help picking something to wear."

He shakes his head. "We'll go shopping. Nothing in your closet matches that description."

My eyes narrow, but I can't argue with him.

"You know you're playing with fire, right?"

My head falls back against the couch, and I stare at the ceiling. "I know."

"I mean, you have a decent poker face. I'll give you that, but you like this guy."

"I hardly know anything about him." It's true. With all our texting and meet ups, I haven't asked him any of my usual date questions. I know nothing about his family, his upbringing, and I have no idea where he sees himself in five years.

"But you still like him."

Just thinking about my time with Chase makes my chest warm, and I know Miles is right. Maybe not knowing enough about Chase is just making me like him more. Because without concrete facts to shape him as a person, I'm left only with how he makes me feel. And for whatever reason, the amount of fun I have around this man is unmatched. Blowing out a breath, I relent. "I do."

"And you're going to get wrapped up in this."

"Or," I say, perking up. "Maybe this will get rid of whatever illusion I have." Sitting up, I turn to face him and tuck my feet beneath me. "I mean, I barely know him. You know how someone always seems great on the first few dates, but then they aren't."

He looks unconvinced. "Yeah."

"Well," I say, getting more eager to share my theory. "This is a great way for me to realize he isn't as great as he seems without having to dump him. We'll go on a few fake dates, I'll get to know him, and I'll probably find out I don't want to be with him anyway."

"You might . . ." he says with a slow nod.

"I will." I *have* to. Because if I don't figure out what will turn me off for good, I *am* going to get wrapped up in this. I might be good at guarding my heart, but Chase has already broken down the barricades, and I've only known him for a few days.

Miles stares at me for a moment. When he speaks, his words come out slowly, like they've been carefully chosen. "I don't think I've ever seen you like this."

To be fair, I've never felt like this, but Miles doesn't need to know that. I open my mouth in a pathetic attempt to defend myself when my phone vibrates on the couch between us.

Miles arches an eyebrow. "Him?"

Reaching for my phone, I turn it over and look. "Yeah."

> CHASE:
> Let me take you out this week.

"What did he say?"

I glance at Miles before looking back down at my phone. "He wants to get together this week."

Pursing his lips, Miles takes another sip. "Of course he does."

> CANDACE:
> For practice?

> CHASE:
>
> Of course. Strictly practice.

"You look disappointed."

Miles's voice makes my head snap up. "No," I say too quickly. "I'm just trying to figure out my schedule."

"Mhm," he mutters, seeing through my lie.

> CANDACE:
>
> Does Tuesday work?

Miles watches me closely, but I also know Chase will answer in a matter of seconds, so I keep my eyes trained on my phone.

> CHASE:
>
> Tuesdays aren't good for me. My boss always makes me work late.
>
> How about Thursday?

> CANDACE:
>
> Sure. Same place?

> CHASE:
>
> No. I'm picking you up and taking you to dinner.
>
> Dress nice.

"What the fuck are you smiling about?" Miles asks, and I let out a laugh.

"Nothing." I let a smile stretch across my face. "Nothing at all."

seventeen

MILES HOLDS up the little black dress he wanted me to wear last Thursday when I met up with Chase for drinks. "It is time." He holds out the small piece of black fabric and nods toward me. "Put it on."

"Are you sure?" I ask as I take the hanger from him and hold the dress to my body. "This seems like a little much."

"Trust me, I've seen you in this dress, and I've seen you in everything else you own. You're wearing the dress."

"Should I take that as an insult or a compliment?"

He crosses his arms. "Both."

I roll my eyes. "Fine." I quickly strip down to my underwear and pull the dress overhead. The thin straps carry a dipped neckline that shows more cleavage than anything else I own, and the slimming waistline gives me a classic figure. It stops just above the knee. It's one of those rare pieces of clothing you sometimes stumble upon that feels like it's tailor-made for your body. I bought it for a friend's bachelorette party a couple of years ago and haven't worn it since—despite Miles suggesting it for every event.

"Damn, Candace," he says as soon as it's on. "I think it somehow fits you even better now."

I stare at myself in the mirror, and I think he's right. I've filled out a little since I first bought it. I was worried it might be small on me now, but it hugs my frame in all the right places.

My hair is down in loose waves, and I add a little more makeup than usual to help dress things up. "And you don't think it's too much?" I ask, turning to face him.

Miles takes a seat on my bed. "I think he's going to try to fuck you, and if he doesn't, I think he might like boys."

"This isn't a real date. Remember?" I turn to look at myself in the mirror one more time. "He's not actually interested in me."

He waves off my comment. "Yeah, I know. He likes blondes who serve coffee." His knees bounce. "I can't wait to meet him."

I give him a warning look over my shoulder. "Just . . . be nice."

He gets to his feet. "Shut up. I'm always nice." He points to a pair of strappy heels—also picked by him. "Put these on." Without another word, he walks out of my room, and I'm left alone to do the finishing touches.

CHASE:

Be there in 5.

For a fake date, this feels real. My nerves and excitement run away with all the hypothetical ways the night might go. Just knowing he'll be here in a matter of minutes is enough to spike my heart rate.

Forcing out a deep breath, I sit on the edge of the bed and slip on the shoes Miles chose, sliding the back strap over my heel. With these shoes and a delicate bracelet, I stand in front of the mirror again for a final review.

I look incredible.

Do I look like myself? I'm not sure, but the girl in the mirror looks fearless. I usually *am* fearless—more than I have been lately, at least.

You are a hot, successful woman in your twenties. Start fucking acting like it.

There's a knock at the door, and the tiny yelp that leaves my lips contradicts my pep talk immediately.

Miles is on his way to the door when I come out of the hallway, and I hold up a hand. "I'll get it."

His hands fly up in the air, and he stands frozen in place. Once I reach for the door handle, I shoot him a glare, and he drops his arms with a laugh. Gathering my bearings, I remind myself to breathe and open the door.

My anxiety and nerves melt away with one look at Chase's disarming smile. He's wearing a white button-down dress shirt, navy blue slacks, and brown leather shoes, and he looks like someone who just walked out of a magazine trying to sell each of those things.

"Hey," I say with an easy smile.

"Hey, yourself."

I step aside. "Come in. I just have to get my purse."

Once he's in the apartment, he looks around, taking it all in—including Miles standing off to the side between the kitchen and entryway. It's always a fun moment when dates realize my roommate is a guy. There's usually a shift in their expression—the mild surprise they try to hide. Sometimes Miles will pretend to be straight just to fuck with them.

Nothing in Chase's expression falters. Taking a step toward Miles, he reaches out a hand. "Hey, man. I'm Chase."

Miles meets his outstretched hand. "Miles. It's nice to meet you." He glances at me before locking on Chase. "So, are we allowed to know where you're taking her tonight?"

Chase moves his hands to his pockets as he leans against our entryway, crossing his ankles. Instead of directing his answer to Miles, he looks at me. "What do you think of Ella's?"

My hand slows as I hold my small black bag to my body. "Ella's?" It's one of the nicest restaurants in the city, and one I never thought I'd find myself sitting in.

Miles lets out a slow whistle. "Aren't they always booked?"

Chase gives Miles a trace of a smile. "I have a reservation." He lifts his gaze to me as I walk toward him. "But we can go somewhere else if you prefer."

"Are you kidding?" I say with a laugh. "Ella's is fine—more than fine." I pause, looking down at myself. "Am I okay in this?" I hope he says yes, because if Ella's calls for something nicer, we'll have to stop at a store on the way.

"More than okay."

My eyes snap up to find him watching me intently, and I'd pay an obscene amount of money to know what he's thinking right now.

I know Miles is eating up this interaction, so I'm grateful when all he says is, "Well, you two better get going. Treat my girl right."

Chase holds out his hand a second time for Miles. "She's in good hands."

"Oh, I have no doubt," Miles says with a trace of laughter, and I know that's our cue to leave—before he says something about the many things he's sure Chase can do with his hands.

I blow Miles a kiss and head into the hall with Chase closing the door behind us. Not even seconds after the door latching, I get a text from my not-so-subtle roommate.

MILES:

OKAY ZADDY!

My lips twist to fight my smile, and I slip my phone back into the small bag.

"Everything all right?"

My head snaps up. "Yes. Sorry."

"No need to apologize."

I wait for him to walk, but he doesn't.

"You look—" He shakes his head slightly. "You look amazing."

Even as my heart hammers in my chest, I crinkle my nose. "Thank you?"

His eyebrows furrow. "Why the question?"

With a subtle lift of my shoulder, I start toward the exit. "I don't know. This whole practice thing makes compliments a little weird."

He catches my hand. "You think I'm lying?"

Looking up at him, I try my best to figure him out, but it's useless. "I don't know what to think."

In one swift movement, he pulls me to him. "Then let me make this very clear." He glances at my hand in his before meeting my stare again. "Nothing I say to you, tonight or any other night, is a lie. I might lay it on a little thicker than if we weren't doing this, but I won't lie to you, Candace." He brushes my cheek with his free thumb, and I could get lost in the warmth of his eyes. "You're beautiful. That's just a fact." He looks down at what I'm wearing, his jaw tensing. "And in that dress, you could break any man—not just me."

He steps away, watching for my reaction, and I'm left with my head spinning. "Well, in that case, thank you."

"You're welcome." His smile has shifted slightly to amusement, and I wonder how obvious it is that I'm struggling to breathe.

"Nice tattoo by the way." He gestures toward my floral half sleeve. I guess all the shirts I've worn around him before have hidden it.

"Do you like tattoos?" I ask, curious if this is a good thing or if, like my brown hair, it's just another thing to make me less his type.

Keeping his gaze fixed on the floral design on my arm for a moment, he swallows and nods. "Right now? Yes. Very much." I let out a burst of laughter, and he grins. "Come on," he says as he holds his hand out for me to take. "Let's go."

The way he looked at me lingers on my skin as his words echo in my head, and I have to force my feet to move forward.

I am in way over my head.

We walk out to the parking lot, and the only car parked this way is a Lexus. *Of course.* He would drive a car that's nice without automatically making him look like an asshole. It isn't too flashy, and it doesn't come with a stigma attached to it—like how everyone who drives a BMW thinks they own the road.

When he clicks the button on the fob and confirms that's the exact car we're walking toward, I'm not sure if I should be relieved or disappointed. I still want to find something I don't like about him. I need to sniff out his fatal flaw like a damn bloodhound and let go of this silly crush.

Keeping my hand in his, he walks with me around to the passenger side and opens the door. "Thank you," I say as I sink into the seat. I think my plan is working as far as becoming desensitized goes. He held my hand for the entire walk to the car, and after the first few seconds, my breathing returned to normal. And a few seconds after that, my shoulders relaxed. I can do this. I can be around Chase as his friend. We can flirt and touch for the sake of keeping his predator of a boss at bay, and I think I'll be able to keep my wits about me.

Resting his forearm on the open doorframe, he looks down at me with that easy smile of his. "How did I get so lucky to have met you?"

Oh, fuck him. With a shake of my head, I reach for the seatbelt. "Get in the car, Chase."

He closes my door, but not before I catch a trace of a chuckle.

eighteen

WE'RE GREETED outside the restaurant by staff opening the doors for us. They seat us right away, and our server just asked me what type of *water* I'd like to start with.

"Um—" My eyes jump to Chase for a fraction of a second. He's sitting with both hands clasped in front of his mouth while he watches me with a trace of a smirk. I don't know why I'm blanking. I know what types of water there are. Right? I've just never been to a restaurant this nice with a man this hot, and the combination is making my brain fuzzy.

"Spring is fine," Chase answers for me, and I could kick myself. A great way to start out the night.

"Excellent," our server, looking refined in a white button-down with a black vest, says with a grin. "I'll have that right out."

My eyes follow the man as he walks away. As nice as this place is, it isn't stuffy. The guy who just took our water order has exposed tattoos on his forearms and bright blue glasses that remind me a little of Miles. It all helps to ease some of my nerves.

Chase catches me staring. "Blonde with tattoos. The only thing he's missing is a beard, and he'd be your perfect man."

I raise my eyebrows playfully. "Two out of three isn't bad. Maybe I'll go ask him what he's doing later." I set my napkin aside like I'm about to get up.

He points for me to sit with a trace of a smile pulling at his lips. "Not so fast. Tonight, you're mine."

Those words pour white heat into me, but I do my best to hide it. Tilting my head innocently, I ask, "You'd stand in the way of love?"

He reaches for his napkin, unfolding it and placing it on his lap. "I would. You might not know me that well yet, but I'm very selfish."

Yet. It's such a trivial word, but in that sentence, it could knock me out of my chair.

The teasing glint in his eyes helps me recover. "Fine," I say with a dramatic sigh. "I guess I'll just have to come back here on my own to seduce him."

"I have no doubt you could." Something new flashes in those eyes, but it's gone in the matter of seconds. If I didn't know better, I'd think it was a hint of hunger—desire?

Our server comes back with two waters, and we order our drinks, salads, and entrees. I choose the chicken piccata and Chardonnay, while Chase orders the prime rib and a glass of bourbon.

He clears his throat once we're alone again. "So, what do you think of the place?"

I look around the dimly lit room with its sleek aesthetic. They've managed to make the place subtly festive. A pianist plays instrumental holiday music in the middle of the room while small bunches of fresh holly adorn each table beside a flickering candle.

"It's amazing," I say, still looking around in wonder. "I hope you know I'm not splitting this bill, though."

His laugh pulls my attention back to him. "I wouldn't dream of it."

The way he's looking at me is too much. Sitting up straight in a desperate attempt to get back to business, I say, "So, tell me about yourself."

He blinks. "What do you want to know?"

"Anything? Everything? Whatever your girlfriend should know about you?"

"Ah, right." He nods. "Not much to know, really. My parents and sister still live in Massachusetts, but I live here. I moved for college and never went back, but sometimes I miss it. My sister has three kids who call me Uncle Cheesy—mostly because my sister finds it funny." He looks up like he's trying to remember if there's anything else. "Oh, and I'm a bit of a workaholic, but I'm sure you've gathered that, and it's not always by choice."

I absorb every detail like a sponge, holding it in as the pieces of my Chase puzzle grow and click into place. "Uncle Cheesy?" I ask with a slight lift to my lips.

He laughs. "Yeah. I think it started as Uncle Chasey, but as soon as one of them pronounced it wrong, the new name stuck."

"They sound wonderful." I can totally see Chase as an Uncle Cheesy now that he's said it. I picture him running around the house with three sets of tiny feet giggling after him. It's adorable. "Will you see them for Christmas?"

Chase shakes his head, and my smile fades. "I haven't been home for Christmas since my boss took on running the Christmas party. I think it's been three years?" He shrugs. "I always try to take a week off in January to go see them instead."

A comment about his boss is on the tip of my tongue, but I know that's not what he wants to talk about, so I bury it and instead say, "At least you get to spend some time with them."

He smiles, but there's a hint of sadness to it. "Yeah." Snapping out of it, he gestures toward me. "But what about you? Any siblings?"

I shake my head. "Nope. Just two loving parents who get a little weirder every year."

"Weird parents are the best."

A smile warms my lips. "They really are."

Seeing me laugh makes his smile stretch further, and something in my chest warms. I consider him. This beautiful man in this outrageously nice restaurant. "Why are you single?" As far as I can tell, he could probably have any woman he wanted. Why waste his time with a fake date?

Our drinks arrive, and Chase turns his attention to the person who dropped them off, thanking them. When he turns back to me, he takes a sip like he's willing to abandon my question altogether.

I raise an eyebrow to prompt him.

"You want to know why I'm single?"

I nod.

He shrugs. "I had a somewhat serious girlfriend a while back, but we broke up last October. I've dated a little here and there, but nothing stuck."

I press my lips together, trying to read between the lines.

Chase chuckles. "I don't mind being single."

"Of course, you don't. As long as there aren't any parties to go to, right?" I tease as I take a sip of my wine.

He narrows his eyes playfully. "Who knew going to a Christmas party alone would be such a mistake?"

"I mean, the number of mistletoes alone should have been a sign." During the holidays you either have couples being cozy or singles looking for someone to get cozy with.

He nods after taking a sip and sets down his glass. "You're right. I should have known."

I let out a sigh and tease, "Such a damsel."

He grins. "I am. I'm a hopeless damsel who needs you, Candace."

"But I'm sure you could find a real date for this party."

He tilts his head, an eyebrow raised in interest. "Well, I was sort of trying to do that when we met."

Realization hits me. Of course, he was. "Oh, the barista would have loved this."

"Layla," he corrects with the corner of his mouth quirked.

"Right, Layla. Well, she's missing out."

His smile stretches further. "I'm sure she's happily doing something with her boyfriend." He crosses his arms on the table and leans closer. "What about you?"

I blink. "What about me?"

"Why are you single?"

"Well, I'm certainly not taking people to places like this."

"I don't think you'd need to."

The way he's looking at me is starting to make me sweat. He's too focused. Too intense. Too determined to see what's beneath the surface. I swallow down the thought. "It wouldn't hurt."

He smiles a little more at that. "I have a feeling it isn't hard to find someone eager to date you."

Crossing my arms on the table, I match his position. "Well, if you ask Miles, I'm too picky."

"And if I don't ask Miles?"

I hold his gaze, my eyes searching his for an answer. "I don't know," I finally say. "I like my life, so unless someone is going to make it substantially better, it feels like a waste."

He nods, taking in what I've said. "Sounds perfectly reasonable."

"It does, doesn't it?" I take another sip of my wine. "Plus, there just aren't enough bearded blonde men with tattoos in the world."

"Tragedy," he says with a sad shake of his head. "That's not the type of guy you usually go for, though."

"It could be." I shrug. "I think how attractive someone is goes beyond the physical." I give him a pointed stare. "I would never limit myself to just blondes."

A teasing smile plays at his lips. "I never said I *only* date blondes. I said I usually go for blondes."

I roll my eyes.

He takes a sip of his drink. "You really don't have a type?"

I stare down the gorgeous but *clueless* man in front of me. Our salads arrive and we both sit up straight to make room for the plates.

"Chase," I say as I stab my fork into the most beautifully plated garden salad I've ever seen.

He pauses before taking a bite, like my saying his name is of the utmost importance.

My cheeks heat. "I did give you my number, in case you've forgotten."

"Oh, I haven't forgotten." He moves his salad around with his fork. "I just wanted to hear you say it."

I glare at his smug expression as he takes his first bite before I go back to eating my own food.

"Am I still?"

I glance up at him. "Still what?"

"Your type."

My chewing slows, and I let my eyes drag over him. From his thick hair to his sharp jawline, his beautifully angled features, kind eyes, and impeccable style. "No."

He eyes me with amusement. "No?"

I stab another piece of lettuce with my fork. "Nope." When I dare to look at him again, he's still watching me. "Look, you're pretty. That's just a fact. But as soon as I realized it wasn't me you were interested in, I only saw you as a friend." I tap my temple with the back end of my fork. "That's just how my brain works." It's a boldfaced lie, but I'm sticking to it for the sake of self-preservation.

He takes another sip, his eyes never leaving mine. "I like you, Candace."

The approval in his tone shouldn't make my body hum. I shouldn't wish this table were smaller, so he'd be within reach. I shouldn't look forward to the end of this extravagant meal because it means he might take me by the hand again. But even though I'd never tell him, I'm doing all those things.

nineteen

"THAT WAS the best meal I've ever eaten," I say as we head down the wide sidewalk lining the cobblestone street. I glance over my shoulder at the black decorative sign that reads *Ella's*, already feeling a little sad that I'll probably never eat there again.

We thought about splitting a dessert, but as soon as we saw there were no options that didn't have chocolate *or* fruit, it was a bust. Chase was perfectly content with the idea of watching me down an entire piece of chocolate cake by myself, but I passed.

As if reading my mind, Chase says, "Just say the word, and we'll go again. They're a client of the firm." He takes my hand in his, and it somehow relaxes me and makes me jittery all at once.

"Is that how you managed to get a reservation?" I've never tried to book a table, but I've heard clients complain about waiting months.

His lips lift as we walk. "I worked on their campaign for a while and had some good ideas, so I pulled some strings. I sometimes have the luxury of *seeming* important."

Letting out a laugh, I take my free hand and pat his arm reassuringly. "Don't worry, you're very important." My hand is met with the hard muscle of his biceps, and it takes everything in me not to wrap my fingers around it. I've only ever seen him with a shirt on, but the sudden desire I have to tear it off is . . . unsettling. I quickly adjust my purse on my shoulder to give my hand something else to do. "So, where to now?" My voice comes out a little breathless, and I hope he doesn't notice.

"Don't get me wrong, I love Ella's." Chase stops at a crosswalk and looks both ways before pulling me across the street. "But their portions are small."

Once we're on the sidewalk, he slows, and I say, "You're still hungry?"

He glances down at me in disbelief. "Aren't you?"

I hadn't really thought about it, but I guess he's right. I'm content, but I don't feel full.

Reading through my hesitation, he glances at the shops around us and asks, "Do you like beer?"

"What?" I ask with a breath of laughter. "Why?"

"Because I've only ever seen you drink wine, but I could go for some tacos up ahead. The only drawback is that I don't think they'll have your Chardonnay."

My favorite taco place sits up ahead on the right. "Well, I don't like beer." His feet slow before I can finish my sentence like he's already regrouping and ready to take me somewhere else, so I quickly add, "But they have margaritas, so it's fine." I only had one glass of wine with dinner, so the switch shouldn't be an issue.

He lifts an eyebrow. "You like margaritas?"

I nod. "Love them."

He practically groans. "The thought of kissing you while you taste like tequila and lime is doing unspeakable things to me, Candace. I hope you know that."

I'm glad he's holding my hand because without him pulling

me forward, that would have stopped me in my tracks. He said it so casually too, like he could have been talking about the weather. He doesn't even look at me to check for my reaction—and thank God for that because I have no idea what color my cheeks are right now, but my entire body is *burning*.

As soon as the door opens, we're met with a rush of sound. It doesn't matter that it's late and other places are closing, Paco's Tacos is alive and well. The workers yell orders to each other from the kitchen, and the line of people grow louder and drunker the later it gets. We stand in line behind a group of guys who look like they were probably a part of a frat a few years ago, and they can't quite let that part of their life die.

Leaning in toward Chase, I say, "This is my favorite place to get tacos."

His eyebrows shoot up. "Really? How have I never seen you here?"

"I don't know," I say with a light lift of my shoulder. "I'm probably in here at least once a week."

He blinks. "Damn, you've been here all along, haven't you?"

I'm not quite sure what he means by that, so I just tilt my head with a pinch of my brow. "I haven't been far, that's for sure." Nodding to the menu boards hanging above, I add, "This one's on me."

With a shake of his head, he says, "Grab that table in the back corner while it's still open. I'll meet you over there. What can I get you?"

I hesitate, my mouth open and ready to fight him on this. I can't let him pay for everything.

Keeping his voice low, his eyes jump between mine. "There's no way I'm letting you spend a penny tonight."

I arch an eyebrow.

"You don't scare me, beautiful."

A slow smile pulls at the corner of my lips. "You're lying."

His expression mirrors my own. "I am." Straightening, he adds, "But the way I see it, you have two options. Either you can tell me what you want, or I'll get you the same thing I order." He gives me a sideways glance. "I'd love to see you down three tacos and a lager."

My lips purse. "You know I don't like beer."

The line moves ahead of us, and he takes a step. "Which is why you should hurry up and tell me."

With a shake of my head, I purse my lips. "Fine. Get me a chicken double-decker and a margarita with salt."

A satisfied smile stretches across his chiseled features. "God, I love it when you're bossy."

"Unbelievable," I huff with a shake of my head before ducking out of line. I take a seat in one of the chairs he pointed to earlier and try to wrap my head around the night I'm having. I've been in this taco place more times than I can count, and yet, being here with Chase makes it new.

He pays for our food and heads toward me with paper trays, a plastic cup holding a margarita, and his bottle of beer tucked under his arm. We're severely overdressed, and the sight of him in his well-pressed clothes has a smile tugging at my lips.

As nice as he looks, being here with him makes me wish he were in a T-shirt like he was when we got coffee. There's something sexy about seeing him more relaxed. *This* is the version of himself he always has on display. I want access to the lesser-known Chase—the version he reserves for weekends and those closest to him.

But the thought of taking polished Chase and turning him into a disheveled mess of a man is sexy, too.

Catching myself, I blink and refocus.

Chase moves his chair from across the small table so that it's right next to mine before he settles into it. "Not close enough for you?" I tease.

He winks as he places my margarita and taco in front of me and rests his hand on the back of my chair. His fingers send little jolts of electricity across my back, leaving my skin buzzing in their wake. "At the party, you and I will be next to each other like this. I figured it wouldn't hurt to get some tacos and see how it goes."

"Tacos never hurt." I take a bite and close my eyes for a moment as the perfect combination of flavors hits my tongue. When I come back, he's watching me with a twinge of a smile.

"You look amazing."

"It's the power of the dress," I say with a hand covering my mouthful. Swallowing, I sit up straight. "I promise I don't look like this in anything else I own."

"No," he says with that same faint smile. He leans in closer. "Don't get me wrong, that dress is . . ." He blows out a breath. "Certainly something, but you with a taco is where the real magic happens."

A laugh escapes me, but I shake my head and go for another bite. "Eat, Chase."

He does, watching me with amusement the entire time. "When are you going to cut my hair?"

Wiping my hands on a napkin, I stare at his brunette locks. They're starting to have some wave to them. Reaching up, I run my hand through his hair, getting a feel for what he's looking for with my fingertips. It's something I do at work all the time, so I didn't think anything of it. But the way this man melts at my touch brings me too much delight. I let my fingers trail down the back of his neck as I pull my hand back. "Don't you have someone who usually cuts your hair?"

"Yes, but I like you more."

My eyes snap to meet his. "I'm not cutting your hair."

He shakes his head, bewildered. "Why? I'll pay you. I'm not looking for a handout. Let me schedule an appointment, and I'll come to the salon like your other clients."

I take a sip of my margarita to buy time and hope the tequila will hit me in a matter of seconds. He isn't my client. He's a man I'm fake dating for a Christmas party, who I am so undeniably attracted to it scares me. He's someone I won't be able to stay friends with if these feelings don't go away, so the last thing I need is for him to come in every six weeks for a haircut. "I think your hair looks great the way it is, but if you want it cut, go get it cut. It just won't be me who does it."

He gives me a teasing smile, beautifully ignorant of how serious I am. "I guess I'll wait then."

I roll my eyes and take another sip. "Aren't we here to practice something?"

He keeps his eyes on me a beat too long, his expression unchanging. "You're right." Moving his chair a few inches closer to mine, he says, "This is about how close we'll be sitting at the party. It will be a large round table with a few other people from my department. We'll have to sit through some end of the year ceremony bullshit, but there will be plenty of Chardonnay to get you through it."

"Sounds reasonable."

"Good." He nods. "And I probably won't be able to keep my hands off you."

I force out a laugh. "Right. Because these people know you well, and that's what history has proven." I give him a sideways glance.

He holds my gaze. "Something like that."

I go to look anywhere else, my heart pounding, but he leans in closer, and his magnetic force demands my full attention.

His eyes are sincere when he says, "No one would believe I'd be able to keep my hands off you because no one would believe *any* man could keep his hands off you. I've been struggling with it all night, and we're not even really dating." He shakes his head. "If you were mine, there's no way we'd be sitting here like this."

I swallow hard, and when I go to speak, my voice comes out quieter than I intended. "What would we be doing?"

Chase's warm, brown eyes search mine, but I have no idea what he's looking for. "Well," he finally says as he moves his hand to the inside of my knee. "I probably would have had my hand here most of the night." His fingers drag over my skin in slow, teasing circles.

My leg falls open a little wider on instinct, and Chase's fingers slowly circle higher. My breathing shallows, and I clasp my hands in front of my mouth with my elbows on the table and force a steadying breath. This dress won't hide the way he affects me. My chest and back are too exposed, my shallow breaths too evident.

His touch lights a fire through me, and every time his fingers circle higher, the heavy heat between my legs intensifies. When he reaches the middle of my thigh, I've lost all hope of controlling my breathing. My eyes dart around the busy restaurant, and Chase says, "No one's watching."

He's right, of course. Everyone is too busy with their own plans to care about the couple sitting close in the corner. I tilt my head to look at him. "What else?"

His mouth quirks, and he pulls his hand away from my leg. Moving it to the back of my neck, his feather-light touch caresses the nape, sending tingles down my spine. He guides me closer to him, bringing his lips to my ear. "I'd whisper all my filthy thoughts in your ear."

My breath catches in my throat, and when he massages his thumb up the side of my neck, I naturally tilt my head to give him more access. Without so much as a warning, he presses his lips to the spot just below my ear in one slow, torturous kiss. Before I can stop it, an audible sigh leaves my lips, and I feel him smile against my skin. "And you definitely would have made that sound more than once tonight."

He slowly pulls away, and I blink like being roused from a

dream. Shaking my head, I hope my bemused smile hides how turned on I am. "You're despicable."

He grins. "You don't know the half of it."

I believe him. The way he just made me feel, in a matter of seconds, in the back of a taco shop, is probably a fraction of what he could do if given the . . . opportunity. There's no way a man like him doesn't know how to make a woman feel good. Miles's advice to sleep with Chase echoes in the back of my mind, and I take a larger sip of my margarita, swallowing down my temptation with it.

"And are you?"

My eyes dart to meet his. "Am I what?"

"Despicable?" He gives me a roguish smile. "Because tonight you've been acting like nothing short of a saint."

Setting down my drink, I shift to face him and give him a leveling look. "Chase."

"Candace."

Slowly, I lean toward him. "Are you worried I won't deliver?" Before I can even think about what I'm doing, my hand is on his chest, my fingers trailing over every muscle beneath his shirt. We're close enough to kiss like this, and my tongue instinctively wets my bottom lip at the thought. Chase's eyes track the movement and stay locked on my lips. My hand continues to trail until I reach the top of his belt. My fingers lightly brush his crotch as I pull my hand away.

He isn't smirking anymore. He isn't even smiling. If I didn't know better, I'd say he's *flustered*. With a shake of his head, he swallows. "I wouldn't doubt you for a second."

I give him a side-long glance, desperate to touch him more but fighting it. "Good." Smiling at him, I add, "I promise to pull out all the stops for your party." Because if I do much more right now, I won't be able to stop.

Regaining some of his usual confidence, he eyes me up and down without shame, challenge brewing. "I look forward to it."

"I bet you do," I say with a laugh, and his smile only stretches further. "So, how did we meet?" I need to get this conversation back to safer territory.

He gives me a funny look. "I accidentally asked you out, and it was the best mistake I've ever made."

Something comes out of me halfway between a scoff and a laugh. "That's the story you want to go with?"

He looks mildly offended. "It's a great story."

My nose crinkles. "Yeah, if you want to make me look pathetic."

He sets his bottle down mid-sip. *"What?"*

I shift to face him. "What type of self-respecting woman dates a man who not only had no intention of asking her out, but also went back to ask out the right girl the next day?" I lift a dubious brow.

Amusement dances in his eyes like he knows he's playing with fire. "One who can't resist my charm?"

I playfully shove him and turn to face forward again. "You're not *that* pretty."

He brings his hand to his chest with a wounded expression. "First of all," he says, holding up a finger. "I am exactly that pretty. And second"—he holds up another finger—"you could never be pathetic. Look at it this way, a man thought he knew what he wanted until you came along and showed him otherwise. What's wrong with that?"

I shake my head. How can he not see this for what it is? There's no way anyone would think this is a good story. "Says the man who also went back to ask another girl out after meeting me, and when he got turned down, he settled."

A slow smile stretches across his face. "Well, men are stupid."

"*So* stupid."

His lips twist. "Okay, fine. We can meet however you'd like, but I will warn you, I'm a terrible liar, and I'm known for going off-script."

"Noted." I shrug. "We can just meet at a coffee shop then. Let's just leave out the part about the barista." I give him a sideways glance.

"Layla," he gently corrects.

I wave him off. "Yes, yes. I know her name."

His head tilts, those brilliant eyes inspecting me. "Are you . . . jealous?"

My heart hammers in my chest. I'm not sure jealous is the right word. Do I wish he had asked me out instead? Sure. But that's about as far as my feelings toward her go. I lean back to get a better look at him. "The only thing I'm *jealous* of is the fact that she doesn't have to use dating apps anymore."

His eyes narrow like he doesn't believe me. "Okay," he says. "We met at a coffee shop, and you were way out of my league." Widening his legs to make room, he slowly inches my chair closer toward him. "I couldn't see why you would ever be interested in a guy like me. I was about to leave, but at the last minute, I wrote on my receipt asking for your number. And by some fucking miracle, you actually gave it to me."

By the time he finishes, the side of my chair is flush against the front of his. I'm hanging onto his every word, completely in a trance being this close. And who smells this good? Like Christmas trees with a dash of spice. All I want to do is climb into his lap—which wouldn't be a stretch from where we're at, considering I can feel the warmth of his thighs on either side of me.

The corner of his mouth quirks, and he quickly adds, "Then I grabbed your hand, dragged you home, and we had the best sex either of us has ever had."

"Chase!" I push him away from me, laughing. But with our chairs this close, there's only so much space for him to go. "You're . . ." I shake my head, still laughing.

He cocks an eyebrow. "Despicable?"

I nod. "Yes, among other things."

That beautiful, easy smile covers his face. "One day, I'd love to hear all the things you think I am." His fingers brush over my exposed back, and his touch has my heart racing. "But I should probably get you home."

"Probably." I don't want this night to end, but I know he's right. If this were a real date, our night might be just beginning. Maybe he would take me back to his place and—no. I shut the thought down before it runs away with me.

Chase holds my hand for the walk back to his car, he touches my leg twice on the drive home, and by the time we're standing outside my front door, it all feels like it went by too fast. This date has been a dream, and it's not even real, but there's still a chance he might kiss me at the end. My head spins, trying to keep up.

"Thanks for tonight." I reach for my keys. "I don't think I've ever had food as good as that."

"The company wasn't bad either."

"No." I smile. "I guess it wasn't."

He leans in, and even though my heart feels like it stops, everything else is in overdrive. I force myself to breathe, and when his lips find my cheek, I freeze. A kiss on the cheek? Leave it to Chase to be modest now. When he pulls back, he keeps his face close to mine. "I promise to kiss you properly before the event. I'm just afraid if I kiss you now . . ." His gaze is fixed on my mouth.

"It will be too soon."

He blinks. "Yeah." The corner of his mouth lifts. "We might forget."

Despite my disappointment, my mouth pulls upward. "We wouldn't want that to happen." Turning, I unlock the door and slip inside. Before closing it, I say, "Goodnight."

Chase nods. "Night, Candace."

As soon as I'm fully inside, I lean my back against the door for support. Miles is watching some type of gruesome horror movie, but he pauses it when he sees me. "So . . ." he says hesitantly. "How did it go?"

What a loaded question. *How did it go?* Great. Easily the best date I've ever been on. I didn't want it to end. It felt too short, too fun, and for a man I'm not actually dating, he knows how to turn me on way too much.

So, in another sense, the date was terrible. Nothing about him turned me off like I was hoping, I'm no closer to finding his fatal flaw, and he left me wanting more—a lot more.

I walk over to the couch and lie down, my head landing just outside Miles's lap and my legs up on the couch even though I haven't taken my heels off. Staring up at the ceiling, I sigh. "I am so fucked."

He just laughs and pets my head. "I know, honey. I know."

twenty

THE FOLLOWING NIGHT, *Just Friends* plays on our TV because Miles and I watch it every year religiously during the month of December—usually more than once.

"You know," Miles says as he stretches out on our couch like a lazy house cat. "Your favorite Christmas movie isn't *that* Christmassy."

I frown. "Sure, it is. There's caroling, Christmas parties, elaborate light displays."

"Yeah, but that's all frilly shit. The movie is barely about Christmas at all. You're just a sucker for love."

Taking a sip of my wine, I shake my head. "I'm a sucker for Ryan Reynolds."

Miles stares at the screen. "Aren't we all?" My phone buzzes, and he looks at it with an eyebrow raised. "Is that him?"

I reach for my phone. I don't think it's Chase. He already told me he's working late tonight. It's the group chat I have with my parents.

MOM:

We were starting to get down about the house not being decorated, so we decided to pack!

DAD:

The neighbors were asking about the toy shop, and when I told them we were going on a cruise this year instead, they looked devastated.

MOM:

Your father can't live with that type of guilt.

DAD:

I'm tempted to set it up even though we won't be here.

MOM:

Don't be ridiculous! It's too much work!

A chuckle escapes me as I type back my response.

CANDACE:

This is a much-needed break for you two. The neighbors will be fine.

"Hey," I say, bringing my attention back to Miles. "My parents booked a cruise this year and won't be hosting Christmas."

Miles lifts his head. "Where was my invite?"

"Oh, we were both invited," I assure him. "To a week-long wellness detox retreat."

His face scrunches.

"Yeah. We were both busy. You're welcome."

He gives a two-finger salute before letting his head flop back on the couch. "Have fun Bill and Pat."

My phone goes off again.

MOM:

Plus, who knows how many years are left before you settle down and have your own little candy canes. Then we'll have to go big every year!

I don't respond, and neither does my dad. He's probably scolding my mother in person because they *know* how I feel about having kids. It doesn't matter how many times I try to explain how that lifestyle isn't for me, my mom is convinced I'll change my mind, and my dad is hopeful she's right.

With a slight shake of my head, I put my phone down and try to separate myself from what I'm feeling. "So anyway, it will just be the two of us," I say to Miles.

When he doesn't respond right away, I look up and can't fight my smile as I watch him ignore me to text the guy he's been seeing. "So, is this thing between you two exclusive?"

He tilts his head from side to side. "On my end, yes. On his? I don't know. I think so. Like I said, he's kind of new to this, so I don't think he has the boys lined up."

I sigh dreamily and clasp my hands under my chin. "If only I could meet this mystery man . . ."

Miles scoffs. "He's not that much of a mystery. He's an accountant from Apopka, but you'll love him."

"I'm sure I will." I take another sip of my wine.

He raises his eyebrows and quietly mutters, "Not as much as you love Daddy Chase, but . . ."

I nearly choke and have to cough through my last sip. "Would you stop calling him that?" I manage to get out. It's the only way he has referred to Chase since meeting him.

"No," he answers flatly as he sits up so he can look me square in the eyes. "You don't even deserve him at this point. You went on a date with a man who looks like *that*, and all that happened between you was a kiss on the cheek? What are you, twelve?" He shakes his head. "You should have. Ridden. That. Dick." The last three words come out deep and rough.

"I told you, it's not like that."

Miles rolls his eyes hard enough that his whole head rolls with them. "Please. I saw the way he looked at you in that dress." He points a finger at me. "And I've seen you work your magic on guys before. You're fucking hot when you want to be. You could have seduced him."

I know I've been different with Chase—more cautious than I usually am when I'm interested in someone, but that's because I don't *want* to be interested in him. I'm actively trying very hard not to have feelings for him that go beyond thinking he's attractive. "What would be the point?"

We lock eyes and as soon as it registers what he's about to say, I quickly add, "And do not say anything about—"

But Miles has already yelled, "HIS DICK."

I shake my head with a laugh, but he isn't finished.

"His big, thick, Daddy Chase dick that is probably just as beautiful as the rest of him."

I can't stop laughing. "You've thought about this a lot, haven't you?"

With a slow shake of his head, Miles says, "The things I would do to that man."

I snap my fingers in front of his face. "Hey. Accountant in Apopka. Stay with me."

He blinks. "Right. What were we talking about?"

"How about we talk about you helping me find a dress? We're officially one week out from this party."

Miles taps his fingers on his bearded chin. "Sunday?" Looking at me, he adds, "I mean, you're working tomorrow anyway, and I'll be doing dirty things to an Apopka accountant."

"As you should. Sunday is great."

My phone vibrates next to me, and I hope it's not my mother with more life planning advice.

> **CHASE:**
> I have never been so happy to see my couch.
> What are you doing?

I snap a quick picture of our movie night. There's still a half-eaten pizza sitting in the box on our coffee table from earlier.

> **CHASE:**
> You and pizza? I hope Miles knows how good he has it.
>
> Even with the pineapple.

I bite back my smile, and Miles says, "You're so in love it's disgusting."

I grab the pillow next to me and toss it at him before typing my next response.

> **CANDACE:**
> Rough day?

> **CHASE:**
> Somewhat. My boss only cares about planning this stupid party, so everything else is left for me. I had to personally reach out to four clients she's supposed to oversee because they haven't heard from her in weeks.

I can't stand this woman. Chase already said his job was stressful without the added chaos of his boss wanting to become an event coordinator.

> **CANDACE:**
> This woman is quickly becoming one of my least favorite people.

CHASE:

She's not all bad.

But this time of year undoubtedly brings out the worst in her.

"Ask him if you can take him for a ride," Miles says flatly in the background.

My head snaps up. He's being ridiculous.

"Just to get a feel," he adds casually. "You know, before the party."

Ignoring him, I turn back to my phone.

CANDACE:

Of course. I'm sure she's lovely in the summer months.

Thankfully, for the rest of the night, there's no further talk of how well-endowed Miles thinks Chase must be. He puts on an anime show while I scroll through different types of dresses on my phone, but we mostly talk through it all, and by the time I head into my room for the night, I only find it a little weird that Chase never messaged me back.

I mean, it's a Friday night. He could be doing anything—he could even be with a woman for all I know. My stomach tightens at the thought of him with his hand on another woman's leg while he whispers in her ear. I just imagine him venturing his hand up further than he did with me. Maybe I should have played into this whole practice thing more. Maybe Miles is right, and I should have participated just as much.

I swallow hard and swipe my phone open. It's been over three hours since I heard from him. It's not like we text on a constant schedule, but he seemed a little down earlier, and now that I'm alone in my room, it's eating at me. Because if he's not out on the town with some gorgeous blonde woman I imagine being much prettier than me, maybe he's upset. Maybe he took offense to my last comment about his boss . . .

I doubt that's the case. Even if I did upset him, I think he would still talk to me. I'm biting my thumb as a stare down at the screen, debating if I should text him again.

Or I could call him.

The initial thought spikes my panic, but the more I think about it, the more I want to hear his voice. I'll be able to tell so much from hearing him. It's not like we've never spoken on the phone.

Before I can talk myself out of it, I hit the call button.

twenty-one

WITH EVERY PASSING RING, my heart rate rises, but it's too late to hang up. He'll see I've called. Or I could play it off as an accident. Yeah. Maybe I'll just say—

"Candace?"

His voice sends a rush of heat through me, and I'm already a little breathless when I say, "Hey."

"Is everything okay?"

"Of course. No—everything is fine. I was just . . . calling you. Should I not have?"

What sounds like a leather couch cushion shifting in the background catches my attention. "You can always call me. I just . . ." He lets out a breath of laughter. "I probably shouldn't talk to you right now."

"Are you with someone?" I blurt. There's no background noise, but he could have a girl at his place. The realization hits me like a punch to the gut, and I think I might be sick. "I'm sorry. I should have texted. I'll let you—"

"Yes," he chuckles in my ear. "I've been on a date with a bottle of scotch all evening. We've gotten to know each other pretty well, and she's telling me I should definitely not talk to you while I'm with her."

I freeze until I manage to slowly take a seat on my bed. "Are you *drunk*?"

"I prefer the word inebriated. Sounds better."

I laugh. "And why are you inebriated?"

He lets out a groan that gets muffled, like he's rubbing his hand over his face. "I don't know. It wasn't the plan. I just needed a drink after work, which led to thinking about shit, which led to drinking more."

My smile fades. "What shit were you thinking about?"

He lets out a sigh, and when he speaks next, it sounds like he's on the move. "It's just my job. I swear this promotion is going to be the death of me. My boss expects too much. Way too much. And I'm having trouble keeping track of it all because the only thing I want to think about is you in that black dress."

I stop breathing.

The sound of my pounding heart is accompanied by the sound of him rummaging through something. "Where the hell are my Oreos?" he mutters.

The air I'm holding rushes out in a laugh. "I'm sorry, what?"

"What do you need me to repeat?" He sounds distracted. "The part about the Oreos, my shitty situation at work, or the part about you torturing me in that dress."

The fact that he's thinking of me at all has my stomach clenching. My mouth opens to say I wasn't trying to torture him, but he speaks before I get the chance.

"Aha! I found the bastards. At least one thing is going right for me today." The rummaging continues, and I listen with rapt attention. His voice gets a little muffled as he mutters about knowing they weren't all gone, and I imagine he has the phone tucked in the crook of his neck. He groans, and in a louder, but more muffled voice, he says, "Damn it. They're stale." It sounds like he still has a mouthful of cookie. "See? I work too much. I'm not even home enough to enjoy the shit I buy before it goes bad."

"We'll get you more Oreos."

"The mint ones."

"Sure."

"They're the superior Oreo."

"I believe you."

"And you," he says before I hear him collapsing back onto a leather couch. "You are so beautiful. And you and I . . ."

When he doesn't say anything more, I ask, "Are friends?"

"Yeah. You and I are friends." There's another pause. "Why are we friends again?"

I smile even though he can't see me. "Because you asked me to be your fake date for the Christmas party. How much have you had to drink?"

"No. I mean, why are we only friends?"

Time stands still. This being fake was all his idea to begin with. As much as my body buzzes at his words, I have a feeling it's just the alcohol talking. "Because men are dumb. Remember?"

A humorless laugh leaves him. "Right. I'm working on it."

"Are you?"

"Well, I thought I was. But getting drunk and calling you is probably sending me ten steps back."

My lips twist into a smile. "Chase."

I'm pretty sure he still has the stale Oreos with him because his mouth sounds a little full when he says, "Yes?"

"I called you."

"Oh." There's more shuffling, like he's sitting upright. "Why did you call me again?"

"No reason, really. You just seemed a little off earlier."

"Yeah. I guess I was."

"Want to talk about it?"

"With you?"

My lips lift. "I am the one asking."

"It's so nice of you to ask. Did I mention how gorgeous you are?"

"You might have said something along those lines." My voice is quiet. I know he's drunk. I know I can't take anything he says right now for face value, but God, does it feel good to hear him say it.

"And smart, too. As your friend, I feel like I should mention this isn't just about your looks."

A torn smile pulls at my lips. This conversation somehow makes me both elated and disappointed. "You're a good friend."

"No. No. I'm not. I'm pretty sure good friends aren't supposed to think about you the way that I have."

The air gets caught in my throat, and my thoughts betray me. I let myself picture Chase's mouth on my neck, his hands in my hair while he—

"You were right. I'm despicable. A despicable, despicable man. The things I would do to you if given the chance. Fuck, I need to get off the phone."

Afraid he'll hang up, I quickly blurt "But—" even though I don't know what to say. This is definitely the alcohol. And for both our sakes, I should let him hang up. I should even encourage it.

"But?" His voice is low, rough, *husky*, and Chase being turned on might be my new favorite version. Forget weekend Chase with his relaxed clothes. I want bedroom Chase. I want the man whose voice sounds like this just from thinking about me.

Who am I kidding? I want them all.

"But you didn't even kiss me last night," I say quietly as I try to click all the pieces into place.

He lets out a breath caught between a scoff and a laugh. "I didn't think you wanted me to. I was all over you last night, and you barely gave me anything back. Which is fine. I know our deal is for the party."

My teeth sink into my bottom lip. He's right, of course. I know I didn't give him much to work with. He was practicing, and I was . . . focusing on not letting it affect me.

Before I can say anything, he adds, "And I was worried I wouldn't be able to stop. I knew one kiss wouldn't be enough. If I kissed you, I would have kissed you all the way to your bed and had my way with you."

I look at my bed with new eyes, imagining what could have happened in here last night if I had just been a little more—well, *more*. A heavy heat settles between my legs at the thought of him being here with me. I've slept with guys I've liked less than Chase, but maybe that's the issue. I like him too much for this to be casual. On second thought, I'm already in this deep, so if I went a little deeper . . .

"If you wanted me to, of course."

Blinking, I come back to reality. I was so distracted by the sheer thought of him, I'd left him hanging. My mouth has suddenly gone dry, and I swallow. "Of course."

There's a pause, like he's waiting for more, and I know I should say something. This is the part where I tell him I feel the same. This is the part where I let my guard down. Hell, this could be the part where I have a little fun with him and hear his husky voice again.

Fuck.

My forehead falls forward into my palm, and I squeeze my eyes shut. I can do this. I can put myself out there for him. He might not want to date me, but he certainly wants *something*. I can be open to it, right? Maybe?

"I think I should hang up now," he says, his voice a little sloppy, like he's getting tired on top of being drunk. "I've been making a mental tally of all the things I'll need to apologize for tomorrow, and it's getting up there."

I let out a laugh, but it does little to ease the tension in my body. "You don't need to apologize for anything."

"You're too good to me, Candace." There's a hint of a smile in his voice.

My heart races because there's so much I want to say—so much I'm not sure I *should*. But ultimately, I shouldn't say any of it while he's drunk. Then we'd both have things to apologize for.

Letting out a sigh, I clench my fist around my blanket and say, "Goodnight, Chase."

His voice is low as he says, "Goodnight, Candace." Then he disconnects the call, and I ache to have him back on the line.

I think I did the right thing. He may not have meant half of what he said, but I can't help feeling like I just missed the opportunity I'd been hoping for.

twenty-two

IT'S HALFWAY through my workday when I finally get a text from Chase.

> **CHASE:**
> Should I ask what your favorite type of flower is?
>
> Or have you already blocked my number?

His message brings a smile to my lips, and my chest warms. I can't remember the last time someone offered to buy me flowers. I'm waiting for one of my afternoon clients, but I have a few minutes to send him a quick response.

> **CANDACE:**
> I know how you feel about useless products, and there's hardly anything more useless than store-bought flowers.
>
> And there's nothing to apologize for.

When I woke up this morning, I felt better about letting the call end last night when it did. It would have been a bad idea to confess anything while he was drunk, and as tempting as it was to let that conversation run away with me, I'm glad we both called it a night.

CHASE:
My tally says otherwise.

CANDACE:
Your tally isn't needed. I enjoyed every minute of our conversation.

Leaning my back against the counter, I watch the three dots as I wait for his next text.

"Still going to that party with him?" Amanda asks as she sweeps the floor near my station.

I glance up to catch her knowing smile. "That's the plan," I say with a raise of my eyebrows. "Miles is helping me pick out a dress for it tomorrow."

"Ooh. I want in on this. You better send me pictures."

"You've got it," I say with a laugh.

CHASE:
I don't deserve you.

Such benevolence.

I shake my head at the words this man chooses to use.

CANDACE:
Only for you.

CHASE:
Let me at least make it up to you with a coffee.

Southern Roast tomorrow?

As tempting as his offer is, Miles and I need to find a dress, and I have no idea how long that will take. I'm hoping it will be quick, but a lot depends on if the dress is waiting for me, front and center, or if the bitch is hiding.

CANDACE:

Can't. Going shopping with Miles.

A woman walks in, who I suspect might be my next client. I haven't met her yet, but Amanda greets her at the door and asks her who she's here to see.

CHASE:

Shopping?

What's the occasion?

I know he's fishing to see if I need a dress for the party Friday. If he finds out I need to buy something, he'll offer to give me money for it. I don't want his money. My disposable income may be new thanks to my recently acquired group of clients, but I can at least afford to buy a dress.

CANDACE:

We don't need an occasion.

I quickly slip my phone back into the drawer when Amanda points the woman in my direction. Giving her my best smile, I hold out a hand and introduce myself.

Ms. Thompson ends up being another referral from Nicolette, who complains about the riffraff they're now letting into the country club. She was nice enough, though. And the tip she left was almost half of what I charged for the cut and color. The rest of the day goes by in a blur, as Saturdays usually do. The constant bustle of the salon leaves me feeling both energized and drained. Some of the other stylists are still working when I pack up my things at 5:30 p.m. I know Saturday appointments are in high demand, but I try to avoid working late on weekends if I can help it.

Reaching for my phone in the drawer, I see there are a couple of new texts from Chase, so I take a moment to catch up.

> CHASE:
> Well, I hope you two find whatever you're looking for.

Then two other texts that look like they came in a few hours after the last one.

> CHASE:
> Miles says you're going dress shopping tomorrow.
>
> For a certain Christmas party.

My face falls. Miles? When did Chase talk to Miles? Exiting the thread, I go back to my messages and open one from my roommate.

It's a picture.

Miles and Chase are together at an outdoor bar I recognize. Their heads are together, both smiling wide like they've been best buds for years, and even though knowing they're together makes my nerves jump to attention, I can't help smiling at the sight.

> MILES:
> Look who I found!
>
> Come meet us when you get off work.

"What are you smiling about?" Amanda catches me as she puts her purse over her shoulder.

With a lingering smile on my lips, I say, "Miles and Chase are at The Yard together. Want to join?"

Her head tilts. "They hang out?"

"They do now, I guess." I give her a bemused shake of my head and hold up the picture I was sent.

She takes a step toward me to get a closer look and laughs. "Well, aren't they a sight for sore eyes? Count me in."

We head out into the evening air, and I'm thankful to feel the slightest chill, reminding me Christmas is near. I'm just wearing black leggings with a white tank and a denim shirt over it, but at least Florida is giving me a reason to keep my arms covered.

As we start our walk, I quickly send Miles and Chase the same text.

CANDACE:

See you boys soon.

I wait a moment to see if either of them responds before putting my phone away, but no new messages come in. The thought of them having too much fun to check their phones should make me happy, but my anxiety spikes. I don't think Miles would tell Chase how much I like him, but I also don't know how long Miles has been there, or how many drinks he's had at this point. The thought makes my feet carry me down the sidewalk just a little faster.

twenty-three

AS SOON AS we reach The Yard, I spot them. Chase has his back to us, but I notice him first. He's on one side of the picnic style table alone while Miles and another guy sit across from him. My eyes immediately snag on Chase's broad shoulders pulling the material of his dark blue T-shirt, and another jolt of excitement runs through me because I get to see weekend Chase again.

Miles looks up as we walk into the large outdoor dining area filled with wooden tables and blue umbrellas. He flashes me a smile, but then slams both hands down on the table and yells, "You brought Amanda?!" with nothing short of elation.

Amanda skips toward him and Miles gets to his feet, colliding into her with a hug. "Bitch, where the hell have you been?" he says as he squeezes her tight.

They're still locked together when I make my way to the table, and Chase looks up at me with a grin. "Well, hey there, beautiful." He slides over to make room for me on the bench beside him, and I smile as I set my bag down and take a seat.

Miles finally releases Amanda long enough to pull away and look at her. "Did you go more platinum?"

"Yeah!" she says with a smile. "Candace helped me with it about a week ago."

Miles runs his fingers over the ends of her hair. "Love." He glances my way. "You did this?"

"I did," I say, happily clasping my hands under my chin and resting my elbows on the table.

Miles walks back around to his seat with Amanda sliding in next to him. "Good job, Stink."

My smile widens. "Why, thank you."

Chase smiles at Amanda as she takes a seat. "Nice to see you again."

You'd think he just said something a lot more with the way she beams at him, but that's part of his charm. "You too."

Gesturing toward the man sitting on the other side of Miles, I ask, "And who do we have here?"

He's tall. I can tell even though we're all sitting. I only come up to Miles's chest, and he looks to be about the same height. He has strawberry blonde hair with scattered freckles, and I *hope* this is the guy Miles has been so crazy about.

The guy holds out a hand to introduce himself. "Hi, I'm Elvis."

Amanda does a double take. "Your name is *Elvis?*"

"He's my accountant," Miles says, like it will somehow explain.

Elvis lets out a laugh. "Would you stop?" Turning back to the rest of us, he adds, "I am not his accountant."

"Oh, that's right." Miles puts his hand up to block out Elvis and loudly whispers, "He's my lover."

My eyes fly to Elvis. After what Miles mentioned about him needing a little more time, I figured he would look uncomfortable, but he just lets out a hearty laugh and says, "You're stupid." The adoration in his eyes suggests otherwise, though.

Miles looks over at Elvis. "You really should be my accountant. My finances are a *mess*. I hope you know what you're getting into."

Elvis shakes his head. "You don't scare me."

"He should," I say with a laugh. Reaching my hand across the table, I introduce myself. "Candace."

Elvis grins and takes my hand. "You and I need to talk."

My smile widens. "We definitely do." In a playful whisper, I add, "I know all his secrets."

Miles looks between us. "I'm not sure how I feel about this."

Ignoring his comment, my eyes jump between him and Chase. "So, how did you two end up here together?"

"Well," Miles says, taking the lead. He gestures toward Elvis, and says, "We were on a date, minding our own business, when this hunk of a man walked up and asked if we'd ever consider adding a third. I, of course, said yes right away, but when I looked up and saw it was Daddy Chase, I was *shocked*."

Chase gives me a sideways glance, his lips turning upward. "I was getting takeout."

Laughter bubbles in my throat. "Makes sense."

He gives me that easy-going smile I love so much, and I'm overwhelmed by my need to kiss him. He's here. Spending time with my best friend of his own free will. Seeing him put in the time to get to know someone so important to me has me wishing this was more. It's something so small, but it's hitting me too hard. If there weren't so many people around, I'd probably climb him. But instead, I settle on resting my hand on his knee hidden beneath the table, showing my appreciation in a smaller way. It's one of the first times I've made a move to touch him, and Chase's eyes light with delight.

His acknowledgment heats my cheeks, and the feeling of his knee against my fingertips has my heart pounding. Even after he looks back at my friends to jump into the conversation, all I can think about is the way he just looked at me, and the fact that I'm still touching him.

It's enough to make me pull my hand away.

Chase snatches my fingers under the table before they get too far, and firmly puts my hand back on his knee. He doesn't say anything about it, and he doesn't look at me, but he keeps me there, his hand resting on mine, before he lets go and folds his arms on the table.

No one notices our subtle exchange. Amanda asks Miles and Elvis how they met, and without missing a beat, Elvis jumps in and says, "We were both on Christian Mingle."

Miles nods. "We were the only two with shirtless profile pics and knew it was meant to be."

Laughter breaks out among the table, and the sound of Chase laughing next to me, while we're surrounded by my friends, might be more addicting than anything else about him.

Elvis catches sight of the dwindling beer in front of Miles. "Another?" he asks, pointing to the glass.

"Please," Miles says with a nod.

Chase turns to me. "Let me buy you a drink."

I beam at him. "Okay."

His mouth quirks as he stands. Before walking away from the table, he stops by Amanda. "Can I get you something, too?"

She smiles up at him. "Pinot Grigio would be great. Thank you."

As soon as Chase and Elvis head toward the bar, I turn my attention to Miles. "Um, he's funny."

He lifts his chin. "I know."

"And hot," Amanda chimes in.

Miles lets out a laugh. "Amanda, you think everyone is hot."

Her eyes widen. "Not true! I just happen to be sitting at a

table with three exceptionally hot men who are all unavailable to me."

"I mean, Chase technically isn't unavailable." My eyes drift up to meet hers.

"Oh, please." Miles shakes his head. "That man adores you."

I arch an eyebrow and say nothing.

"Don't get me wrong, he might still be a fuckboy. But if he is, he's a fuckboy who adores you."

A breath of laughter leaves my lips. "Thanks for the vote of confidence."

He flashes me his best smile. "Anytime."

Amanda puts her hand on mine. "Just see how things go after the Christmas party. It's less than a week away. If you're really not sure where he stands, see what happens after Friday."

Chase returns with our drinks a minute later, saying, "Ladies," as he sets a glass of Chardonnay in front of me and hands Amanda her Pinot.

We thank him and Elvis slides back into his seat next to Miles.

"So, we know Elvis is an accountant, but what do you do for work?" Amanda asks Chase.

He takes a sip of his beer. "Nothing exciting."

"I'm an *accountant*." Elvis emphasizes by putting a hand on his chest.

Chase smirks. "Okay. Maybe my job is a little more exciting than accounting, but not by much." He turns his attention back to Amanda. "I work in advertising."

Her eyes grow wide. "Ooh. Would we recognize any of your campaigns?"

He thinks for a moment. "Yeah, maybe. The one I did for Lexus has gotten a lot of airtime."

Amanda gapes at him. "The one with the woman who hates all the noise at the gas station?"

A humble smile stretches across his lips. "That would be the one."

I know the exact commercial they're talking about. A woman is pumping gas and everything around her is so loud. Someone blaring music, a toddler demanding something from his mother, construction and horns blaring in the distance. But when she gets into her car, everything goes quiet. It ends with words coming up on the screen that read, *Find Your Serenity in a Lexus.*

The ad always stood out to me because it was *good.* It had me wanting the peace and quiet of a Lexus even though there's no way I could afford one.

I blink, looking over at Chase. "That commercial was your idea?"

"Yeah," Chase says simply, like it's nothing to gloat about. "It was fun, and it all worked out because they ended up cutting me a great deal on my car."

"That's amazing!" Amanda says with genuine excitement. "I feel like I know a famous person."

Chase lets out another laugh with a shake of his head, but I can't stop looking at him. Why did I never ask him about his job? About the work he's done? I know I've been trying to keep him at a distance, but how could I have been so selfish to never even ask about his accomplishments? I've been talking to this man every day for over a week, and in a matter of minutes, Amanda connects with him on something he truly cares about. And in a matter of minutes, I feel like I wouldn't deserve him even if he wanted this to be real.

twenty-four

CHASE AND AMANDA have been talking about this new band, American Thieves, for at least twenty minutes while Elvis peppers me with questions about the new man in his life. Even as I laugh and play along, I'm keenly aware of Amanda and Chase the entire time. They're animated and laughing with smiles on their faces, and it's hard not to look over at them every few minutes.

I think I'm succeeding. My eyes stay fixed on Miles and Elvis, giving them at least ninety-five percent of my undivided attention.

"I'm so glad you're here tonight," I tell Elvis with a smile. "I've been asking Miles if I could meet you since I knew you existed."

"Nosy," Miles teases, and I narrow my eyes at him. On a more serious note, he leans toward Elvis. "I told her how this is all a little new."

Elvis nods. "Yeah." He looks around before leaning toward me like he's about to share a secret across the table. "I'm not out with my friends at home yet."

I zip my lips shut and flick the key away. "Well, you're welcome to our side of town anytime."

He gives me a subtle wink. "Thanks."

Miles gets to his feet and stretches his arms overhead. "All right. Well, I'm done sitting on this wooden bench. We were going to meet up with a few people at Stem and Leaf. Want to come?" He looks around at the rest of us.

Amanda jumps to her feet. "I'll join, but only if I'm not crashing."

Miles waves away her concern. "Absolutely not."

My eyes jump to Chase, but I've already started shaking my head. Looking up at Miles, I say, "I'll probably turn in. Long day."

"I'll walk you," Chase says, and having his eyes on me sends a jolt down my spine.

"Oh. Um. Okay." I nod. "Sure."

We all stand and gather our things, and my heart starts to race at the thought of walking back with Chase alone. Miles snaps me out of it when he says, "Hey, Stink," and I look up at him. "Did you bring your shears home with you?"

I grimace. "I didn't. Why? Want a haircut?"

"Yeah. I figured if we're hanging out all day tomorrow, you could clean up this mess. It's fine, though."

"I'll stop at the salon on the way home and grab them."

"Wait." Chase has been watching our exchange open-mouthed. He balks at Miles and me. "She cuts your hair?"

Miles gives me a sideways glance like he's not sure why this is weird. "Yeah . . . ?"

Chase shifts his focus to me. "You cut his hair?"

I let out a sigh, knowing exactly where this is going. "Yes. I cut his hair."

Looking back at Miles, he runs his hands through his brunette locks and grips them the way I knew he would. "I've been asking her to cut my hair since I met her, and she won't do it."

Miles glances at me with uncertainty written in his eyes, but I just shake my head. We might be able to communicate a lot of things telepathically, but there's no way I can describe my reasoning with a single look.

Miles looks back at Chase with faked sympathy. "Well, she loves me more. Sorry."

Chase cracks a smile and points up at his hair, still sticking up from where he gripped it at the roots. "Well, this is getting out of hand, Candace."

I roll my eyes and dismiss him by looking at the other three. "Have fun tonight."

"You too," Miles says with a laugh, like even *he* knows Chase won't let this haircut thing go.

We say our goodbyes and head out in opposite directions.

The night air feels dry and cool against my skin. Year round, the city has string lights over the cobblestone streets, but for the month of December, the trees are wrapped in red and green twinkling lights, too. The whole scene makes our little downtown feel more magical at night.

As Chase and I walk, we're practically shoulder to shoulder. Our arms brushing now and then, and each time they do, I take in the clean scent of him.

"Didn't want to keep the party going?" I ask.

He gives me a warm smile. "I am keeping it going."

I let out a breath of laughter that comes out sounding more like a scoff. "Right." Before he can say more, I offer, "I know I joked to stay away from Amanda, but you guys seemed to hit it off. If you like her, I'm sure she'd be interested."

He stops in his tracks, and by the time I turn around, I'm a few paces ahead of him. "You think I like Amanda?"

"I think you two have things in common, and she seems like your type."

He shakes his head. "Oh, Candace." Walking back toward me, he tsks the whole way, "Candace, Candace, Candace."

"What?" I ask with a laugh. "She's adorable."

He nods. "She is."

"And sweet."

"Very."

"And blonde."

His lips press into a tight-lipped smile as he holds up a finger. "Ah, there it is."

I let out a laugh. "What? I'm trying to help you."

He sticks both hands in his pockets. "That's not how you can help me, and we both know it."

Now it's my turn to stop in my tracks. Something about his response hits differently. Something has shifted. I don't know what, and I'm not sure when, but this is more than fake dates and practice. It has to be.

He doesn't stop. He doesn't turn around. He just keeps walking, and says over his shoulder, "Come on. Your salon is up here."

Is he mad? I've never seen Chase upset, but the subtle change is noticeable. I scramble to catch up with him, but he still makes it to the salon door before me. Leaning up against the front of the building, he waits for me to get my key.

"Let me make one thing clear," Chase says as he watches me fumble with the lock. "I stayed and hung out with Miles tonight for you, and I got to know Amanda tonight for you."

I give him a sideways glance as I unlock the door. "I never asked you to do either of those things."

He shakes his head as I pull the door open. Catching the edge with his hand, he holds it open for me, his arm above my head. "That's not my point," he says as I walk past him. I go to my station and get the small case with my shears inside the drawer, but I can feel him watching me. "My point is that as great as your friends are, it's not about them. It's about you. It's always about you."

twenty-five

IT'S ABOUT ME? I stare at him, not sure what to say back to that. Part of me wants to call him a liar. It hasn't always been about me. It's not like I'm the one who needs a stand-in date for my company's Christmas party.

But the way he looks at me makes me want to believe him. I think I *do* believe him. At least when it comes to this. The word *why* is on the tip of my tongue, but I pull it back. The way he's intently watching me is too much for me to keep this conversation on the track it's going. Something in my gut tells me I shouldn't dig for what he means because we're wandering into dangerous territory. When I first met Chase, everything about him screamed that he plays the field and would only want to keep things casual, but the way he's looking at me now has me second guessing myself. He has no business looking at me this way, and I have no business tripping over that look.

Changing the subject, I ask, "So, how fancy are we talking for this Christmas party? I want to make sure I get the right dress."

He looks down like he's collecting himself before answering. "You'll look amazing in anything you wear. You could show up in a T-shirt, and you'd still steal the show." His mouth lifts, and I'm grateful for the familiar playfulness behind his eyes. "Just get something you like, and let me pay for it."

"That is . . . wildly unhelpful but thank you." I drop the case with my shears into my bag and cross my arms. "What about the decorations? Are we talking chandeliers and ice sculptures or cozy with greenery?"

"I don't know. Expensive?" he says slowly as he looks around the salon for inspiration. "I'm sure there will be garland and Christmas trees of some variety or another." His eyes lock on me before trailing to the ceiling above. "Mistletoe."

I look up, and sure enough, I'm standing directly under one of the many mistletoe scattered around the salon. I swallow before sliding my gaze back to find him studying me.

"That's still not exactly helpful." My voice comes out quieter than I expected, but that probably has something to do with it being harder to breathe.

He smiles faintly and walks across my station until we're both under the mistletoe.

"What are your thoughts on mistletoe?" he asks, his voice low.

I look up again. "I like them as much as any other Christmas decoration."

Chase lets out a low laugh, pulling my eyes back to him, but he's still looking above us. "Oh, come on. They're easily the least useless of all the decorations. They at least serve a purpose."

My lips turn upward, and I try to desperately hide how hard my heart is hammering in my chest when he brings his gaze back to mine. "I guess that's a fair point."

"I think so," he agrees quietly.

Our eyes lock, and for a moment we're both just standing toe-to-toe, looking at each other. He's close enough for me to feel the heat coming off him. Close enough for me to smell the scent of fresh linens and his usual spice. If either of us shifted an inch, there'd be no space between us.

How much I crave to close that space is terrifying.

My breathing shallows, and Chase's gaze dips to my mouth for a fraction of a second. There's a seriousness about him again. Lost is the playful quirk of his lips or the mischievous glint in his eyes. The man standing before me looks like he's full of heavy thoughts and deliberation. He glances up at the mistletoe again before settling his unwavering gaze back on me. "We should probably—" His focus shifts to my mouth again. "You know, we might as well . . . so we know what we're doing."

My voice is soft when I ask, "For practice?"

His eyes jump to meet mine. "Yeah."

"Are you sure?"

"I think we should practice."

"Okay," I whisper, my voice all but completely gone.

But he doesn't kiss me right away. His hand weaves into my hair, and that alone is enough to make my breath catch in my throat. His tongue wets his bottom lip, like just the thought of what he's about to do has his body physically reacting.

I'm completely still. I think I've forgotten how to move. I barely remember how to breathe.

His thumb runs along my jaw, setting every fiber of my being ablaze. It isn't until the seconds passing without his lips on mine turn to torture that I breathe out his name.

His stare jumps from my lips to meet my gaze.

"This is the part where you kiss me."

And just like that, his eyes fall back to my mouth again. "I know," he says, his voice rough. He swallows. "But if I fuck this up . . ." He shakes his head.

I open my mouth, but whatever I was about to say gets wiped away when his lips find mine. All hope of him being a bad kisser is also wiped away—along with every other thought

I could have. I soften into him. All the tension I've held in my body, trying to keep this man at a distance, melts from solid ice to a puddle.

His warm, perfect lips drag over mine. And as they do, he somehow pulls me with him. I push up on my toes, not wanting this to end—trying to keep us connected in this magical moment for as long as I can.

When our lips threaten to part, I waste no time going back for more. I need it—*crave* it. If this is the only time I'll kiss him while we're alone, I want to make the most of it. My lips pull him back to me in a matter of seconds, and the way it unleashes some of his restraint only fuels me more.

Chase places his free hand on the other side of my face, cradling my head, and I let him tilt my face to kiss me deeper. I let him take control again, and I melt for him a million times over. His tongue expertly parts my lips, pulling a soft moan from the back of my throat, and that small sound has him kissing me deeper. When his tongue slides over mine, a heavy, wanting heat settles between my legs. It's been so long since I've felt this . . . this feeling of hope . . . this feeling of surrender . . . this *turned on*. My hands are in his hair, and I might as well be a teenager with how desperate I am for more.

I have no idea how much time has passed when we eventually pull apart. With heavy breaths, I imagine what I must look like in this moment: swollen lips, skin chafed from his weekend scruff, and I'm sure my hair is an absolute mess.

When Chase finally drops his arm and creates a crack of space between us again, he's breathing hard, too. He's disheveled, and something about knowing I'm the one who undid this perfect man has me dying to kiss him again.

"I don't think you fucked it up," I manage to say.

There's no cocky smirk or playfulness to his voice when he says, "No. That was—" He swallows and nods. "That was good."

I take a step back despite everything inside me screaming to jump him. I was hoping the distance would clear my head, but getting a better look at him definitely makes the fog worse. God, the things I would do to him if I didn't think things would go downhill from there.

Chase clears his throat, and it's only then that I realize my eyes were dragging down the scope of his body. I blink, and a fresh wave of heat washes over me. Spinning around, I look for something to keep me busy. I grab a comb from my station and tuck it into my bag for no particular reason, and then walk over to my cabinet and act like I'm searching for something, but I can feel his eyes on me the whole time. "So, no advice for the dress, then?" I ask over my shoulder.

"Candace."

Something in the way he says my name sends my heart into a frenzy. Pausing my pointless search, I slowly turn to face him.

"That was a good kiss."

"Yeah," I say, suddenly out of breath again. "It was."

His warm, brown eyes look darker than I've ever seen, but he doesn't make an attempt to move or speak. He just looks at me, and the weight of his gaze could drop me to my knees. And once I'm on my knees—nope. Not going there.

I close my cabinet and force myself back to reality—the reality where this is practice for a performance. "Think we'll be able to convince your coworkers?"

He doesn't answer right away. He just stands with his back against my station, but in a fraction of a second, his demeanor shifts. He blinks, snapping out of whatever thoughts he just had and as he pushes off, he says, "Yeah. I'm not worried about it. Got everything you need?"

I nod, looking around the salon one last time. As terrifying as it was to have his full attention a moment ago, I deflate at his shift. "Yeah."

"Great. I'll walk you home."

Now it's my turn to scrutinize him. He's still pleasant, but the closeness we shared has vanished. We're back to being us—friends. He turns and opens the door, and I thank him as he holds it open. "You don't have to walk me home."

Chase shakes his head before looping his arm over my shoulder. "It's late. I'm walking you home."

And as much as I want to fight him on it, I don't. Because he's touching me again, and all I can do is replay the kiss we shared and think about my newfound appreciation for mistletoe.

twenty-six

MILES MAKES A FACE. "ABSOLUTELY NOT."

I stare down at the long black dress on the hanger in front of me. Miles has turned down every single one of my finds, but he hasn't suggested a single dress. He just browses through the racks with a face of determination and an unwillingness to consider anything with sleeves.

"How is it hideous? It's just a black dress."

He answers without looking. "My point exactly."

I stare at him, waiting for more of an explanation, but he continues his search. I let out a groan and stare up at the ceiling, collecting myself before I tackle the next row. We've been at it for almost an hour, and I haven't tried anything on.

"Should I just wait for you to find whatever you're looking for?" I point a thumb over my shoulder at the pair of chairs where disgruntled husbands usually sit.

"No . . ." Miles drags out the word. "*You* should be looking for something sexy instead of trying to dress like a scandalous nun for this thing." He picks up one dress and considers it for a moment before tossing it over his forearm. "You set the bar with that black dress you wore on your date, and I know this occasion calls for something a little different, but the man has expectations now."

I scoff. "I doubt it. He wasn't exactly helpful when I asked him for specifics." My mind wanders back to Chase listing off decorations before finally landing on *mistletoe*. That was easily the best first kiss I've ever had, and I'm still trying to figure out if that should disappoint me, or if I should be elated by it.

"Which dress did you just pick up?" I point to the material draped over his arm.

Miles glances down at the dark piece of fabric before waving me off. "It has potential, but I'm not convinced it's the one."

"At this rate, we'll never find *the one*. Let me try it on."

He holds up the dress in my direction like he's trying to imagine it on me. "I guess it can't hurt," he finally says, handing it over.

Happily snatching it from his hand, I head to the dressing room with Miles at my heels.

"I'll wait here for the big reveal." He takes a seat in one of the chairs outside the women's fitting room, and I slip inside. I know he wants Chase's jaw to hit the floor when he sees me Friday night. I want that too, but I don't think I have to go for solid sex appeal the way Miles is thinking. I'm sure if I find a nice dress that's flattering for my body, he'd have the same type of reaction.

Slipping on the sleek maroon dress, I quickly realize I can't wear a bra because of how low the back goes. I take off my bra and position the fabric. Staring at myself in the mirror, I can't deny the dress is gorgeous. It's simple with its thin straps and overlapping fabric, creating a dip at my chest. My chest fills out the dress nicely, but what really makes it eye-catching is the slit gliding up and stopping mid-thigh. I'm sure my leg would look incredible through that slit if I were wearing heels.

Once I step into view, Miles perks up. "God damn. That looks better than I thought it would."

"Yeah?" I ask, looking down and smoothing my hands over the fabric.

He raises his eyebrows. "Uh. Yeah. You two might not even make it to the party with a dress like that, and that's exactly what I was going for." I roll my eyes, but he ignores me and circles his finger in my direction. "Spin."

I do and look over my shoulder to see his response. "Damn," he says again. "I'm good. I am really fucking good." His eyes dart up to meet mine behind his neon glasses. "You know you can't wear panties, right?"

"Yeah, I saw that. I might have a thinner pair at home I can try."

He shakes his head slowly. "Eh, I wouldn't risk it. Why mess up a dress like this with a panty line?"

He's probably right, but I'll still look when I go home. "So, you think this is good?"

He nods. "I think he's definitely going to want to fuck you."

I let out a laugh. "Why is that always the goal?"

"Consider me a matchmaker," he says with a grin. "A true believer of Christmas miracles."

My eyes narrow. "You just want to know if he's good, don't you?"

He nods, unashamed. "Very much so."

I turn to study myself in the mirror, pushing up on my toes, so I can imagine what it will look like once I have heels on. "Well, if it's anything like how he kisses, it's bound to be good."

Miles sits up straighter. "You kissed him?"

I catch his eyes in the reflection of the mirror and nod.

"And I'm just hearing about it now?"

I turn around to face him again. "It happened last night." I shrug. "He thought it would help if we got it out of the way."

Miles groans, rolling his eyes with his whole head like he does. "Oh, fuck this practice shit. What happened?"

I laugh at how invested he is in all of this. "He kissed me at my salon, and then he walked me home."

Miles blinks, but the fact that he's not saying anything tells me he's waiting for more.

". . . And that's it."

He gapes at me. "That's it? You didn't pull him into our apartment and have your way with him?"

"I did not."

His forehead falls into his hand, and he rubs his head like a disappointed coach might. "Candace," he says quietly.

"Yes, Miles?"

"Sleep with the man. You're attracted to him, and he's attracted to you. Who cares if it doesn't last? Have *fun*."

My teeth sink into my bottom lip. He's right. In some roundabout way, he's *always* right, but I still feel like if I sleep with Chase, I'd be selling myself short.

Dropping my arms by my side, I let out a sigh. "Okay, fine. Maybe." Raising my eyebrows at him, I ask, "The dress?"

Miles lets out one of his deep laughs I adore so much. "Never mind. Don't sleep with him. You look like I just suggested getting a root canal with no drugs." He stands and gets to his feet. Looking over his shoulder, he adds, "And if you like the dress, I think you should get it. Your boobs have never looked so good."

My lips twist into a smile as he leaves the fitting room area. With a shake of my head, I turn on my heels and head back into the dressing room. Pulling the curtain shut, I stare at myself in the mirror. I feel good. Glancing down, I check the tag and that good feeling disappears. *Holy shit.* I mean, the dress is gorgeous, but $300? I grimace and study myself in the mirror again. It's hard to justify spending that amount of money regardless of how good I look. My mind is already running through my schedule for the next couple of weeks to help justify the cost. At least it's always busy around the holidays. Even Nicolette and all her friends push up their appointments to make sure they're looking great going into the new year.

And this dress looks like it was made for me.

Taking a deep breath and facing forward again. I run my hands over the soft fabric. I can do this. I can buy myself an expensive dress.

And it took so long to find it. I know Miles would be a good sport if I went out there and said we needed to keep looking. He'd probably shop all day if it meant finding something perfect, but the last thing I want to do is start this search all over again.

My shoulders drop as I resign to keeping the dress. I don't know if Miles is right about whether I should sleep with Chase, but he is right about one thing. My boobs do look amazing.

twenty-seven

MY WEALTHY WEEKLY REGULAR is back, and even though I was grateful for her when I put that dress on my card, I'm having trouble holding onto that feeling now. She's driving me nuts. I've spent the last hour foiling Nicolette's hair for the highlights she insisted she needed, even though her brown roots were barely visible. Today was supposed to be one of her regular blow dry days, but she came in frantic, insisting she had to have her color touched up before the weekend. So, I've been running around the salon at maximum speed, trying to get this shit done before my next client comes in a couple of hours.

Checking the large digital clock on the salon wall, I turn back to Nicolette. "Now we just wait for you to process. I'll probably have time to dry you, but I might not have time to curl your hair."

A dramatic frown tugs the corners of her mouth down. "Oh, but I need you to curl it, too. I'm sure you could use the extra money." She eyes me in the mirror, and in a sing-song voice, adds, "I'll make it worth your while."

I nod to hide my teeth gritting. "Of course. I'll make it

happen." I know for a last-minute job like this, she'll tip even bigger than she normally would, but she doesn't have to be so condescending about it. She acts like she single-handedly keeps the lights on for me, and okay, maybe the payout I get from her and her friends helps—a lot—but that doesn't mean she should act like she owns me. "I just may have to do it after I get my next client situated."

I hate being double booked. If I had my own space, it would be one thing. But with so many other stylists sharing the floor, it can be tricky to figure out where to put someone while I have a second person in my chair.

"Great," she says happily. "Only you get my blonde just right."

Fake blonde.

Her roots are dark. It's why she comes in here every six weeks on the dot. Sometimes she'll even bump it up to four or five, depending on who she's trying to impress.

My phone vibrates in my back pocket, and I look at it since I'm just waiting for the chemicals to do their thing.

> CHASE:
> Have I mentioned how much I hate Tuesdays?

> CANDACE:
> I was just thinking the same thing.

Three messages come in from him, back-to-back.

> CHASE:
> We should run away together. Every Tuesday.
> We'll tell no one and hide out.
> Bring snacks.

His idea sounds amazing, but then again, doing anything with him sounds amazing.

> CANDACE:
> If only.

"Who has you smiling like that?" Nicolette asks, pulling my attention back to the mirror. She's watching me with that cat-like grin, and I quickly tuck my phone in my back pocket.

"Oh, no one. Just a friend." I start cleaning up the color bowls I used and wash my brushes in the sink.

I can feel her eyes still on me when she says, "That's not the type of smile you give for a friend."

I shake my head. "It would never work. I'm just . . . I'm just in a bit of a predicament, I guess."

She audibly gasps. "Ooh, is he married?"

Letting out a baffled laugh, I say, "What? No. Not at all."

She's quiet for a moment, like she's trying to decide if she believes me. "Trying to pick between two?"

I shake my head with a bemused smile still on my lips.

Nicolette sighs. "If your boyfriend is the one who pays the bills, I understand why you'd stay with him. I know a lot of women who won't leave their husbands for the same reason. That's why I climbed the corporate ladder myself."

Oh, how badly I want to roll my eyes at this woman. You would think she's never done anything for herself with the way she acts sometimes. I swear she's a country club wife at heart. I take a deep breath, and before turning around, I put on my best smile. "I could probably learn a thing or two from you." When all else fails, go with flattery.

Lifting her chin, she says, "Oh, I have no doubt." Eyeing me in the mirror again, she lifts a feline brow. "If you're trying to decide who to sleep with, go with the guy who earns less than you—they're usually better in bed. If you're trying to be taken care of in other ways . . . well, then find a man who earns more." She shrugs casually. "Some women end up having both."

I let out a breath of laughter. "Right." Peeking at one of her foils, I say, "Let's get this hair washed," and hope that's the end of this conversation.

It's not. She goes on about how men who earn less usually feel the need to *prove* themselves in bed, and by the time my other client, Brianna, arrives, I'm desperate to greet her and get started. Fortunately, Nicolette has some sense of self-awareness around people who aren't me, and the small talk she makes with Brianna stays within the safe confines of nail polish colors and designer handbags.

I end up getting home late thanks to the last-minute hair emergency and settle into the couch as I catch Miles up on Nicolette's fucked up philosophy on men.

"Damn." He shakes his head. "I mean, I guess she has a point. If she's just looking for a good time, why not date younger?"

I huff. "Not *younger*, just someone who earns less." I turn back toward the TV where Miles and I are watching all the Christmas episodes from *The Office*.

"Oh. Yeah, that's fucked. Is she hot?"

"Gorgeous, but talking to her is exhausting, and I'm only with her for a couple of hours a week. I can only imagine how the men she dates must feel."

My phone lights up on the couch between us.

CHASE:

Candace.

Miles drops his gaze to the phone before raising his eyebrows with a pleased look on his face. "Speaking of men you are dating . . ."

I shoot him a warning look and grab my phone.

CANDACE:

Chase.

His response comes in right away.

CHASE:

I need a haircut.

My breath comes out more like a scoff.
"Something wrong?" Miles asks.
"He wants a haircut," I say as I type my next message.

CANDACE:

Then go get a haircut.

CHASE:

Let me clarify.

I need you to give me a haircut.

Miles shakes his head. "Why don't you just cut the man's hair? You just did mine, and now I look fabulous." He flips a piece of invisible hair over his shoulder.

CANDACE:

Let me also clarify. Again.

I'm not cutting your hair.

"Because," I say as I type back my response. "I don't need him becoming a client. I don't know if I'll want to see him every six weeks after this."

CHASE:

Candace.

I'm about to take out the kitchen scissors.

Don't think I won't do it.

"Now he's threatening me with kitchen scissors," I say flatly.

"I'm glad I know the context behind that statement." Miles

shakes his head. "Just cut his hair. If things end badly, or if you don't want to see him again after this, *then* you can tell him no. But there's no point in not cutting his hair now."

> CANDACE:
> Don't you dare.

Looking up at Miles, I sigh. "If he comes to the salon, he's going to draw attention. He brought me coffee the other day, and Amanda could hardly walk a straight line. The more people in my life who meet him and think there's something going on between us, the more questions I'll have to answer when this is all over."

A picture comes in from Chase, and I pause before opening it. He's never sent me a picture, and for some reason, I'm thrilled by the new development. Tapping on my screen, a full-sized picture of Chase standing in his bathroom comes into view. He's leaning toward the mirror, his eyes trained on his reflection while he holds a pair of black kitchen scissors near the top of his head. His tongue pokes out between his lips in concentration and . . . he's shirtless.

"Holy shit." Miles snatches the phone from my hand to get a better look. "Daddy Chase is fucking ripped."

"Would you give that back?" I ask, trying not to sound flustered.

He does, but he moves in closer, so his eyes never have to leave the photo. "Candace."

I stare at the picture and swallow hard. "Yes, Miles?"

"Go cut that man's hair."

I nod, in a trance from the sight of Chase's bare chest. "Yeah. I should probably do that."

"And when you're done . . ."

"Yes, Miles?"

"Lick his fucking skin off."

I laugh and push him away before trying to type my next

text. My thumbs hover over the keyboard when another message appears.

CHASE:
Should I take your silence as full support?

I'm tempted to write back saying the only thing I fully support is him never wearing a shirt again, but I don't think that would be helpful for either of us.

CANDACE:
Send me your address, and don't do anything stupid before I get there.

twenty-eight

A HALF HOUR LATER, I'm standing in front of Chase's high-rise apartment. If anything is clear after the conversation I had with Nicolette today, it's that he makes more money than I do. When Miles and I were shopping for apartments, we didn't even look in this area because we couldn't afford it—and that's with *two* incomes.

Inside, the espresso doors contrast with the cool white walls, and the whole vibe of the place makes me feel like I'm in an art museum. I had to stop by the salon to grab my shears and a few other things on my way here. I thought about turning back and changing my mind at least five times, but I know Miles wouldn't have it. He's right about Chase not becoming my client. I can always tell him I don't want to cut his hair later. I just wish we weren't opening this door in the first place.

Contradicting my thoughts, I raise my knuckles to the dark wood and knock. It only takes a moment for Chase to answer. Even though he put a shirt on, he still looks hot. His gray sweats casually hang on his hips and the white T-shirt paired with them stretches over his frame in all the right places.

"Candace," he says with a grin, like he wasn't expecting me. "Come on in." He steps aside.

"Hey." I try my best to give him a convincing smile, even though I'm still not sure if I should be here.

His apartment is stunning. Modern. Sleek. Clean. A large black leather couch takes up the open concept family room and faces a massive TV mounted to the wall. Behind it sits a large kitchen where an impressive island houses the sink.

"Chase," I say quietly as I marvel at the high ceilings and dark accents against the light floors and walls. "Your place is gorgeous, but . . ." I turn to face him. "There's no Christmas tree."

He moves his hands to his pockets and leans up against the entryway like watching me take it all in is fun for him. He shrugs. "It's just me. Seems kind of pointless to decorate."

I gape at him. "But it's *Christmas.*" Staring around the beautiful, but sterile room, I add, "Florida hardly feels like Christmas. Literally all we have are decorations."

He points over his shoulder. "Say the word and I'll fill the place with fake snow."

I give him a warning look before my eyes trail over the sleek fireplace made of dark tile, and I point to the mantle. "You could hang some stockings."

"It's just me," he reiterates.

"Or garland."

"I'd be vacuuming up plastic pine needles every hour."

I give him a sideways glance. "You do seem a little . . . *meticulous.*" Turning to face him, I take in the entire scene, assessing Chase, not for the first time. "And put together."

The corner of his mouth lifts. "I like things a certain way."

Taking a few steps toward him, I stop to examine him a little more closely. He's watching me with mild apprehension behind those beautiful eyes, and even though his posture stays relaxed, I have a feeling he's reconsidering letting me come here.

My fingers run through his locks before pulling the strands out at an angle to check the length. "It's been driving you crazy not to cut your hair, hasn't it?"

"Yes, but every time you run your hands through it, it's worth it."

My hand stills in his hair, and we lock eyes. "Why not just get it cut where you'd usually go?"

"You're prettier than my barber."

Dismissing his comment with a shake of my head, I pull my hand from his hair and look around. "Well, where do you have the best light?"

Moving away from the doorframe, he cuts to the other end of the living room and flips a light on near his kitchen table. The lighting is still a lot softer than what I'd have in the salon, but it will do. Chase pulls out a chair and takes a seat. He's so beautiful in his element this way. Seeing him in sweats, sitting in his apartment, might even beat the version of him I love seeing on weekends. It's like the more casual he becomes, the more attracted I am. I brace myself for my next sentence. "You should probably take off your shirt."

He raises his eyebrows, that adorable smirk pulling at the corner of his mouth. "You want me to take my shirt off?"

"Unless you want hair in it. I forgot to grab a cape."

"How convenient." He lets out a laugh as he pulls his shirt over his head. He methodically folds the shirt before setting it on the table.

I'm in a trance.

I don't snap out of it until he takes a seat again and nods toward me. "Ready when you are."

"Right. Sorry." I blink and move from my spot in the living room to join him. Setting my bag down on the kitchen table, I organize my things with the distinct feeling of his eyes on me the entire time.

I shoot him a sideways glance and tease, "Are you worried I'll mess something up?" I grab my spray bottle.

"Are you kidding? I've never been more confident about being in the right hands."

Shielding his eyes and face with my hand, I dampen his hair. "But you like things a certain way."

"I'm quickly realizing having you standing in front of me wearing leggings and a Rolling Stones T-shirt is how I like things."

Gliding my fingers over the strands of his hair, I prepare for the first cut. "Right," I say with a breath of laughter. "Let's hope you still feel that way when I'm done." The scissors snip and the first few strands fall to the floor. I know what I'm doing when it comes to hair, and since I already have a feel for how he likes his, I have no problem making the first cut and getting to work. Maneuvering around him, I take turns using my comb and shears to cut and texturize. He's been quiet the whole time, and I hope he isn't regretting this decision.

I stand in front of him as I finish. "I don't think you've ever been this quiet."

"I don't think I've ever seen you this focused."

Leaning back slightly, I run my comb through his hair to see how everything falls. "I'm working."

"Well, it's turning me on."

The words come out of his mouth so casually. I almost don't catch what he said, but as soon as it registers, I lean back to look at him again. "What?" I ask with a laugh.

His eyes jump up to meet mine. "Are you really that surprised?"

"Yes," I answer automatically.

A ghost of a smile teases at the corner of his mouth. "Candace, you're practically straddling me, and I think I should sit on my hands, so I'm not tempted to touch you in ways that I shouldn't."

I look down, and sure enough, my wide stance hovers over his leg. My heart stutters in my chest, and the room suddenly feels too warm. I should tell him to sit on his hands. I should step away from him. Flirting with Chase feels like playing with fire, but before I can stop myself, I say, "Since when do you hold back on touching me?"

"Always," he answers too quickly. "I always hold back when it comes to touching you."

Every warning siren goes off in my brain, but everything I've been trying to do for the sake of self-preservation wanes under the intensity of his stare. "Why?"

A humorless laugh leaves him, and he drops his gaze to where his hand rests on his thigh. All it takes is a lift of his pinky, and he's grazing the inside of my knee. "Because there's no limit for me. I could do everything with you and not regret a single thing." He keeps his eyes trained on his hand as he smooths his palm over my thigh and hooks his fingers around the back of my leg. "But the last thing I want to do is make you uncomfortable. If I ever did something to make you say Jack Frost, I'd be . . ." He shakes his head.

My pulse quickens, and it takes all my willpower to keep my knees from buckling. I try to brush it off with a smile as I look over my work, running my hands through the shorter hair.

His mouth quirks, but he says, "It's not funny, Candace."

"It's a little funny," I admit with a shrug, and hope he can't see how much he's affecting me. The way my heart is in overdrive, but the rest of my body has slowed. The way the warmth of his hand has me wishing he could touch me everywhere. And how the thought of him touching me everywhere has a heavy heat pooling between my thighs.

I continue to check his hair even though I've finished. He means he could do everything *physical* with me. That he wouldn't regret a single thing if we crossed the lines of friendship over to something more.

But I'd want more than physical. I'd want all of him. So as much as I'd love to indulge myself in Chase, I know better. I know what sleeping with him would do to me, but he's so damn tempting. My gaze dips to his mouth. Why couldn't he have been a bad kisser?

"Candace?" Chase asks, pulling me from my thoughts.

I dare to look at him. "Hmm?"

His hand is still on my leg, my knees weakening with every brush of his thumb. "Are you done?"

My eyes dip to his lips again. I don't want to be done. If anything, I hope I'm just getting started.

twenty-nine

I BLINK. "AM I DONE?"

Both his hands are on my legs now, and I have no idea when the other one mirrored the first. "You were cutting my hair."

"Right." I nod. "Yeah, I'm done."

He's watching me carefully. "Look, if I overstepped with something I said, I didn't mean—"

"No!" I say, and it comes out louder than I meant it to. "No. Don't . . ." My words come out breathless. "Don't stop talking."

He cocks an eyebrow. "Don't stop talking?"

My cheeks flare. "I just mean—" I wet my lips. "I like when you say things."

Both hands move up a little higher, his thumbs grazing the inside of my upper thighs. "Like when I say you turn me on? Because, Candace, I . . ."

His thumbs creep dangerously close to where I'm aching to be touched, but I panic. I sit in his lap, straddling him before he can get that far. As soon as I sit, I can feel how true his last statement was. He's hard and thick between my legs, and it takes all my self-control not to rock against him. Even without the added movement, Chase sucks in a breath, his hands wasting no time sliding up to cup my ass.

"I like the things you say." I'm rethinking this position now that I can feel how perfectly he fits between my legs, but I try to stay focused. "I like spending time with you, but I can't sleep with you."

He lets out a breath as he adjusts to me on top of him. "I wasn't asking you—"

"I know, but you don't want me to say Jack Frost, so I'm letting you know what would make me say it."

He nods, looking more serious. It isn't until he says, "Can't or don't want to?" that he looks more like his usual self, up to no good.

My heart pounds in my chest. "What do you mean?"

His mouth pulls into a half smile. "They're two very different things. You said you can't sleep with me. Is that because you don't want to? Or is something else preventing us from both getting what we want?" His fingers trace along my lower back as he waits for me to give him an answer.

"Despicable," I say with a light laugh and a shake of my head. His entire body radiates heat, and my hands explore the lines and grooves of his muscled stomach.

There's a wicked glint behind his eyes. "So I've been told." He holds my gaze for another beat before relenting. "Okay, fine. We won't sleep together." He gives me a playful lift of his brow, and I brace myself for whatever he's about to say. "But you still want me to say whatever thought pops into my head? No thought is off limits?"

My lips twist. "No thought is off limits."

He sits up straight, pulling me flush against him. Feeling the bulge of him pressed against me pulls a gasp from my lips, the added pressure creating a delicious ache between my legs.

His voice is low and husky when he says, "Good. Because I'm going to need you to move those hips for me, beautiful. Give me something to think about when I fuck my hand later."

He presses his lips to my throat, and I suck in a breath. My hands weave through his still damp hair, pulling it at the roots and forcing his mouth up to meet mine. He tastes like mint, and when his tongue sweeps over my bottom lip, I gladly open for him to kiss me deeper. His tongue drags over mine, and my hips roll. I'm desperate to create friction between us for my own selfish reasons, but when he groans and says, "Fuck. Good girl," I almost self-combust.

My mouth moves to his neck where I leave an open-mouthed kiss, and then another, and another—all while slowly grinding against him. I nip at his jawline, and the sound of his breath catching will forever haunt me in the best way. This kiss was a terrible idea. I can already feel my resolve slipping. The back of my mind desperately tries to come up with excuses to go back on my words, even though I only said them minutes ago. Thank God we're confined to this kitchen chair. There's only so much damage we can do here.

We're all tongue, teeth, and lips, and every tiny new thing I discover sends a wave of excitement through me. Like the way he grips me tighter when I take his bottom lip between my teeth. Or the way he weaves his hand in my hair when he wants to kiss me deeper. Even the way he grips my hips to still them, as if the movement he asked for is too much to bear. They're all fragments of a bigger picture clicking into place, and I'm dying to see the finished result even though that's the one thing I said I wouldn't do with him.

Eventually, Chase's kisses slow before he leans his head back and stares at the ceiling, breathing hard. "Is the dress you got for the event ugly?"

Through panting breaths, I let out a bewildered laugh. "What?"

Rolling his head to look at me, he says, "Please tell me the dress you're wearing Friday is hideous. Because if it's not, I think it might put me over the edge. You could kill me, Candace."

"What are you talking about?" I say with another laugh. "You saw me in a dress when we went on our 'not date.'"

His eyebrows furrow. "That was definitely a date."

"A fake date."

He holds my stare like he's considering whether to argue with me. "Fine. Yes, I saw you in a dress for our 'fake date.'" He releases his grip on the back of my neck to put air quotes around the words. "But I had no idea how you tasted or moved . . ." His hands slide up my thighs on either side until his thumbs hook at my hips. "I had no idea how you *felt*." He shakes his head. "I was so naïve. So blissfully ignorant of what I was missing."

Resting my arms on his shoulders, I brush some of the hair off him before running my fingers through the short hair at the nape of his neck. "To be fair, you'll still be able to do all those things at the party. That's kind of the whole point of this."

His gaze locks on mine, and those warm brown eyes look like they have so much to say. He opens his mouth, but his lips shut too soon. He nods. "You're right."

The silence that falls between us feels weighted, so I move to get off him. "Why don't you check your hair before I leave?"

Chase wipes his hands on his pants and lets out a breath before pushing himself up. "Don't trust your work?" Looking over his shoulder, he smirks and gestures for me to follow.

I'm relieved when he leads us to a bathroom in the hall and not his bedroom. If I saw Chase's bed right now, there's a good chance I'd pull him onto it and make him forget I ever said I couldn't sleep with him.

"I don't trust the picky guy who hired me," I tease.

We both stand in front of the mirror, and all it takes is one look at my mussed hair for me to break into laughter.

Chase raises an eyebrow at my reflection. "Are you laughing at my hair?"

"No." But when I look at his hair, I start laughing again. "Wait. Yes. Wet it a little. It dried crazy from me tugging at it."

That easy smile crosses his face as he runs his hand through his dry hair. "I like that you messed me up."

I work on taming my crazed hair into a messy bun. "Yeah. I wish I could say the same."

He grins and rests the palms of his hands on the counter next to me, still watching my reflection in the large mirror. "Well, I like that I messed you up."

My breath catches. I like it too. Maybe a little too much. Once I'm done tying up my hair, I turn to face him, leaning my hip against the side of the counter. "Should I ask why?"

His smile broadens. "Because you put up a good front. Too good, actually." He stands up straight and steps in front of me, easily pinning me in place and turning me to face him with his arms on either side of the countertop. "The only time I see you crack is when you're flustered," he says in a low voice.

Before I can say anything back, he covers my mouth with his, and I could crumble to the floor. Chase lifts me up onto the bathroom counter, my legs on either side of him. He kisses me without reservation, and it steals the breath from my lungs. All my senses are consumed by him, and when his tongue claims my mouth like it's his for the taking, I blush at the sound it draws from the back of my throat.

Pulling back, he wipes his bottom lip with his thumb, and the corner of his mouth lifts. "And the fact that you let me kiss you like that is your biggest tell of all." He brushes his thumb across my bottom lip, and I have to fight the urge to take it into my mouth and suck. Chase leans in close. "The fact that you let me make that pretty mouth of yours so swollen and red thrills me like you wouldn't believe." My teeth sink into my bottom lip, but he pulls it free. "So, I have to ask. Why is it you can't sleep with me?"

My heart hammers in my chest. I can't tell him I won't sleep with him because I like him too much. That regardless of how much my body is begging to be whisked away so Chase can have his way with me, I'm cemented in the fear that it would mean more to me than it would to him.

"I don't think of you that way, remember?" My voice comes out like a whisper, but conviction carries every word.

His head falls forward with a shake, and I have to fight the urge to run my hand through his hair again. When he looks up at me, amusement shines behind those eyes. "That's the story you're sticking with?"

My hands grip the counter on either side. "What do you want me to say, Chase? That sleeping with you would make this too real for me? That I don't want to deal with the aftermath of that decision when this ends? You asked me to stand in as your date, and that's what I'm going to do. Yes, I find you attractive. I think any woman would. But we don't need to sleep together. That would make this whole thing . . . messy."

His eyes never leave mine. "Messy?"

I nod, but I don't dare breathe. That's the closest I've gotten to a confession. I've kept my feelings for him tucked away inside a jar, and now the seal has been cracked. Now, it's going to be a lot more difficult putting the lid back on.

The corner of his mouth twitches. "Sometimes messes are fun."

Hiding my disappointment with a laugh, I playfully push him out of my way so I can hop down. "Unbelievable." Without looking back, I head toward the kitchen.

Chase's footsteps follow close behind. "You don't have to leave," he complains with a laugh.

I put my spray bottle back into my bag. "I'm leaving because it's late, and we both have to work tomorrow."

He carefully picks up my shears from the table, putting them neatly back into their case.

"Thanks," I say, tucking them back in my bag.

A dangerous smirk flirts at the corner of his mouth. "What are friends for?"

thirty

BREATHING in the aroma of freshly ground coffee beans, I stand in line at Southern Roast for an afternoon pick me up. It's busy today. I think there's something about mildly cooler weather that makes everyone want to seize the opportunity for a cozy drink.

Chase made sure I got home safe last night, but I haven't heard from him since.

It's starting to eat at me.

He's been the one to reach out on most occasions, but while I'm standing here in line, I might as well see how he's doing.

> CANDACE:
> Do you hate your haircut?

Maybe I should have stayed a little longer. I should have wet his hair and styled it so he could see the finished look instead of messing it up and leaving. My teeth sink into my bottom lip at the thought of what happened between us last night. His hands and mouth exploring every exposed part of me.

The buzzing of my phone makes me jolt.

> CHASE:
>
> Absolutely not. Best haircut I've ever had.
>
> No awkward grow out phase necessary.

Relief eases some of the tension I've been walking around with all day.

"What can I get for you?"

I look up to find the blonde barista staring at me with big, blue eyes and a dazzling customer service smile.

"Sorry," I say as I step up to the counter. "A medium peppermint mocha please."

"Sure," she says happily. "Can I get a name?"

"Candace." I pull out my wallet and fish out some cash from one of my clients earlier today.

"You were in here with that guy recently, right?"

My eyes dart up to find her still holding the marker and cup. "Uh. Depends on which guy you're referring to. Maybe?"

She looks young. Maybe early twenties, and it annoys me even more that Chase tried to ask her out. He's a grown ass man. Even if he and I don't turn into anything, he should at least be with someone closer to his age.

She frowns before writing my name and passing my cup off to the other barista. "I think I saw you in here with Chase, right?"

I rock back on my heels. "Ah, that guy. Yes, I do know him." I hand her the cash, but she doesn't count it right away.

She's still just looking at me thoughtfully. "You're not dating him?"

Unsure how to answer, I eventually settle on saying, "No. No, we're just friends."

She nods and lets out a nervous laugh. "Probably a wise

choice." When I stand there, waiting for her to say more, she adds, "Your drink will be right up."

Eyebrows furrowing, I mutter, "Thanks," and step to the end of the counter. Has he been coming in here and trying to convince her to leave her boyfriend or something? I want to roll my eyes at the thought.

There's another text from Chase when I look down at my phone.

CHASE:
What's your favorite Christmas song?

Some variation of Frosty the Snowman plays overhead, and all I can think to say is *not this*.

CANDACE:
John Lennon's Happy Xmas. Why?

The second barista places my drink on the counter, and I thank him. My eyes dart to the girl one last time, but she's already back to her bubbly self and smiling at the next customer. Turning and walking to the exit, I push the door open with my back and read the messages from Chase.

CHASE:
I feel like it says a lot about a person.

That's probably the least Christmasy of Christmas songs. Are you the Grinch?

I huff and walk toward the salon.

CANDACE:
Says the man who has no decorations in his apartment.

It takes him a few minutes to respond.

CHASE:

I guess I deserve that.

CANDACE:

Not even a snow globe.

CHASE:

You know how I feel about useless products.

AND it has fake snow.

I let out a laugh, but then another piece of the never-ending Chase puzzle clicks into place.

CANDACE:

Do you think all Christmas decorations are useless?

This time, he answers in a matter of seconds.

CHASE:

I think they serve their purpose.

Just not in my apartment.

I shake my head, stopping in front of my salon to text him back.

CANDACE:

What's your favorite Christmas song?

My phone vibrates as I pull open the salon door. My client isn't here yet, so I take my time getting settled with my drink.

CHASE:

The one where grandma gets run over by a reindeer makes me laugh.

CANDACE:
Why am I not surprised?

My fingers hover over the keyboard. I'm tempted to tell him about my weird interaction at Southern Roast just now. I still can't figure out why she would suggest not dating Chase be *probably for the best*. What could she know that I don't?

CHASE:
On another note, I was hoping we could get drinks tomorrow, but I don't think I'll be able to see you until the party. I didn't finish all the work I brought home on Tuesday for some reason.

It's almost like I was distracted or something.

Shit. I totally forgot Tuesdays were bad for him. I was so focused on giving in and finally cutting his hair, I didn't even pay attention to which day it was.

CANDACE:
I'm sorry! You could have told me to come over a different night.

CHASE:
And risk missing out on all the fun we had?

I let out a breath of laughter.

CANDACE:
Your job is more important.

CHASE:
That's debatable.

> But the boss wasn't pleased. She's stressed about the party, and now she's breathing down my neck on top of it. I'll probably have to put in some late nights these next couple of days. She wants proposals for three different pitches by end of day Friday.

My heart sinks. Partly for him dealing with his boss, and partly because not seeing him until the party feels like such a long stretch of time. The deeper I fall into Chase, the more anxious I am to be around him again. I'm like a junkie who needs her next fix, and it's borderline pathetic.

CANDACE:
> Take care of what you need to do.

I add a heart emoji and press send.

Next time I see him will be the performance, except for once, I won't have to act at all.

thirty-one

MY FINGERS RUN under the delicate maroon straps that rest over my tattooed skin. The inked flowers are visible the same way they were for our date. My head tilts as I study myself in the mirror. It certainly doesn't leave much to the imagination. From the low backline to the sleek material that clings to my every curve, and the slit stretching up to my thigh, more of me is on display than ever before. And somehow, amidst all those things, the dress remains elegant. It has a sophistication to it that makes it easily my favorite thing I own.

Miles walks out of his bedroom after finishing work for the day, and I catch him in the reflection of the mirror doing a double take when he passes my open door. He's wearing sweatpants with no shirt, his colorful tattoos clearly on display.

In the time it takes me to turn around to ask him what he thinks, he's already slammed his back against the hallway, both hands gripping the wall on either side like he was blasted backward.

I let out a laugh and pop my hand on my hip. "I take it you approve?"

He cranes his head forward to get a better look without separating himself from the wall. "Who. Are. You!"

With my best dazzling smile, I hold out my hand and say, "Oh, I'm Chase's girlfriend. It's so nice to finally meet you."

Laughter bursts from his lips. "You're going to kill it tonight." He looks me up and down. "You're going to destroy him, aren't you?"

A light laugh leaves me as I reach for my phone on the bed. "I'm going to play the part he asked me to play."

"I like your hair like that."

I glance in the mirror before looking back at him with a smile. "Thanks." It isn't much different from how I normally wear my hair, but instead of styling it with loose waves, I went for a more defined curl.

His lips twist like he's trying to fight his smile. "He's coming to pick you up again, right?"

"That's the plan." I grab a delicate pair of black heels—also picked out by Miles—and slip the strap over the back of my ankle.

He grins but says nothing.

"What are you so happy about?"

He wistfully leans against the doorframe. "I just want to see the look on his face. This feels like a wedding."

I force out a laugh. "This is the furthest thing from a wedding." I slip on my second shoe. "The groom and I aren't even together." Gesturing toward the hallway behind him, I add, "And I doubt anything will beat your reaction just now."

Miles weighs his head from side to side as he thinks it over. "I mean, it's hard to top me on most things." His gaze settles on me again. "Do you think you'll sleep with him? You should totally sleep with him."

"I already told him that can't happen."

He closes his eyes like he's trying to suppress his disappointment. "Why would you do that?" Before I can answer, he shakes his head. "Just do the thing already!"

"Don't get your hopes up." I pat him on the chest as I walk past him to the living room.

He groans behind me. "Quit being a baby and fuck the man. If all goes to hell after, it will at least make for a great story."

"That's one way to look at it." He's a terrible influence, and he knows it. Of course, I want to sleep with Chase. I haven't stopped thinking about what it felt like to have him underneath me since I left his apartment Tuesday night. I'd give anything to feel wanted by him again, and again, but I can't shake that feeling of how it would probably end in disappointment.

A knock puts a stop to our conversation. I don't think I've felt nervous all day, but knowing he's standing on the other side of that door has my heart pounding. It isn't until Miles grins and ushers me toward the door with both hands, mouthing, "Go, go, go," that I take a step forward.

Prancing backward, he peeks around the corner so he can spy like the nosy bitch he is, and I take a steadying breath before opening the door.

Chase has his head down as he messes with the cuff of his white shirt poking out of the sleeve of his black jacket. Everything about him looks sharp. I liked his hair a little longer, but the cleaner look is phenomenal on him. Every article of clothing looks well pressed, and the way it all hugs his muscled frame could easily make me drool if I stood here long enough.

His eyes lift first, his hands freezing. That gaze works its way up my entire body, and it's only when our eyes lock that he stands up straight. "Candace."

I smile. "Chase."

He looks me up and down again without shame. *"Candace."*

I fight the urge to bite my lip. Tonight is about pulling out all the stops. Tonight is not the night to be shy. "Do you want to come in?"

Lifting his fist to his mouth, he shakes his head. "No."

I let out a bewildered laugh. "No?"

"No."

I'm tempted to look back at Miles, but instead I say, "Can I ask why?"

He looks me in the eye again. "You're . . . You look . . ." He shakes his head. "If I come in, I'll mess you up, and we'll never make it to this party."

"You're welcome!" a loud whisper sounds behind me as Miles walks past us on the way to his room. I guess he's seen all he needed to see.

Chase laughs, but his eyes only flick to Miles for a second before falling back on me. "I knew you'd try to kill me tonight."

I shake my head with a smile. "Okay. Stay here, then. I just have to grab my things." As soon as I turn around, Chase lets out a groan.

When I come back a moment later, his head is leaning back against the wall. "Do you know what you look like from behind?"

Lifting an amused brow, I say, "I know what the back of the dress looks like."

"And you thought I was strong enough to resist such a thing?"

Walking up against him, I put a hand on his chest, the warmth of him radiating through my fingertips. "You don't have to resist anything tonight." I kiss him, and another faint groan drags out of him. "Tonight, all our practice pays off."

I go to pull him with me, but he snatches me back, holding me flush against him. "Thank you for doing this."

"Of course," I breathe. "What are friends for?"

thirty-two

SEASONS COVE IS one of the grandest hotels in the area. I've never stayed here. I've never been here. I've never even *considered* coming here because of the price tag associated with it.

Everything about this place is extravagant.

The tiered fountain in the center of a circular driveway.

The large white columns framing the entrance with matching palm trees on either side.

The bustle of the valet drivers as people arrive for the event.

I know my eyes must be huge when I look over at Chase as he pulls up to the valet, but I don't care. "*This* is where your company is having their Christmas party?"

He grimaces like it's a bad thing. "I know. It's ridiculous, but I promise we'll have fun."

"Chase," I say as I look between the stunning entrance with what looks like marble stairs leading to the large doors with brass handles. "This looks like it could be a *gala*, not a company Christmas party."

He shrugs as he puts his car in park. "It's a company Christmas party held at a place they sometimes have galas."

"Chase!" My voice bubbles with laughter, and the corner of his mouth lifts when I say his name.

"Stay there," he says as he gets out of the car, and I can't take my eyes off him. He hands the keys to the valet, exchanging a quick nod and pleasantries, buttons his jacket as he walks around the front of the car, and by the time he makes it to my side, I'm buzzing with anticipation for him to touch me.

Opening the door, he holds out his hand. "Ready for this?"

Smiling at him, I let him help me out of the car. "As ready as I'll ever be. Are you?"

Chase grins before immediately tucking me to him and kissing the side of my head. His voice is low in my ear when he says, "You make this part easy." His words feel molten, running down my spine and spreading warmth to every part of me.

I thought the lobby had a lot to look at with its sculpted architecture and massive chandeliers, but as soon as we enter the room for the party, I'm met with even more elaborate decorations. At the far end of the hall stands a Christmas tree as tall as the ceiling, covered in glittering ornaments and extravagant ribbons. The scattered tables are covered with white linens and dark green runners. Each table has garland draped over the center with soft lights sparkling throughout, giving the entire room an enchanting glow. The six sets of double doors that line the right side of the wall must lead to a full-length balcony, and above each doorway is, of course, mistletoe.

My mind jumps to the annual white elephant party we have in the salon with all the stylists, only solidifying my awareness that Chase and I are not the same. The stark difference is the first time I feel a twinge of relief that this isn't real.

Because outside of being Chase's fake girlfriend, I don't belong here.

People pack the room in every direction, and I lean in closer to Chase while I take in the scene. "You work with everyone here?"

"Not all in the same office," he clarifies. "We have a few firms in the area, but we all get together a few times a year at events like this."

"Well, it's great to see the company is doing well."

A man approaches us with his stunning and very pregnant wife. "Hey! You made it!"

Chase lets out a laugh as he shakes hands with the man. "I'm more surprised to see you here." Releasing the man's hand, he moves to hug his wife. "I figured you'd be having a baby by now."

"Not yet," the stunning blonde says with a tired smile as she runs a hand over her swollen belly. "Any day now, though."

"Let me introduce you to my girlfriend, Candace." He places his hand on the small of my back. "Candace, this is Jeff and Sherry."

Shaking each of their hands, I give them both a polite smile. "It's nice to meet you."

"It's so nice to meet you," Sherry says, suddenly looking more awake. "Seeing Chase happy with someone is long overdue."

"Yeah, I hardly complain about anyone working *too hard*, but I was starting to think he'd work himself to death in that office," Jeff adds with a laugh.

I feel like I'm missing something, but Chase just squeezes me tighter and smiles down at me. "See, you practically saved me."

He's so convincing in the way he looks at me. I almost get lost in his gaze until I remember to play the part. "Please." I wave off his comment and wrap my arms around him. "I'm the lucky one."

Chase dips his chin. "Well, if you two will excuse us, we still need to find our table."

"Of course," Jeff says with a nod. "We'll see you once you have more awards than you can carry."

"You'll help bring them to the car, won't you?" Chase asks with a playful smirk.

"Only if he's not carrying me," Sherry adds with a laugh. "Have fun, you two!"

"It was lovely meeting you," I say again. "And congratulations."

The couple beams and continues to work their way through the crowd. "Not your boss, I take it?"

Chase forces a laugh that sounds more like a scoff. "No, but she's around here somewhere." He does a quick scan of the room but doesn't react to anyone.

"Your friends?" I ask as soon as it's just the two of us in a room of strangers again.

A faint smile pulls at the corner of his lips. "Yeah. They were just colleagues for the longest time, but after so many years, they've become good friends."

"What did they mean by your happiness being long overdue?" It feels like too personal a question, but if him bringing me here is a *big deal*, I should probably know.

Chase grips the back of his neck before slowly rubbing his palm over the nape. He looks around the room. "Here, let's sit."

We find our names on the seating chart and settle into our chairs. Turning to face me, he leans his arm on the back of my seat. "It's been a while since I've had a girlfriend."

"Oh?" I remember all the women who tagged him in photos on social media, but I guess that doesn't mean he actually dated any of them. Technically, it's been a while since I've had a boyfriend.

He shakes his head. "Things didn't end well with my ex,

and ever since, I've sort of been . . . coasting." He levels me with a stare to make sure I'm following.

"Coasting," I say with a slow nod.

"You know, go to work, and go home. Tried going out with people when they asked, but I didn't want to be there. I'd been in a fog, but after seeing how things went last year without a date, I needed to find someone."

A placeholder. That's what I am. I *know* that's all I am, but I still have to fight the urge to shrink when I cautiously say, "Well, you found me." Leaning my elbows on the table, I add, "I'm glad you were looking."

I said it because it's true. I've had more fun with him during these past few weeks than I have in a while, but the way he looks at me, like I've just spilled my biggest secret, has me fighting a smile.

I shake my head. "Don't gloat."

He holds a hand to his chest and leans forward. "Me? Gloat about the fact that I've somehow snuck through your defenses?"

"You haven't snuck through anything," I say with a playful sideways glance. "These defenses were built for you."

Chase gets to his feet, and when I look up at him, he hooks a finger under my chin. "Now *that* is something I will gloat about." He presses a kiss to my lips, and my entire body warms. "Let me buy you a drink."

"From the open bar?"

Chase grins. "Yes, but buying you a drink sounds better." He turns to go, and over his shoulder adds, "I'll tip well to make up for it."

As he walks away, I can't shake my smile.

No one else has found their way to our table yet, so I sit alone and take in the scene around me. There are couples kissing under mistletoe, excited greetings with warm hugs, and they have an actual pianist in the corner playing Christmas classics. I never imagined I'd be at a party this fancy with a man like Chase, but I'm glad I'm here. I'm glad I get to step into these shoes, just for tonight.

After a few minutes, Chase slides into the chair next to mine and places a glass of Chardonnay on the table. "Have I told you how incredible you look?" Toying with one of my curls, he leans in closer. "I'm afraid you're way out of my league, Candace." I could laugh at how absurd that comment is considering I feel like I'm the one who doesn't fit in here, but he moves to kiss my neck, and I tilt my head without thinking. It's like my body already knows how to react in a way that will make it easier for Chase to touch me.

"I hope we're not interrupting anything," a voice across the table says, and my eyes fly open.

thirty-three

TWO GORGEOUS GIRLS stand before us as they set their drinks on the table. One with sleek, long, brunette hair that, I'm assuming, she tried to fade into a blonde, but because she's starting from a level five, it ended up pulling more of an orange tone. She still manages to pull it off. The other girl has red curls styled to perfection, and I wonder if it's her natural color.

Chase leans back in his seat but keeps his arm on the back of my chair. "Candace, I'd like you to meet Chloe." He gestures to the redhead. "And Brittany," he says, gesturing respectively to the brunette.

I try to match them up to the many girls who tagged him online, but it's been so long since I looked at those pictures. I have no idea if these are some of the women he's spent time with.

The girl with auburn hair assesses me. "So, you're the one who's been keeping him from us," she says with a hint of sarcasm.

Darting my eyes to Chase, I lean in a little closer. "I guess I am," I say with a smile. "I didn't realize I was keeping him from anything." My hand finds Chase's leg under the table, and I take another sip of my drink.

"You're not," Chase says simply. "They're just upset because I won't drive their boat around anymore."

Thinking back to his social media, I vaguely remember seeing him tagged in photos on a boat. He looked good sun-kissed and windblown, and part of me is a little jealous these girls got to see that side of him. By the time summer rolls around next year, who knows if we'll still be . . . whatever we are.

"Has the big boss lady met her yet?" Brittany asks Chase like I'm not sitting here.

"Nope," Chase says happily. "We haven't had the pleasure of running into her."

Brittany scoffs before finally turning her attention to me. "She's going to hate you." I arch an eyebrow, and her eyes go wide. "It's not you. She would hate anyone Chase is dating."

"Good to know," I say with a laugh. They're not telling me anything new. His boss is the reason I'm here, but these girls don't know that.

Chase's fingers trace the nape of my neck. "If she has an issue, I'll deal with it." He gives me the easy smile I love so much before saying, "Come on, let's go for a walk." Standing from the table, he holds out a hand for me to take before looking at the girls. "Ladies, if you'll excuse us."

Trying to contain my obvious relief, I say a quick goodbye and take his hand so he can lead me through the crowd. He heads straight toward one of the many double doors, nodding to the occasional person but never stopping. Pausing before opening the door, he looks up at the mistletoe overhead and breathes out the word, "Perfect," before covering my mouth with his. He kisses me through the doorway, and once we're on the balcony, he doesn't stop kissing me. He spins us around, pressing me up against the small sliver of wall between sets of doors so no one inside can see us. His hand on my back holds me flush against him while his free hand is braced against the wall by my head.

"Chase," I breathe when he moves to my neck, his lips trailing down to my collarbone. When his mouth lands on my cleavage, I inhale a sharp breath. "You're going to mess me up, and the party hasn't even started."

He stands up straight and leans his forehead against mine. "Maybe messing you up is the party I'd rather be at."

As we catch our breath, I can't help studying him in the glow of the coach light a few feet away. There's a hunger behind his eyes, but also a hint of desperation I've never seen in him—not in this way, at least. "You don't like being here, do you?"

"Not at all."

Playfully, I whisper, "Then why are we here?"

The corner of his mouth quirks. "Because I never show my face with them, and this is the one function I feel like I *have* to go to. They all get drinks on Tuesdays, and I blow them off every week. I stay and work late." I open my mouth to ask about the extra workload he mentioned before, but he cuts me off. "Partly because I have to, but even if I didn't, I wouldn't want to go."

"But Chloe and Brittany's boat?"

Chase's smile broadens. "You're not the reason I stopped hanging out with everyone from the office. I only hung out with them for a few months after my breakup. I was fucking depressed, and at the time, I felt like my options were to take them up on their invites or sit around in my apartment all day. I always offered to drive so I wouldn't have to talk to anyone."

"It must have been a bad breakup," I say quietly.

He rubs his hand over the back of his neck. "It was nothing special. We were together for three years when I found out she was cheating on me. She said it was because I worked too much, which maybe there was truth to that. I don't know."

"Even if you did work too much, that's no excuse to cheat on someone. I'm sorry."

He blinks, the clarity coming back to his eyes. "Don't be. I'm glad it didn't work out."

I've never seen him like this, and I think I've been wrong about him. This missing puzzle piece somehow changes the whole picture. He was committed, then he was hurt, and then he tried to distract himself from that hurt. Nothing about that makes him a fuckboy.

I don't know what comes over me, but I kiss him. I kiss him, and for the first time since meeting him, I let my emotions slip into it. I let myself feel everything. All the hope, fear, and straight adrenaline that comes with falling for someone new.

When we pull apart, Chase lets out a slow whistle. "Damn, Candace. If I had known you'd kiss me like that, I would have told you my sob story a long time ago."

A light laugh leaves my lips, and I trail my finger down his torso until I gently hook it into the front of his belt. "Tell me all your secrets, Chase. There's no telling what I might do."

He blinks, his wide eyes dropping to my finger before jumping up to meet my stare. God, he's beautiful. I'd pay money to see this turned-on look of surprise on his face every day.

"When I was fourteen, my girlfriend dumped me in front of my friends in the cafeteria."

Placing my hand on his chest, I gently push him away from me with a laugh.

I walk toward the door, and he adds, "In college, my shorts somehow ripped, and I had no idea until my roommate pointed it out to me that night."

I reach for the door handle. "Are you coming?"

"My ass was out all day!" he says as he starts after me. "I flirted with girls!"

I look over my shoulder at him. "Something tells me you still made quite the impression."

He grips the side of the door as he follows me back into the party. "Of course I did. But that's not the point."

I shake my head. "So humble."

"You want to see me humble?" His hand wraps around my wrist and he pulls me to him. We're standing under the mistletoe again, and I can't help looking up at it before I meet his gaze. "The fact that you're here with me humbles me. The fact that you let me touch you, kiss you, and act like you're mine at all, humbles me." He hooks his finger under my chin, and I forget how to breathe. "*You* humble me."

"This is you humble?"

He grins. "Believe it or not, yes." He gently weighs his head from side to side. "Humble and a little determined."

"Determined?"

"Yes."

My lips twist. "Determined to do what exactly?"

A dangerous smirk pulls at the corner of his mouth. "To make sure you have a great time tonight."

I smile. "I am having a great time."

"Good." He kisses my forehead. "Because it's just getting started."

thirty-four

THERE ARE two additional people seated at our table when we return. A middle-aged married couple by the names of Dawn and Rick. His black hair is starting to turn salt and pepper, and her laugh lines are adorable every time she grins at him. They make a cute couple, and they're pleasant to talk to. Even Chloe and Brittany are more agreeable after the initial shock of meeting me. They love the fact that I'm a hairdresser and have a million questions regarding the best products available to them without a license.

Chase keeps his hand on my leg, which is mostly exposed thanks to the slit of the dress. As much as I talk and laugh with the people around us, I can't stop thinking about everything he said on that balcony. His past, how he doesn't want to be here, how he's *humbled* by me. For someone I've been talking to every day since meeting him, he's different from what I thought. There's more to him than the confident flirt of a man who makes me laugh, and I should have known that. I'm disappointed I didn't dig deeper sooner. Who knows what I would have uncovered by now?

The conversation at the table shifts to a more work-related

topic, and I welcome the break. Taking a sip of my wine, I listen to the chatter and let myself enjoy the steady movement of Chase's fingers tracing circles along my inner thigh. Heat settles between my legs, and every time his hand inches a fraction higher, my breathing halts. If he keeps this up, I'm going to be completely at his mercy. I've never been this turned on by an innocent touch, but every chance I get, I shift to give him more access. And every time, he takes it. It's a secret dance we've been doing ever since we sat down, and it's been wearing away at my restraint with every torturous brush of his fingertips.

He gives nothing away as he casually sits next to me with his eyes trained on the people in front of me. Occasionally he takes a sip of his drink, but his hand never stops working its way up my leg, and all I can do is sit here and try to keep my breathing even. He has to be at the top of the slit, but I don't dare move my eyes to check. The table and linens hide anything he's doing, but my heart rate spikes when his hand moves further. He's so dangerously close to feeling how much he's affecting me, and when his pinky grazes my hip, he chokes on his drink before looking me up and down with wide eyes.

He's figured out I'm not wearing anything underneath.

A series of emotions flash behind those eyes. Shock, curiosity, and a molten heat all gleam before me in a matter of seconds before he tosses the rest of his drink back in one large gulp.

Keeping his voice low, he says in my ear, "Well, I'm getting another drink since you're trying to kill me. Would you like one?"

I try to bite back my smile but fail. "I would. Thank you."

He stares at me for a long moment, his knee bouncing slightly like he doesn't know what to do with me, and I love seeing him unravel. With his voice low again, he says, "Keep sitting there looking sweet and unsuspecting. I'm the only one who gets to know how wicked you are."

"No promises," I say with a hint of a smile.

Chase keeps his eyes on me for another beat before blowing out a breath, adjusting himself, and getting to his feet. He walks away, as I shamelessly enjoy the view, and when he looks back at me, he just shakes his head again and runs a hand through his hair.

"You two make the cutest couple," the woman, Dawn, says fondly. "How long have you been together?"

I blink, trying to remember what Chase and I agreed on. I figured he'd be able to answer these questions, but I'm on my own for this one. "Oh. It's new. I met him a few weeks ago."

"Well, he looks absolutely smitten." Her smile is warm, and I have to admit, it feels good to have someone rooting for Chase and me in this hypothetical relationship.

"He's a great guy," I say with a nod, suddenly feeling shyer than I have all night.

"He is," Brittany says. "I think every single woman in the office has hoped to catch Chase's attention—maybe some of the married ones, too. I mean, it's not every day you find a successful, single guy who looks like that." She nods in the direction Chase went, and I look over my shoulder to find him returning with our drinks. He sets my wine down in front of me as he slides into his seat, his eyebrows slightly furrowed.

"Everything okay?" I ask quietly, and I'm grateful to hear a new topic of conversation pick up on the other end of the table.

He glances between me and the cup in front of him. "Yeah . . ." The corners of his lips dip. "Have you talked to anyone else here tonight?"

I shake my head. "No. I've been here with you the whole time."

He nods. "That's what I thought. It's just . . ." He shakes his head. "My boss thinks you made an interesting choice?"

I frown. "What interesting choice did I make?" Is she judging my dress?

"I think she was referring to me, but she made herself busy before I could ask."

"You're my interesting choice?" I ask with a breath of laughter.

He doesn't answer, just stares at his drink, turning the glass on the table as he tries to piece it all together.

I put a hand on his leg, and he finally looks at me, his hand stilling. "It doesn't matter what she thinks, right? I'm just here so she can't drunkenly corner you."

His mouth quirks. "Oh, you're doing much more than that." He lets out a light laugh. "I haven't decided which is more dangerous. Being cornered by her"—he nods in the direction he came from—"or wanting to be cornered by you."

I raise an eyebrow. "You want to be cornered by me?"

"Yes," he says quickly. "Especially now that I know . . ." He gestures toward me with his drink still in hand, pausing when his eyes drop to where the slit of my dress rests. He shakes his head. "I would like that very much." Taking a sip of his drink, he sets it down on the table in front of him before resting his arm on the back of my chair and bringing his lips to my ear. "I hope you know I won't be able to think straight for the rest of the night."

Instead of explaining *why* I showed up here wearing nothing under my dress, I kiss him. It's a kiss like any happy couple might share at a table, but the way Chase's hand grips the back of my neck makes me wish it could be more.

"Good evening! It's so lovely to see you all here," booms a woman's voice over the microphone.

Wait. I know that voice.

I turn to see the speaker at the front of the room, and my

heart jolts in my chest. I know that face—that hair. I know that feline elegance and subtle arch to her brow. I know the dissatisfied purse to her lips right before she knows you're about to cave and give her whatever she wants. I know the power she loves having over people—people like me. People like Chase.

Every bit of heat from that last kiss turns to icy dread. I look at the man next to me. Gone is the playful demeanor I've grown to love. In its place, I find a clenched jaw and stern gaze as he looks toward the front of the room.

Nicolette stands in front of the mic wearing a stunningly elegant gold dress practically made of glitter, and even though she just addressed the whole room, her eyes are locked on me.

"That," Chase says, leaning in, "is my boss."

thirty-five

MY CLIENT. My best paying *client* is his boss. Of course, she is. The universe would have been too generous to make this simple. Chase's fingers trail over my exposed back as she talks, but I can barely feel it. This new realization demands all of my attention.

Nicolette. Nicolette is the one who gives him extra work, who tries to control him by keeping him at the office, who got drunk and pounced on him at last year's Christmas party. Does she know she makes him so uncomfortable he had to bring a fake date? Would she even care? Or would she laugh it off as part of the game?

I don't even add my clients on social media because I try not to mix business with my personal life, and yet here I am, putting on a show for the client who single handedly changed my life.

This was a bad idea. Nicolette only thinks about herself, and the last thing I want to do is give her a reason to see me as the enemy. Then again, I thought I had Chase pegged until a few moments ago. He's different than I thought he was, so maybe Nicolette is different too. Maybe there's a chance she isn't going to use this as a reason to make me dread our appointments more than I already do. After all, it's just a date at a company Christmas party.

Despite my pep talk, Chase appraises me and asks, "Are you okay?" The warmth of him next to me only adds to the sudden sweat prickling my forehead.

Taking a breath, I nod. "I'm fine." But what if Nicolette's *not* different? What if she's every bit as vindictive as I suspect she could be?

His eyebrows furrow, and he glances at the stage again before looking back at me. "What's wrong?"

"I just . . ." My eyes dart to Nicolette again, her harsh gaze still appraising me like I've disappointed her. When I look back at Chase, I try to collect my scattered thoughts. "This might be a bad idea."

Nicolette wraps up her speech with an enthusiastic, "So let's have a great night!" and everyone stands to applaud.

The room breaks out into movement as people no longer feel confined to their tables like someone breaking a rack in pool.

"A bad idea?" Chase asks, confusion clearly displayed on his face.

"Not *bad*." I shake my head. "I don't know the right word. I just . . . your boss." My eyes scan the room, and it isn't difficult to find the woman I'd rather avoid. Her dress might as well make her a walking neon sign, and I have no idea how I missed her until now. I really was wrapped up in Chase. He completely blinded me. All I could see tonight was him, but that's all changed. Nicolette heads straight for us, and now, all I can see is her.

Too soon, that cat-like purr of a voice grates down my spine. "Well, aren't you the last person I thought I'd see here?"

Chase looks past me to his boss, the crease between his brows deepening. "You two know each other?"

I force myself to put on my best smile. "Hi, Nicolette."

"We *do* know each other." Nicolette's eyes are practically glittering as she looks between Chase and me. "The question is, how do *you two* know each other?" She points a well-manicured finger between the two of us.

Chase raises an eyebrow, still looking clueless and beautiful. "Candace is my—"

"Date. I'm his date." I step closer to Chase, and his hand immediately finds the small of my back. He would have said *girlfriend*. It's what we've been saying all night, but *date* feels like a safer bet right now.

With her lips parted, she does a slow nod. "Well, that's . . . surprising. How did you meet?"

"At a coffee shop," I answer pleasantly. If there's anything being a hairdresser has taught me, it's how to appease people until I'm blue in the face. "I was behind him in line, and we got to talking." I glance up at Chase, but his eyes are fixed on his boss.

He inhales, and his hand on my back starts to trace small circles. "Yeah. As soon as I saw her, I knew I was done for." He grins down at me, and it's so fake. All of this is so, *so* fake, and yet I'm hanging on his every word. "But how do you two know each other?" he adds, snapping me from my daze.

Nicolette lets out a humorless laugh. "Oh, she's my stylist," she says with a wave of her hand and an air of importance. "In fact, I've brought in quite a few of her clients." She turns to me. "Haven't I?" Before I can answer, she shifts her attention back to Chase. "Poor thing could barely keep the lights on until I showed up."

I note the subtle jab, but she won't crack my mask. I've been wearing it every time she sits in my chair for months now. Looking at Chase, I say, "Nicolette was nice enough to refer some of her friends to me, and I have to admit, they've become my favorite clients."

He nods but still looks like he's trying to piece together what we're not saying.

A server carrying hors d'oeuvres passes, and Nicolette stops her, holding out a twenty-dollar bill. "Could you be a doll and get me a martini from the bar? Make sure they use the good stuff."

The girl looks mildly confused, like she's debating telling this woman that fetching drinks isn't in her job description, but she eventually takes the money and says, "Of course, ma'am," before disappearing into the crowd.

Nicolette lets out a light laugh as the girl walks away. "Money," she scoffs. "Such a dreadful thing." When she turns back to us, her eyes unmistakably lock on me. "But it certainly does keep people loyal." Her eyes flitter up to Chase. "Like this one and his impending promotion. He's been such a hard worker." She puts a hand on Chase's arm, her thumb rubbing over his biceps, and his body tenses next to me. "Putting in all the nights, weekends, and after-hour phone calls. I don't know what I'd do without him."

I still smile. I still keep my shoulders relaxed and my body soft. But I hate this woman. I hate what she does to him. Minutes ago, he was an easy-going, confident force of a man, and now it's like something in him has switched off. I could stand here all night and bullshit with Nicolette if he needed me to, but I don't think that's what he needs. I think he needs to get away from her.

"Well, it was such a pleasant surprise running into you here." I intertwine my fingers with Chase's, and his grip tightens around mine. "You'll have to excuse us for a moment. I think I may have left my phone in the car."

"Right. Your phone," Chase says like that was the plan all along. He gives a tight-lipped smile to his boss in the sparkly dress. "Have a great night, Nicolette."

He turns away without waiting for a response, but that silk-like voice calls him back. "Oh, and Chase?"

His body goes rigid before he turns to face her again, and I wonder if she notices. I wonder if she has ever seen a happy, relaxed Chase or if this is the only version she's known. "Yes?"

"I'd like you to come find me later, so we can chat." Her eyes flitter in my direction before she adds, "Alone."

"Alone?"

"Yes." She smiles my way, but there's nothing nice about it. "Candace will be fine. She can find something to keep her busy. I'm sure the girls in the office would love to get to know her. Either that, or maybe they could use an extra set of hands behind the bar."

I blink, the shock of her comment fracturing my composure. Nicolette knows I used to bartend after work. She knows because she was the reason I could quit and start doing hair full time.

Luckily, Chase speaks up before I've fully processed her comment. "Are you suggesting my guest—*my girlfriend*—works the bar?"

Well, so much for just being his date. "Chase," I say quietly, but he only looks at me for a fraction of a second before his attention is forced back to Nicolette.

"Your girlfriend?" Tossing her head back, she cackles. "Please. Candace is *not* your girlfriend."

His jaw ticks into a frown. "What makes you say that? You don't think I'd have a shot with her?"

It takes everything in me not to let my head fall into my hand. That's not what she's insinuating. She and I both know it.

Nicolette smirks. "Oh, I have no doubt she's *desperate* for your attention. Tell me, how did she get you to bring her here?"

Chase bristles next to me, and I give a tiny squeeze of his

hand. I don't care if Nicolette insults me. She's been dishing me backhanded compliments for months.

Ignoring my silent plea, Chase lets go of my hand and takes a step toward his boss. "Desperate?" he asks in disbelief. Pinching the bridge of his nose, he shakes his head and drops his hand. Leveling a heavy gaze on her, he says, "Look, Nicolette. The only one desperate here is me." He gestures back toward me but keeps his eyes fixed on her. "I'm desperate for anything this woman will give me. I want all of her. I'm so fucking lucky that she's with me, and I won't stand for you treating her as anything less than the incredible woman she is."

Nicolette's wide eyes jump to me. I'm not sure which she's more surprised by, Chase finally standing up to her, or the words coming out of his mouth, but I'm sure my expression doesn't look much different from hers.

"This is never going to happen," Chase continues, gesturing between the two of them. "I've told you again and again that this won't work, but you're relentless. I'm done with the late-night calls and the suggestive comments. You and I have a working relationship. Nothing more." He glances back at me, and something in him softens before he looks back at Nicolette. "I only want her. Do you understand? It will only ever be her."

Without waiting for a response, Chase turns and grabs my hand before pulling me through the crowd of people. Some nervously wave to him, others try to stop him, but every time he politely excuses himself. It isn't until we're outside the large double doors of the grand entrance that he starts to relax. Running a hand through his hair, he looks over at me, his eyes wide. "You do her hair?"

I let out a bewildered laugh, because of all of the things for him to say right now, that's not what I was expecting. "Every Tuesday."

His speech to Nicolette is still muddled in my head. Words and phrases echoing out of order.

"Tuesdays . . ." The word drops out of him, slow and thoughtful before he shakes his head and scoffs. "Of course."

My own eyes widen. "That's why you always work late on Tuesdays. Because your boss leaves early."

"Yeah." The word comes out with a bitter breath. "I never knew why. She always made it sound important." He shakes his head. "Work-related."

I rub my hand over my arm to fight the chill. The sun has long since set, and the gentle breeze of the cool night passes right through me. The lights illuminating the decorative fountain are red and green, and I'm overly aware of the fact that I'm wearing a thin, strappy dress to a Christmas party. I should have brought something to wear over my shoulders, but Miles would have killed me for trying.

"Are you cold?" Chase asks, already removing his jacket.

"I'll be fine once we go back inside."

He hands the jacket to me. "Do you want to go back inside?"

"Thanks," I say as I pull it on. My eyes drag over him, appraising this new version of Chase without the jacket. Every subtle change about his appearance makes me pause and appreciate him in a new way. He still looks impeccable, but as soon as he starts to roll up the sleeves of his white button-down, I know I'm done for. "It's your party," I manage to get out.

His eyes flick up to meet mine, his fingers still expertly working on rolling the second sleeve. "It's our night."

The way he says those three words makes me feel like the possibilities are endless. Chase makes me feel like I could do anything, and I wish feeling this way with him would never end. "Do you want to leave?"

The corner of his mouth twitches. "Yes." With his sleeves

rolled up, he crosses his arms before gesturing toward me. "But you did get all dressed up for a special occasion. I'd hate to disappoint you."

My lips twist, and with a slow shake of my head, I say, "I didn't get all dressed up for the party."

His eyes lock on mine, and there's a hint of surprise behind them. "So, we could go back to my apartment?"

"I would love to go back to your apartment." I'm dying to be alone with him, to speak freely, to have privacy. I need more than sitting with him at a round table in a banquet hall.

Chase closes the space between us, and my entire body buzzes happily with the contact. He presses his lips to mine, and I melt into him. When he pulls away, he keeps me held against him. His hand tucks a loose curl behind my ear. "Okay, beautiful. Let's get you home."

thirty-six

CHASE SETS his keys on the kitchen counter and gestures to one of the barstools. "Have a seat."

I have full intentions of doing exactly what he says, but I stop short when the sight of something small, green, and decorated with tiny candy canes stares back at me on the countertop. A miniature Christmas tree—probably only two feet tall—sits like an unsuspecting houseplant.

"Chardonnay?" Chase asks over his shoulder as he reaches for a bottle tucked away somewhere.

"You got a Christmas tree."

"What?" he asks, turning to face me with a bottle of my favorite wine in his hand.

I look from the tiny tree to him. "You got a Christmas tree," I say again.

"Oh." Chase sets the bottle on the counter gently as he looks from me to the tree. "Yeah. I did."

"I was here four days ago, giving you a hard time for not having any decorations."

"You were."

"And now you have this tiny Christmas tree."

"I do, and it's already left pine needles all over the place. Do you see this?" He walks over and lifts the tree with one hand to reveal a mess of needles underneath. "I hope you're happy," he adds with a weak smile.

My lips twist, but it's impossible to fight my smile. He went out and got a tiny tree for me? "I am," I say, nodding toward the bottle he set down. "You have the wine I like, too."

Chase sets down the tree and goes back to opening the bottle. "It came with the tree. They called it the Candace Special."

I laugh. "That was convenient."

His lips lift. "It was." He gets two empty glasses from the cabinet and sets them in front of us. "Especially since I had no idea you'd ever be back here. It definitely wasn't planned."

A slow smile pulls at my lips as I take a glass from him. "Of course not. You wouldn't try to seduce me with wine and an adorably short Christmas tree."

Chase clinks his glass with mine. "I would do no such thing."

I let out another light laugh before taking a sip. "Despicable."

Chase grins and leans his elbows on the counter across from me. "Well, we survived the Christmas party." He pulls out his phone, staring at the screen for a moment before he turns it face down on the counter.

"Did someone realize you left?"

He blows out a breath before saying, "Yeah. She isn't very happy with me."

I sit up straight. "We can go back if you need to. Or you can go back on your own if having me there wasn't helpful."

He nods toward me. "Drink your wine, Candace. Neither of us are going back to that party." He rubs a hand over his face. "She's just upset that I won't be there to accept their little plaque for signing the most accounts this year."

I clap a hand over my mouth. "I totally forgot that guy mentioned you were getting an award!"

He chuckles. "Calling it an award is generous. It's not a big deal. She'll just have to accept it on my behalf and put it in my office, which she finds . . ." He turns his phone over. "Disrespectful and embarrassing."

I put a hand on my chest. "Oh, that poor woman."

Chase shakes his head with a beautifully relaxed smile. "She'll manage."

I tilt my head, my curiosity getting the best of me. "Has anything ever happened between you two?"

His eyes stay fixed on his glass as he swirls its content. "The short answer is no, but that's not for her lack of trying." He points a finger at me. "She did land a kiss on me at last year's party. But other than that, she just sends ridiculous emails or calls me late at night, claiming it's about work when it's not."

"Okay." I nod and hope the relief I feel isn't too obvious. "Ridiculous emails?" My voice comes out small when I ask. I'm not sure how much he's comfortable telling me.

Chase rolls his shoulders before rubbing the back of his neck. "She likes to comment on how I look and what I'm wearing. Sometimes she asks me to wear certain shirts she knows I own, or to button them a certain way."

By *button*, I can't help but wonder if he really means *unbutton*. A frown pulls at my lips as I study him, but before I can say more, he continues.

With a shake of his head, he adds, "But nothing physical. I would never sleep with someone I work with, and I've told her that. That's a good way to make things awkward and . . ." His eyes lock with mine. "Messy."

I smile at his use of the word. "Avoiding messes is good."

"I know. That's why I'm standing over here," he says before holding up a finger and walking to the furthest corner of the kitchen, where he leans his back against the cabinets. "Actually, this is probably safer."

Laughter tumbles out of me, and I try not to think about how good he looks, gripping the edge of the counter with one hand while he holds a glass of wine in the other. "You haven't been that far from me all night. What's different now?" As soon as the words are out, I swallow down the fear of him being done with our agreement. The Christmas party is over. He was able to use me to put Nicolette in her place. Maybe this is his playful way of making sure nothing else happens between us. Sure, he invited me back here, but that might be because he feels bad that I just got berated in front of a room full of people. It doesn't mean he wants anything more. He might not even want another kiss. My heart sinks, but I guess there would be no need for it now. We've done everything we've agreed to do.

"The difference now is that I know you aren't wearing anything under that dress, and if you think I've stopped thinking about it for a single second, you'd be severely overestimating my self-control." His eyes trail over me. "And you're still wearing my jacket, which somehow makes you look small and innocent even though you're not wearing any panties, and the whole thing . . ." He shakes his head. "I've never wanted to mess you up more."

My entire body stills, and heat flushes to the surface of my skin. "That's why you're standing over there?" I ask quietly.

"That's why I'm standing over here."

I hold his gaze. Everything I've learned about him over the past few weeks has made me like him more. I like him too much to casually sleep with him, and I like him too much to *not* sleep with him. The thought of never being with him is already heartbreaking. The thought of tonight being the last time I'm sitting in his kitchen, watching him drink wine has me missing what's right in front of me. At this point, the damage is done, and I don't want to miss a single opportunity this night gives me. Getting to my feet, I make my way toward him. "Because you're afraid I'll say Jack Frost?"

He tracks my every movement. "Terrified."

When I reach him, I'm careful to leave some space between us. "Want to know something?"

His eyes dip to my mouth for a fraction of a second before meeting my stare again. "When it comes to you, I want to know everything."

My lips pull into a smile as I set my glass down and reach for his tie. My fingers slide over the silk-like fabric as I delicately loosen it. "I won't."

He doesn't move. He just watches me as I undo his tie and place it neatly on the counter next to him. "Two days ago, you said you would."

My fingers work to undo the buttons of his dress shirt. "Two days ago, you were against getting a Christmas tree." I shrug. "Things change."

His eyes stay steady on mine, but the hunger in them is unmistakable.

With the last of his buttons undone, I push up on my toes and press my lips to his. Chase's body relaxes at my touch, and without hesitation, he takes control of the kiss. He sets down his glass and weaves his hands into my hair as he walks me backward through his apartment. I would have been happy to stay in the kitchen, but I let him lead. I'd let him do anything.

thirty-seven

THAT HUNGER in his eyes matches the intensity of his mouth claiming mine. At this moment, he's everywhere and everything. He's taken over all five senses, and even though my body is in overload from the kiss alone, I need more. I won't be satisfied until I have all of him, and finally giving into the temptation has me feeling more buzzed than any of the wine I've had tonight. I let out a soft moan when his tongue drags over mine. I thought he would tear my dress off in a matter of seconds, but he hasn't. The way he's kissing me makes my legs weak, and it isn't until he turns and pulls me toward the bed that I finally look up.

He sits on the edge of a large bed, and I stand between his legs, my hands running through his hair as he looks up at me. God, I love seeing him like this. Holding me in place with one hand, his other grazes up my leg and slips into the slit of my dress. His touch is slow and teasing, yet bold at the same time. When he reaches the top of the slit, he slides under until his whole hand can grip my bare hip, and I have to fight the urge to widen my stance to give him easier access.

"Candace."

My eyes fly open, and I hadn't even realized I'd shut them.

"You are gorgeous. You know that?"

I smile because those words leave a warm bubbly feeling in my chest.

Chase returns the gesture, and in one swift motion, he pulls me onto the bed next to him and props himself up on his elbow to look at me. "Absolutely gorgeous."

He moves to kiss my neck, and I say, "You sure know how to flatter your fake girlfriend." I internally wince as soon as the words leave my lips. Why am I saying the wrong thing? Why can't I just let him fuck me and deal with the rest of this later? I don't want to think about how casual or temporary this is for him. I don't want to think about how this might not last.

Chase moves so he's hovering over me. All I see is him, and all I feel is his thumb grazing over my nipple through my dress. My back gives a tiny arch in response, and he does it again. Leaning in close, he says in a dangerously smooth voice, "What about this isn't real to you, beautiful?" He kisses me just below my ear, and I whimper. He presses his hips to mine, so I can feel the bulk of him against me, and my hips roll without warning, my eyes fluttering shut.

My chest rapidly rises and falls, and I'm dazed with lust and heat. Chase drags his thumb over my bottom lip before taking it between his teeth, and the sound he pulls from me makes me blush.

The corner of his mouth quirks, and he moves his lips to my ear. "This is real, Candace. But if you need more convincing, throw those pretty legs over my shoulders and let me bury my face between them."

My only response is to kiss him—hard. I'm desperate for him to touch me, taste me, fuck me. I'm completely at his disposal if it means I get to watch him come undone.

Chase yanks my dress over my head before throwing it somewhere in the corner of the room. Those warm, brown eyes take me in shamelessly, but I'm too worked up to wait. I hook my ankle behind the back of his leg and nudge him forward. "I thought you said you wanted to do something," I say, and my voice comes out breathless.

A slow smile pulls at the corner of his mouth before he lowers it to my breast. "I've been thinking about this too long for you to rush me." He takes my nipple into his mouth, and the feeling of his tongue on my pebbled skin has my head falling back. He swirls and gently bites, and when he's had his fill, he leaves torturous kisses over my breasts and stomach.

"Chase," I plead.

His lips pull into a smile against my skin, but he says nothing.

Finally, he moves lower, and my legs fall open. His arms hook underneath my thighs, and in one swift movement, he pulls me to him. When his tongue slowly runs over my center, my hips buck at the contact. He gently sucks on my clit, and my eyes threaten to roll back. How is he so good . . . *fuck*. Holding me firmly in place, he dips his tongue into me, before dragging over me slow and sweet with a soft groan.

"Fuck, you taste good."

I whimper and reach for his hair, desperate for him to give me more. When my fingers knot in the strands at the roots, he lets out another groan and presses his mouth against me again. He delivers slow, steady strokes, keeping me on the edge. It's like he has all the time in the world, and that realization has my legs shaking. As soon as my body starts to tremble, Chase sucks and licks, adding and removing pressure in a way that has me spiraling. My entire body tightens, and my hips squirm because this is too much. This feeling is too strong. His hands grip my legs, forcing pressure where I can't take it. He ravishes me, and I lose it. My entire body convulses, my toes curl, and I cry out as a blanket of white heat tears through me.

Chase's tongue slows as he waits for me to come down

from my high. Once my legs relax and my breathing regulates, he lifts his head and leaves a trail of kisses down my thigh. Sitting up, he wipes his thumb across his bottom lip. "Seeing you come might be more addicting than anything else."

The corner of my mouth twitches, but I'm not satisfied yet. If anything, I only want him more. Moving to straddle him, he lets me push him down on the bed. I can feel him hard underneath me, but it's not enough. I need his clothes off.

His hair is a disheveled mess, his pupils are blown, and when his tongue dips over his bottom lip, I clench.

I need his clothes off. *Now.*

His white dress shirt is unbuttoned to reveal a white undershirt beneath. His black pants and belt are still on, but they look a mess, too.

A mess.

A beautiful fucking mess.

My lips find his neck while my fingers undo his belt. He tilts his head and sucks in a breath when my teeth gently sink into his ear. I work his belt free, my fingers moving to the button of his pants. As soon as his zipper is down, he pulls my mouth to his. The way he kisses me should be enough of an indicator that he's ready, but that doesn't stop me from slipping my hand inside to feel his solid length straining against his boxer briefs.

Chase's head falls back as soon as I touch him. "Fuck, Candace. You don't know how many times I thought about how it would feel to be touched by you."

"Same." The word comes out breathy and full of need because he's hard, and smooth, and thick in my hand.

As soon as the word leaves my lips, he quickly takes off the rest of his clothes. His dress shirt and undershirt get thrown on the floor along with his pants and belt, and I let my eyes rake over his muscled frame. I want him. I want him more than I think I've ever wanted anything.

My mouth works down his chest and abs, and once I press

a kiss to the base of his stomach, I hook my fingers into the band of his briefs and free him of them.

More desire and heat pools between my legs at the sight of him. I could probably look at him like this all day.

He looks at me, but then his head falls back on the pillow like seeing my face hovering so close to his cock is too much.

I kiss his stomach, dangerously close to where the bulk of him lies, and Chase curses under his breath. I love seeing him lose his grip like this.

"Chase."

"Yes," he breathes.

"Look at me."

He does, and as soon as our eyes meet, I slowly run my tongue over the bead of moisture at his tip. His eyes flutter shut, and he curses under his breath, but when he looks at me again, there's a fresh wave of need behind those eyes. "Go ahead, beautiful. Let me see what that pretty mouth can do."

It feels like my entire body purrs at those words, and I do as he says. I take him in, and when it feels like there's nowhere else for him to go, I take him in more. I work my tongue around him and let my hand wrap around his base. He hits the back of my throat, and I love the feeling of being gagged by him.

He takes in a sharp breath. "Fuck, Candace. That's . . . *fuck*." His breathing turns uneven as I work my mouth up and down his shaft again and again, sucking him in deeper each time. "If you . . ." He grips the sheets. "*Shit.* If you keep . . . I'll come."

My movements slow, but I don't stop. I'm not done with him yet. I savor him, taking him in over and over again.

He sucks in a breath. "Jesus Christ."

With one last slow suck, I ease him from my mouth and crawl up the length of his body. What I feel for him goes beyond desire or lust, or any of the things I've felt with men before. When it comes to Chase, my body physically *needs* him.

He kisses my mouth. "You," he practically growls. "Beat all my expectations." He kisses me again, pulling me flush against him by my hips. "Every damn time."

I gasp at the feeling of him, raw and real against me. I'm slick for him, desperate for him to fill me. "Condom," I breathe.

Chase nods as he reaches into the nightstand drawer next to us. He expertly opens the foil and rolls it on in a matter of seconds, and I gently push myself up to let him. As soon as he's done, I reach down and wrap my fingers around him, putting his thick head at my entrance.

Chase's eyes darken, and his hands guide my hips again. This time, easing me onto him. I stretch around the size of his hard length, my eyes squeezing shut once it feels like he couldn't possibly hit deeper. There's still more of him, though. And he continues to slowly guide my hips as he says, "Good girl. Take all of me. I want you to feel me long after tonight."

A whimper leaves me, and I take a steadying breath once he's fully inside before slowly rolling my hips. I curse under my breath, my hands bracing on his chest. With every rock, he meets my movement, and I didn't know it was possible for him to feel this good. I didn't know it was possible for *sex* to feel this good. I'm so deliciously full, and with each movement, Chase pulls me against him so he can hit deeper. My head falls back, and I chase the feeling with every . . . steady . . . thrust.

"Damn, Candace, seeing you in that dress tonight—" He squeezes his eyes shut and hisses as I rock down on him. "Shit." When his eyes open, there's a fire behind his gaze, and his grip tightens on my hips. "I never would have believed you could look more gorgeous than you did tonight." His next thrust is a little deeper. "But seeing you with my cock inside you—you fucking own me," he growls, thrusting harder and making me cry out.

I whimper, my breathing hard. I'm so close, and when Chase sits up so he can hold me with one arm while his thumb works on my most sensitive spot, my mouth is frantic on his. The way he kisses me back lets me know he's feeling everything I am, and when our lips break apart, we're both panting.

I increase my pace, fueling the fire he's ignited in my core. Chase holds me tighter as he fucks me from below. With labored breaths, he nips at my jaw. "You think you can come for me again, beautiful?"

A nod is all I can manage because my body is already inching closer to the edge. I'm so tightly wound, and every clench around him brings a satisfying wave of pleasure through me.

He groans. His hand grips the back of my neck as he thrusts, and my eyes flutter shut. All I'm aware of is how good he feels inside me, and when he growls, "I'm going to fucking lose it when I feel you come," my body trembles. His thumb increases the pressure on my clit. "That's it. Let me make a mess of you."

I shatter. I implode. I bite. I claw. I cry out. I've never felt an orgasm so intense. And the feeling of Chase's own release as he stiffens beneath me is better than I could have imagined. He stays buried deep as he pours into the condom, and I pulse around him.

As soon as he lies back, I collapse onto him, gasping for breath.

Well, he succeeded. If there's anything Chase is good at, it's making an absolute fucking mess of me.

thirty-eight

WE MUST HAVE FALLEN asleep at some point because when I wake up, the room is still dark. I reach for my phone on the bedside table to find it's only a little after one in the morning. The sight of Chase sprawled out on his stomach with the lines of his muscular back and shoulders visible in the dark has my chest aching.

I care so deeply for this man I didn't even know existed less than a month ago. In a matter of weeks, he's managed to sneak his way into my life and completely turn it upside down. He's become an unmistakable force, and I don't know how deep this goes for him. I know he feels *something* for me, but I can't shake the fear that he made this fake from the start for a reason.

I stare up at the ceiling and let out a slow breath. I shouldn't have crossed that line, but at the same time, I don't regret it. How could I regret sex like that? And that was with me mostly in control. I can't imagine what sleeping with him would be like when he's the one who calls the shots. Glancing at him again, I swallow at the thought.

I should go. It's still early enough. Miles wouldn't question me walking through the door before two, but he'll have plenty of questions if he wakes up and I'm still not home. I try to move as slowly as I can, my arm gently pulling the blanket back, so I can slink out of bed and leave without him noticing. Finding my dress might be a little challenging, but I think he threw it somewhere near his dresser.

I sit up on the edge of the bed and try to locate my one skimpy piece of clothing in the dark.

"Candace," a sleepy Chase murmurs behind me.

I close my eyes, disappointed I woke him, and look over my shoulder. "Yes?"

He reaches for me, his hand landing on my hip, and his thumb brushing across my lower back. "Stay. I'll take you home in the morning. Let me wake up next to you . . . just once."

Just once.

I close my eyes and drop my head. How can I say no to that? How can I say no when a huge part of me doesn't want to leave at all. "Okay." I breathe out the word without a fight, even though his last two words cut into me deeper than any of the others.

I lie back in bed, and Chase pulls me to him. His body is warm, strong, and safe. He gently brushes his fingertips over my skin in soothing patterns until I drift off to sleep, knowing being awake with him here is far better than any dream.

The next time my eyes flutter open, soft sunlight peeks through the windows, and I stretch my arms overhead. The first thing that hits me is the feeling of the bed being too big—the feeling of being suddenly alone. Sitting up, I hold the blanket to my chest and look around the room, but it's empty. Only then does the quiet sound of cabinets closing catch my attention.

Getting to my feet, I wrap his soft comforter around me and head into the bathroom for a mirror. To my surprise, I don't look as rough as I thought I might. My curls have fallen, and my lips are back to their natural color, but I don't look *bad*. I look like a slightly faded, washed-out version of the girl I was last night. With the pad of my thumb, I gently rub away some of the eyeliner that smeared overnight.

Looking around, I take in the dark slate that covers the floor and bottom half of the wall. His entire walk-in shower matches, and it all beautifully compliments his black cabinets and white countertop. I pick up a tube of toothpaste neatly set on the counter and put a little on my finger as a makeshift toothbrush to freshen up.

Feeling ready to face him, I grab my phone and head back the way I came. There are four messages from Miles, but each is only one word.

MILES:

BITCH

WHERE

ARE

YOU?!

I let out a breath of laughter and quickly send him a text.

CANDACE:

> Yes, I'm still with him. Yes, it was that good. Yes, I will tell you about it.

My phone buzzes in my hand, but I ignore it. With my hand on his bedroom door handle, I breathe to try to get rid of any lingering nerves. *Please don't let this be awkward.*

The door opens, and the sight makes me pause. Chase is shirtless, wearing nothing but navy sweats as he cooks breakfast with his tiny Christmas tree perched on the counter like a loyal assistant. I don't think I've ever appreciated anything more. Everything about him, from his bedhead hair to his bare feet makes me want to pull him right back into this bedroom and repeat what happened last night.

He looks up, and relief fills me when that easy smile pulls at his lips.

My own smile stretches across my face, and it's only then that I realize I was biting my bottom lip. Crossing the room, I head into the kitchen and stand next to him so I can peer into the pan. There are eggs, bacon, toast, and fruit. All sliced, cooked, and prepared. My eyes widen. "You've been busy."

"I figured this was the most productive way to distract myself from you being naked in my bed."

I give him a sideways glance and steal a blueberry from the bowl on the counter. "If I wasn't so hungry, I might complain about that." We're flirting. It's the morning after our deal has expired, and we're flirting in his kitchen. Maybe it's just hard to break the pattern we've fallen into.

Chase lifts his brow as he turns off the different burners. "Does this mean you haven't had enough of me yet?"

My heart pounds in my chest, but if I don't put myself out there now, it will never happen. Turning him toward me, I push up on my toes and kiss him.

Once I pull back, I dare to look up at him. His eyes are wide like I've surprised him. How can he not know I'm completely at his mercy? "Chase, you could fuck me in every room, and I still wouldn't have enough of you."

In an instant, his mouth is on mine, and I'm overwhelmed with the taste of mint from his toothpaste. He hoists me onto the counter, and the blanket I've been holding falls open. He pulls back and lets his eyes drag over me. "God, I love seeing you naked." He kisses my neck. "Never wear clothes around me again."

I tilt my head, leaning into him, and the blanket falls free, collecting around my hips. Chase lets out a groan, his hands palming my breasts, and my legs fall open. Too soon—too *abruptly*—he pulls back, and I watch in shock as he spoons some scrambled eggs onto a piece of toast.

"What are you doing?" I ask with wide eyes, suddenly overly aware of how naked I am.

He holds the toast up to my mouth. "Eat, beautiful. I can't fuck you when I know you're hungry."

With a light laugh, I take a bite, my eyes widening. Covering my mouth with my hand, I say, "Chase, that's good—like really good."

"I know," he says, holding the toast for me to take another bite. "I'm not much of a cook, but I've mastered breakfast."

My lips twist, and I roll my eyes. "So modest." Nodding toward the toast, I add, "You have to eat, too."

The corner of his mouth twitches, and he takes a bite where I left off. "I think you're underestimating how badly I want to watch you come again."

My phone buzzes on the counter somewhere nearby, but I ignore it and keep eating. I laugh as he misses my mouth and some of the egg lands on my upper thigh. My phone buzzes again as he leans down to eat the food off my skin, his tongue slowly trailing over the spot after, licking me clean. Chase reaches for a blueberry, popping it into my mouth, and my phone buzzes again when I take his fingers into my mouth and suck. I palm him outside his sweats, feeling him hard and ready, and my hands grip his hair as he slides one finger inside me, then another.

Buzz.
Buzz.
Buzz.

Chase takes a break from devouring my neck to pull back

and look at me, breathing hard. "Maybe you should check that."

I kiss him, not wanting any of this to stop. "It's probably just Miles," I say against his lips between kisses.

Chase pulls his fingers out of me, and I whimper in protest. "Well, tell him I'm not done with you yet." A dangerous smirk flirts at the corner of his mouth as he sucks the same two fingers.

He has me in a trance because that might be the hottest thing he's ever done. When I don't move right away, he nods toward my phone. "Go on, gorgeous. We've got things to do."

I blink, remembering where I am. "Right." Reaching behind me, I locate my phone face down on the counter. It's weird for Miles to text me this much, but if he's excited about this, I wouldn't put it past him.

Turning my phone over, my face falls. Yes, a few messages are from Miles earlier, but the bulk of the notifications are from Nicolette. I swallow hard before swiping my phone open. This can't be good.

thirty-nine

BEFORE I CAN EVEN READ the slew of messages, my eyes dart to Chase. "It's your boss."

He pauses before taking another bite. "She texted you?"

My eyes widen as I scroll to count how many messages I've received in the span of a few minutes. "Only six times."

He sets his food down before walking over, so we can read them together.

> NICOLETTE:
>
> Last night was appalling.
>
> Coming to a work function for my office? With my colleague?
>
> I don't know if Chase made you aware, but he and I have had this sort of back-and-forth thing going on for a very long time.
>
> He probably hasn't told you about our plans in January.
>
> The girls would hate to know our hairdresser got in the way of that.

> I'm sure they'd be devastated to have to find someone new.

I gape at Chase to find him more serious than I've ever seen. His jaw and eyebrows are set as he stares down at the phone. "She's threatening me," I say in disbelief as I set my phone down to wrap the blanket around my shoulders again.

He picks up my phone. Reading and rereading the messages with his elbows propped on the counter next to me. "She's out of her mind is what she is."

"What is she talking about in January?" I doubt Chase agreed to date this woman, considering how desperate he was to have a decoy for the Christmas party, but she obviously thinks something will happen after the New Year.

"Nothing," he answers adamantly, still glaring down at my phone. When I wait for more, he looks up at me, his eyes softening. "Nothing," he says again. "She kept asking when I'd get drinks with her, and since she doesn't seem to understand me when I turn her down, I told her it might be better to figure that out after the promotion when I'm no longer her subordinate. I didn't agree to anything. It was just a way to get her off my back."

Hopping down from the counter, I wrap the blanket around me tighter. "Well, if you don't go now, there's a good chance she'll blame me."

He stands up straight and runs a hand through his hair. "And that's a problem?"

I give him a sad smile. "I was still working two jobs before she referred all those new clients for me. If she takes them away all at once?" I shake my head. "I don't know what I'd do."

He nods, looking deep in thought. "So, what do you want to do?"

I know what I *don't* want. I don't want to lose almost a third of my income if we're not on the same page. I don't want to jeopardize my job if he isn't looking for more.

"I mean . . ." I fiddle with the blanket between my fingers. "We did everything we were supposed to do, right?" I look over my shoulder at his bedroom before wincing. "Maybe a little more than we were supposed to."

The corner of Chase's mouth quirks. "A lot more."

I playfully narrow my eyes at him, and he laughs. He's right. We did *a lot* more than we were supposed to, but it still doesn't feel like enough. I meant what I said to him earlier, I don't think I could ever have enough of him.

But I guess this should be it.

I stare down at my phone again, reading and rereading. "She's acting like I went to that party knowing she'd be there."

Chase scoffs. "I'm not surprised. That woman thinks the sun rises and sets for her."

"You never mentioned me?"

Chase tries to think. "She called me while I was out with all of you, and I told her I couldn't talk because I was with my girlfriend. I think that came as a shock to her. She was in a bad mood for a few days, but she bounced back." My lips dip at the corner as the weight in my chest intensifies. Chase must read my expression because he adds, "You don't have to do anything you don't want to, Candace."

A humorless laugh leaves me. "She's threatening my livelihood."

His lips press into a thin line. "What if you slowly work on adding more clients to replace what you'd lose, and we'll just hide this from her?"

He's trying to be helpful, but I bristle. Why is this all on me? Even if I don't take the pay cut, I'd have to jump over hurdles, and for what? "Hide what from her? What exactly would you and I be doing?"

He stares at me. "I—I don't know. This. More of this."

I frown, my eyebrows pinched as I search his face. "Getting carried away after I agreed to be your fake date to a Christmas party? Because that's what this is."

The words hurt to say out loud, but they're true. They're an oversimplified version of whatever this is between us, but the bottom line is, they're true.

His expression hardens. "That's what you think this is?"

"Am I wrong? You're the one who made this fake from the start, you tell me."

"But is that what you want?" His eyes drop to the floor before daring to find mine again.

Something about the way he's looking at me softens the tension in my shoulders. Letting out a breath, I shrug and surrender to the truth. "I think I don't want to go back to working two jobs."

He runs his hand over his mouth and nods, his body turning rigid. "Okay. Yeah."

His response feels like a blow to the chest, but at the same time, it's what I expected. Last night, he said this was real, but a lot of men say things they don't mean when they're about to have sex. I give a sharp nod. "Do you think I can borrow some clothes? I'll bring them back."

Chase runs a hand through his hair. "Yeah. Let me see what I have."

I follow him into the bedroom and awkwardly stand in the doorway like this place should suddenly be off limits. Part of me is afraid that if I walk in there, one of us will pull the other onto that bed again, and I don't think my heart can take making the same mistake twice.

Chase digs through one of his drawers until he finds what he's looking for. Handing a folded pair of clothes to me, he says, "You can keep these."

Ouch.

Is he letting me keep his clothes, so we don't have to face each other after this?

"Okay." The word falls out of my mouth on autopilot. I point to his bathroom. "I'll just change and be right out." It feels ridiculous considering ten minutes ago, he was eating food off my naked body. But that side of us has quickly shifted into . . . well, this.

"Take your time," he says with a tight-lipped smile before leaving the room.

As soon as I'm alone, my chest heaves and my eyes burn. I want to fall apart, but I can't let myself turn into a puddle—not yet, anyway. Not without Miles here to mop me up.

When I walk into the bathroom, it's hard to look in the mirror. I look worse than I did when I first woke up, but I guess that's what holding in sudden heartbreak will do to you. It shouldn't feel sudden. I knew this would happen. Maybe not the part with Nicolette, but I knew whatever dream I was living would be met with a bucket of cold water eventually.

Before I even drop the blanket from my shoulders, I reach for my phone and order an Uber. I can't sit in his car with the tension between us right now. Just the thought of painfully sitting in silence with him for the short drive home has my chest tightening. The car will be here in less than ten minutes, so I quickly change into the clothes he gave me. I have to roll up the blue and gray plaid boxer shorts a few times to avoid them falling off my hips, and the sleeves of the white undershirt go to my elbows, but it will work. They smell like him in the best way, and I try not to think about it.

I pick up my dress from the floor and hook my fingers into the straps of my heels, holding them by my side. Then, taking a steadying breath, I walk back into the living room.

He's back in the kitchen, but he isn't eating or cooking anymore. He's just standing with his elbows propped on the counter, looking deep in thought. When the door opens, he lifts his head. And when our eyes lock, I know my cheeks betray me. His gaze dips, taking in the sight of me wearing his clothes. Chase definitely finds me attractive. I just need more.

"Candace, I . . ."

"I ordered an Uber."

He blinks. "You did?"

"Yeah." I look down at my phone. "They'll be here in less than five minutes, so I should probably head down."

Chase stands up straight, and I hate how the sight of him shirtless has such a dizzying effect on me. I need to keep my head focused if I'm going to get out of here.

"I could have driven you." He runs a hand over his head. "We could have talked or tried to . . ." He stares at me for a beat too long before shaking his head and rubbing his hand over his face. "I'm sorry."

I don't know what he's apologizing for, but I gave him a weak smile. "It's okay. I knew what I was signing up for."

"Yeah. Me . . ." He hesitates, his eyes searching mine for something. Maybe to check if I'm okay? Eventually, he just sighs. "Me too."

I try to hold my faint smile because it's the best I can do right now. No physical goodbye feels right. A kiss feels too intimate, a hug just feels weird, and a handshake might as well be a slap in the face. So, I don't walk toward him. Instead, I walk to the front door, and he follows but hangs back a little like he isn't sure what to do either.

The holiday is still a few days away, but I say, "Merry Christmas," because it's easier than saying goodbye and a little more heartfelt than saying *see you around*.

The corner of his mouth quirks, but not in its usual way. There's a hint of sadness behind his eyes too, but he says, "Merry Christmas," and I know this chapter has ended.

forty

THANKFULLY, the Uber driver doesn't give me a second glance. I've been holding it together, and I think a lot of it has to do with how little this woman regarded me. She didn't even give me a knowing look in the rearview mirror for wearing men's boxers and holding my heels. I don't think I've ever screamed *walk of shame* this loud with my appearance, but she didn't even question it. I don't Uber often, but I'll make sure to leave her a high rating. She deserves all the stars.

On the way over, I sent Nicolette a response saying she had nothing to worry about and that Chase and I were just friends. I haven't gotten a response. I guess she doesn't have much to say about her victory, but I know someone who will have *plenty* to say about this situation. And he's on the other side of the door. The empty hall of our apartment feels like the one thing going my way today. At least the neighbors won't see me like this.

Taking a steadying breath, I unlock my apartment and walk inside. The space is clean and quiet, and I let out a sigh. I'm ready to collapse on the couch and wallow for the next hour before I go into work. I'm still working a half day today. I figured we might be out late because of the party, so I didn't book anyone this morning, but if I had known things would end like this, I might have taken the day.

I drape my dress over the back of a kitchen barstool, but I don't make it to the couch before Miles rounds the corner, his face brightening as soon as he sees me. "Hey, slut!" I must look as bad as I feel because before I can respond, his face falls. Rushing over, he wraps me in a hug. "What did he do to you?"

There's something about being hugged by someone you love when you're on the verge of falling apart that makes the floodgates open. My face crumples against his chest, and even though I *knew* this would eventually happen, it hurts to say the words out loud. "It's over."

Miles pets my hair, his arms squeezing around me tighter. "I'm sorry." He pulls back to look at me but keeps me in a tight embrace. "Did he at least make you breakfast, or do I need to put on an apron?"

I huff a laugh and break away to wipe a fallen tear. "He did, but we were interrupted."

Miles cocks an eyebrow. "Are you still hungry? I was about to whip up some avocado toast if you want to spill the tea while I cook."

"That sounds great," I say with a sigh as I take a seat on the empty barstool. I don't have much of an appetite, but if I don't eat before work, I'll regret it.

Miles claps his hands and starts gathering everything he needs from the pantry and fridge. With the first cut of his avocado, he glances in my direction. "Do I need to fight him?"

I laugh and wipe my eyes one more time for good measure. "No. It's not his fault really." Smoothing my hair back, I try to collect my thoughts. "His boss is Nicolette."

He pauses. "Who the hell is—" He locks eyes with me,

understanding dawning on him. "*Oh!* Bougie Lady? *Your* Nicolette?"

I nod. "The one and only."

He mirrors my nod but slower. "So . . . who cares?"

His reaction gets a feeble laugh out of me. "The whole point of Chase needing a date was because his boss has a thing for him. Nicolette has been trying to win him over for a while, I guess." I rub my hands over my face. "I don't really know all the details, but she threatened me and basically told me to back off."

Miles lets out a scoff. "What are we, twelve?"

"Apparently. She threatened to take away all the friends she referred as clients."

This makes him lift his head from the tomato he's dicing. "Fucking bitch."

"Yeah."

He goes back to cutting. "Is he worth it?"

I don't answer right away. Could I sacrifice that many clients if it meant I could be with Chase? Maybe, but not if we were just casually sleeping together. I'd need more, and he didn't offer it. "He would be if this were real."

He lifts a skeptical brow. "I've seen you two together. It looked pretty real to me."

"Real chemistry and attraction maybe, but if he doesn't want to give this a real shot, none of it matters."

Miles sets a plate of bright green avocado toast in front of me, and I thank him.

"Did you ask him?"

Taking a bite, I shake my head and try to stop thinking about the other toast I was being hand-fed earlier. "No, but that man is not shy. If he wanted something more, I'd know."

Miles eats his toast, deep in thought. Eventually, he just shakes his head. "I'm sorry."

His acceptance of the situation somehow makes me feel

better. I'll get over this. It might suck for a while, but as long as Chase is out of sight, he'll eventually be out of mind. And that will happen a lot faster if Miles accepts this and doesn't bring him up.

"Nicolette sucks for using her power over us in all this, but it's probably for the best. You know?"

"Why? Because you'd keep sleeping with him if that wasn't the case?"

My shoulders drop in resignation. "Yup."

His lips press together, and his eyes narrow. "What about all that talk of not wanting to get in too deep?"

I take my last bite of toast before answering. "I don't know what it is about him, but if he showed interest, I probably would have done whatever he wanted for as long as he wanted."

Miles gives me a pointed stare. "No, you wouldn't have. You've never taken any guy's bullshit after Greg. You would have eventually gotten sick of him fucking around."

"But he has this way of making his fucking around seem like he's not fucking around at all. There's something about him that always comes across as genuine." I groan and let my head fall into my hands. "I need a shower."

Miles takes my plate and sets it in the sink. "Go shower. You'll feel better."

I rub my hands over my face and try to muster all my energy to take on the rest of the day. "Yeah. Okay. Thanks for breakfast."

He smiles a sad, tight-lipped smile, and I fight the urge to fall apart all over again as I get to my feet and head into my bathroom.

The only way to keep everything I'm feeling at bay is to keep myself busy. As soon as the bathroom door shuts, I don't linger in front of the mirror. I rip Chase's shirt and boxers off, so my body is completely bare and my own.

Stepping under the water, I turn my face up. Every time I close my eyes, another flicker of his hands and mouth comes into view. I shouldn't let myself go there. Grabbing the soap, I scrub frantically. Each part of me lathered and washed is another part of last night erased.

forty-one

HAVING to make up the time I take off is usually my least favorite thing about being my own boss. Sure, I have the freedom to make my schedule, but as great as it is to not schedule any clients on a certain day, it is equally terrible having to book myself solid on a day I usually have off to make up for it.

That's the mindset I used to have, anyway.

In the days leading up to Christmas, I'm fully booked. Sunday ends up feeling more like a Saturday, and Monday is busier than my usual weekdays with everyone trying to get their hair done before Christmas Eve on Tuesday.

I've been so busy. I've hardly had time to think about the fact that there's one person on my schedule I'm dreading more than usual. In fact, I don't even realize the time until Amanda walks into my station while I'm cleaning my mixing bowl.

"No sign of her yet?"

"Who?" I ask absently before my eyes jump to the clock in the salon. How is it already 2:45? It feels like I just got here. As soon as I see the time, I register who she's talking about.

Glancing back at Amanda, I keep my voice low. "She didn't call?"

"Nope. No cancellation, and no last-minute call, begging to bump her time up."

Drying my bowl, I set it on the counter. "Interesting."

When our eyes meet again, Amanda gives me a sympathetic smile. She knows everything that happened. I was in a funk yesterday. Hell, I'm still in a funk now, but even if I were my usual self, she still would have cornered me with a million questions after that party.

Turning to rest my back against the counter, I look in the direction of the front door. "Think she'll show?"

"She better," Amanda says with a huff. When I look at her, she adds, "The whole reason you're not with Chase is because you need to keep her as a client, right?"

I tilt my head from side to side. "More or less."

Glaring back at the front door, she mutters, "Yeah. So, she better fucking show."

She's right, of course. I want Nicolette to remain a happy customer. That's the whole point, but as I scan the busy street and sidewalk out front, I can't help hoping she doesn't come. I haven't had enough time to build up my armor again, and I feel exposed.

"Have you heard from him?" Amanda asks quietly, her voice like a gentle nudge.

I pull my phone from my back pocket and glance at the empty lock screen before tucking it away again. I didn't think I'd have any new messages from Chase, but checking has become a habit that's hard to break. "He texted me yesterday."

Her eyes widen. "What did he say?"

I take a breath, desperate to make my shoulders relax. "Just that he's sorry, and he wishes things were different." Glancing at Amanda, I shrug. "I feel the same." She smiles sympathetically, and it tugs at my heartstrings a little too much. Shifting my gaze back to the street outside, my eyes land on a blonde with large sunglasses and a leopard-print blouse making her way across the street. Nodding in Nicolette's direction, I say, "Even if I phase her out, it could take months. It wouldn't be worth it."

"Do you really believe that?"

Pulling my eyes away from my very own Cruella De Vil, I lock eyes with Amanda. "I don't know."

The bell chimes as the door opens, and Amanda quickly rubs my arm and whispers, "Good luck." She turns to address Nicolette with her best customer service smile. "Good afternoon! Candace is ready for you."

Nicolette gives her a tight-lipped smile, but there's something off about her. She's rigid. This isn't the tornado of a woman who always barges in with a big entrance. This woman makes an entirely different statement. I wonder if this is corporate Nicolette. The one she uses as a front between harassing Chase in his office. I try to remember what she was like at the party, but I was too shocked to pick up on details. Just her being there was enough to put me on edge.

But her being here now is having the same effect in an entirely different way. It's like now that I've seen her in her natural element, her mask has slipped. She can't be whoever she wants to be around me anymore, because I know exactly who she is, and she's probably wondering how much Chase told me.

Just the thought of him sends a pang to my chest. I didn't want to cut *his* hair because I didn't want the constant reminder of him, but that's exactly what Nicolette will be. She's a reminder of Chase. She's my only remaining tie to him.

"Nicolette," I say with my best smile. "It's great to see you."

She doesn't say anything at first. Instead, she reaches into her purse to pull out a hard case for her sunglasses. Once she's slipped them off her head and carefully tucked them into the case, she snaps it shut and looks at me with a sympathetic tilt to her head. "Candace. How are you holding up?"

I'm usually good at hiding my reactions from her, but my eyebrows pull together before I have the chance to stop them. "Fine?" I say, not bothering to hide the question in my voice.

Nicolette sets her bag down on a nearby table, making herself at home in my salon. "Well, it's just that I *hated* how you found out about Chase and me."

"Ah." I give an understanding nod, but I don't want to indulge her. Even if hearing someone say his name feels both like a breath of fresh air and a suffocation attempt. Walking over to my cabinet, I ask without looking her way, "Same thing as always today? Wash and blow-dry?"

She doesn't answer right away, and I know this is a power trip to make me look at her. It's fine. I can put on a mask. I can look at her. I let myself close my eyes for a brief moment before glancing over my shoulder.

"Are you sure you're okay?" she says with mock concern, her bottom lip jutting out.

"Nicolette, I'm fine, but I'm on a tight schedule today, so if you want your hair done, you need to tell me what we're doing." The words shoot out of me like a firecracker, and I'm tempted to clasp a hand over my mouth as soon as they're out. I'm tempted to actually *apologize,* but I clamp my lips shut, refusing to let it slip.

Her eyes blaze but only for a second. By the time I blink, she's back to her mask of mock sympathy. "And you poor thing. The way Chase handled that situation was downright awful. He and I had a long chat about it and sorted everything out."

"That's great," I say as I turn my attention back to my cabinet and reach for a fresh cape. I try not to let the thought of her having *a long chat* with Chase get to me. I wonder what his version of this story is.

Maybe I'll never know.

Staying busy, I fasten the cape around her and hope she'll stop talking. Of course, she doesn't.

"I just wish you would have told me. This whole mess could have been avoided if you had been honest with me."

My hand tightly grips the shampoo bottle, but I don't look at her. I stay focused on her hair, lathering the shampoo longer than I need to. "If I had known, I would have told you."

She scoffs. "Chase really never told you about me?"

This time, I do meet her piercing gaze. "No. He didn't."

Our eyes meet, and a beat of silence passes between us like she's trying to decide if I'm lying. She waits until I've resumed working to let out a huff and mutter, "Well, I find that surprising."

I'm sure she does. I'm sure she can hardly fathom a world in which Chase doesn't go around telling everyone about his sexy boss he's dying to sleep with. Instead of dignifying her comment with a response, I try to block all thoughts of Chase and Nicolette from my mind and just focus on the task at hand. Rinsing out the shampoo, I reach for the bottle of conditioner on the shelf above her head.

Even as I massage the product over her silky strands, I can feel her eyes on me. It doesn't matter that I keep my head down and work, she's watching me with the intensity of someone trying to achieve telepathy.

Eventually, her silence breaks. "You know, once Chase gets promoted, there's nothing to keep us from being together."

"That's great," I answer absently as I try to fight every ounce of tension in my body. This woman has lost her mind.

"And you're sure that won't be an issue? Considering your recent . . . history with him. I mean, I know it meant nothing. But still, I feel I should ask. The last thing I'd want is for you to sour our professional relationship."

I pause, her words taking an extra second to process. She'd hate for *me* to ruin our working relationship? Is she serious?

Heat flares down my spine, making me rigid. I can't do this. I can't listen to this toxic woman open her mouth every Tuesday for the rest of the foreseeable future.

Finally, I dare to meet her gaze, and my hands slowly go back to work, rinsing the conditioner. With a slight shake of my head, I let out a breath that might be mistaken as a laugh. Nicolette's eyes blaze, but I don't care.

"Nicolette, stop," I say as I wipe my hands on my apron. She opens her mouth to say something, but before she gets the chance, I turn off the water and wring out the extra moisture in her hair. With my best smile, I say, "I don't think anything will happen between you and Chase." She opens her mouth again, and I lift a single finger to stop her. "But if I'm wrong, I would *never* let it affect our professional relationship. I would never be that petty."

She blinks, and the dumbstruck look on her face is more satisfying than anything she could have said.

I may have to keep her as a client, but I'm done letting this woman walk all over me.

forty-two

MILES HAS our apartment in full festivity mode now that it's Christmas Eve. "You're a Mean One, Mr. Grinch" plays in the kitchen as he manages to cook with a steady swing of his hips.

My elbow leans on the kitchen counter as I sit at one of the barstools and turn my phone around to show Miles the selfie my parents just sent. Their wide smiles warm my heart, and just seeing them happy makes it feel a little more like Christmas.

Miles squints at the picture. "Is your dad growing a goatee?"

Flipping my phone around, I zoom in and groan. "Is he? I thought it was the lighting."

Tossing a dish rag over his shoulder, he walks around to look at the photo with me again. "Honey, that's a soul patch," he says with a laugh.

Shaking my head, I back out of the photo. "I'll let you be the one to have that conversation with him."

He heads back to the stove to finish sautéing something that smells amazing. "Gladly."

When I go back to my inbox, my eyes catch on Chase's name. I doubt I'll hear from him today. I know he said he doesn't visit his family until January, but I'm sure he's doing *something*. I'm almost tempted to ask him. Because as much as it hurts to talk to him, the thought of him sitting alone in that fancy apartment with nothing but that tiny Christmas tree to keep him company hurts worse.

I scroll through our messages from the past few weeks. I was so happy texting him in the beginning. Every time my phone gave me a notification, I'd be a bundle of nerves, excited to see what he said. Now every time I get a text, all I feel is panic. Panic it's him. Panic it's *not* him. There's no winning.

Miles spins with outstretched arms in the middle of our kitchen. "You're sulking."

My head snaps up, and I turn my phone face down on the counter. "I am not."

He keeps dancing. "Just invite him over tomorrow. Elvis will be here."

"You invited Elvis over for Christmas?"

He stops mid-twirl. "Did I not tell you?" He must take my vacant stare as a resounding *no* because he goes on to say, "It was before your shit hit the fan. I thought it would be fun if we both had our people over, since we both have dates for the holidays this year."

"But you knew my thing with Chase would end."

"I was optimistic it wouldn't."

I stare at him, unamused.

"What?" he says in defense. "So, I wanted both of us to get laid on Christmas. What's so bad about that?"

"What are we serving?"

Now it's his turn to give me a look. I never cook. He's the only one who uses our kitchen, and I pull my weight by periodically providing takeout. Miles puts a hand to his chest. "I'll be making a garlic roasted chicken with potatoes and asparagus."

My eyebrows shoot up. "So, we're hosting Christmas dinner? For Elvis?"

He nods. "We are hosting Christmas dinner for Elvis." He turns, his back facing me so he can organize our already clean kitchen. "And if you wanted to invite Daddy—"

"No."

His hands go up in surrender, and he dramatically turns around. "It was just a suggestion! Damn."

Changing the subject, I ask, "What can I help with?"

He sets his elbows on the counter in front of me. "No sulking."

I give him a sharp nod. "Done." I'm actually feeling excited about the holiday now. Having someone here on Christmas will force me out of my funk.

"And today," Miles continues with a subtle quirk of his lips. "You're going to let me practice making Christmas cocktails while we watch whatever Christmas movie your heart desires. Even if it means I have to listen to Anna Farris sing about forgiveness for the fourth time this month."

I practically melt into that statement. "God, I love you."

He grins. "I know."

For the rest of the day, I feel better than I have since leaving Chase's apartment Saturday morning. Things settle into how they were before Chase, and how they will be after him. Miles keeps me laughing with his jokes while we taste test his different concoctions, and the buzz helps to distract me from everything that's happened recently. The best one is made with sparkling wine, rum, orange, and cranberries. I hope he knows what he's gotten himself into because I'll probably ask him to make it every year for the rest of eternity.

We don't talk more about Chase.

We don't talk about Nicolette even though I'm already dreading the appointment she scheduled next week.

Christmas Eve with Miles is light and vibrant, and I feel a little more like the version of myself that I was before.

forty-three

AS MUCH AS living in Florida makes Christmas feel different from the movies, I love this holiday. There's something wonderful about getting together with those you love, and even though our table may be small this year, I couldn't imagine spending this day with anyone other than Miles and Elvis.

It's the first year I'm not with my family, and as much as I love them, this has been the most relaxing Christmas yet. No rushing out the door looking presentable. No waking up early to make a pie that I probably won't eat later because I'll be too busy. No last-minute gift wrapping I should have done the night before but didn't.

Instead, I'm still wearing the leggings I slept in, my hair is up in a messy bun, and I'm wearing an old T-shirt that reads, *Jolly AF*, with a reindeer design surrounding it made to look like the stitching you'd find on a sweater. To be fair, Miles is wearing a shirt with a plate of cookies that says, *I Put Out for Santa*. I haven't been outside today, but Elvis showed up wearing a sweater, so it gives me hope that maybe the temperature has dropped for the occasion.

I sit on our couch with my feet tucked beneath me as I sip my second cocktail. Elvis sits a few spots away with his arm casually around Miles, and the sight alone makes my heart feel full. It's been a while since I've seen Miles this invested in anyone. He's happy. That's all I need for this Christmas to be great.

Yesterday was the first day Chase and I didn't text since meeting. Late last night, after the clock struck twelve, I sent him a text wishing him a Merry Christmas. It was a moment of weakness that I succumbed to thanks to the help of Miles and his many cocktails. Plus, even if I want to keep my distance from Chase, he was still a huge part of my Christmas this year. Not acknowledging the holiday with him somehow felt wrong—unfinished. I had waited for those three dots to appear, wondering if he was home or staying with family. Wondering if he'd thought about me at all that day. Eventually, I gave up hope. I pushed him away, and I succeeded. Why would he answer a late-night text from me?

This morning, I woke up to a text from him. All it said was "Merry Christmas," but it was sent just past two. Did he go out on Christmas Eve? Or was he home? Maybe he already found someone else to keep his bed warm. My chest aches.

So, all day, I've been pushing down those feelings. I've been fighting the urge to send a text asking him why he was up so late. I've been fighting the urge to text him at all. This morning, I deep cleaned the apartment in preparation for the arrival of Elvis while Miles took to the kitchen. Everything he's prepared so far has been incredible. How a man can somehow make a charcuterie board that tastes better than other charcuterie boards, I will never know.

Elvis tosses his head back in laughter before his sparkling blue eyes settle on me. "Candace, how do you live with this man?"

"Um, excuse me?" Miles says as he pulls back to look at his boyfriend. "Living with me is a *gift*."

I wasn't paying attention to the first half of their conversation, but even though I'm a little lost, I say, "He's right. It is."

Miles gives Elvis a pointed look as if to say, *See?*

I laugh and take another sip of my drink. "He does talk about bringing home a cat at least three times a week, but other than that, he's great."

Miles's face turns serious. "It will happen."

Elvis lets out a chuckle. "Not a cat person?" he asks me.

"Not a litter box person. I've tried telling him to just get a small dog instead, but he won't have it."

Miles looks at Elvis. "I need the fluff."

"Dogs don't have the fluff?" Elvis asks.

Miles shakes his head. "Not the same." He shrugs. "Every time I see a kitten, I just want to put its whole face in my mouth." He holds up an imaginary kitten. "I just can't handle it," he says through gritted teeth.

Laughter bubbles through his voice as Elvis says, "Aggressive."

A knock sounds at the door, and I look at Miles. "Did you invite anyone else?"

"It's probably that lady down the hall who brought us cookies last year."

"Okay. I'll get it." Setting my glass down on the coffee table, I get to my feet and head toward the door. I hope it isn't the same woman bringing us cookies again. Last year, they were terrible, and she insisted we try one in front of her. She was sweet, though. A lot sweeter than her cookies.

I pull open the front door, and my lips part, my mouth unsure how to form a single word. Chase stands with a bottle of wine in one hand as his free hand runs through his hair. Something about him looks . . . broken. Maybe it's the way he's holding his shoulders or the way he's looking down. Maybe it's his suit being less pressed than usual, or maybe I'm just looking for him to be broken. Maybe a small part of me wants to see in him what I feel in myself.

My assessment is fast, the mere seconds it takes for him to realize the door in front of him has gone from shut to open. Chase looks up, his beautiful brown eyes meeting mine. It's too much. The way he looks at me is too much. Him being here is too much. I can't do this. I can't be around him right now. He opens his mouth to say something, but before he can get a word out, my panic takes over. I yelp, "Jack Frost!" and slam the door.

forty-four

WHEN I TURN AROUND, Miles and Elvis are both looking at me over the back of the couch with wide eyes like I'm deranged. My heart can't decide if it wants to drop out of my chest or stop altogether and let me die. He's here. He's *here?*

A thud followed by a light knock on the door makes me jump, and I imagine he has his forehead pressed against the barrier between us. "Candace." Chase's smooth, deep voice slips under and around the cracks until it has enveloped my entire body with a rush of warmth.

I stare at the door. I know I should open it. I have to, right? But still, I look between the door and Miles with frantic eyes. Finally, I let my stare settle on Miles long enough to ask, "What is he doing here?" in a sharp whisper.

He whisper-yells back. "I don't know. Maybe open the door so you can ask him!"

I bite my thumb just as Chase lets out another, "Candace." The strain in his voice has me melting and wanting to bolt at the same time.

"Quit being a baby, and open the fucking door!" Miles whispers a little louder.

I shoot him a glare before biting the inside of my cheek and turning to grip the door handle so tightly my sweaty palms slip against the metal. Looking up, I take a deep breath before slipping out into the hall.

Chase takes a few steps away from the door to give me space. We're standing across from each other in the small hallway, my back against the door, and his against the opposite wall.

He runs a hand over his face. "Jesus Christ, Candace. You decide to say, 'Jack Frost' *now?*"

"It was the first thing that came to mind," I mutter as I look down the hall, desperate to avoid meeting his stare. "What are you doing here?" A young couple a few doors down lock up with a pie in hand like they're about to head out for their holiday plans.

"Miles invited me last week. He didn't tell you?"

I look at him. "Does it look like he told me?" Of all the things for Miles to do, this has annoyance prickling through me. "Wait. How would he even invite you? You haven't seen him since we all went out."

Chase tilts his head slightly. "He follows me and sent a message."

My laugh sounds more like a scoff. "Of course." I wonder if Miles has been following Chase on social media since he showed me his profile. Probably. My eyebrows furrow as I study him. "Why would you still come here?"

"Because sleeping together meant something, and you know it."

My eyes dart around the hallway, and I hiss, "Can you keep your voice down?"

"No."

I roll my eyes before pulling him to follow me. "Then let's talk outside. I have a very nosy roommate whose ear is definitely pressed up against the door right now."

To my relief, Chase willingly follows. As soon as we step through the lobby doors, the wind whips stray strands of hair from my bun, and I wrap my arms around my torso to shield myself from the sudden chill. I would normally love this. All I ever want is for the temperature to drop on Christmas so it can give me an excuse to wear a sweater, but since I had no intentions of leaving my apartment today, this T-shirt isn't giving me much to work with.

Chase takes in the sight of me and immediately shrugs off his jacket. "Here."

"I'm fine."

"You're cold."

"We're in Florida. It's not that bad."

"You're right, we're in Florida, and it's not that bad." He holds my stare. "You're still cold."

The last time I wore his jacket comes to mind. The way he looked at me as he kept his distance in his kitchen. The way he said it made me look innocent. The way he wanted to . . . I shut down the thought and grit my teeth. "I don't need your jacket, Chase."

He's made up of harsh lines. I don't think I've ever seen him so stern, and that alone has me losing my bearings. With all seriousness, he says, "Candace, either you put on this jacket, or I drop it at your feet. At least your toes will be warm." He holds out the jacket again, his eyebrows raised. "Well?"

I glance down at my bare feet before snatching the jacket out of his hand and slipping it on. "You are so dramatic."

He lets out a humorless laugh. "I'm dramatic?" He holds my stare, waiting for some type of confirmation, so I cock an eyebrow. With a shake of his head, he runs a hand over his face. "You won't even talk to me, but I'm dramatic."

I shove my hands in the pockets of his jacket to stop myself from wringing my fingers until they're sore. It's warm, and it smells like him. I wish I could bring the fabric to my nose and breathe him in, but I fight the urge. The right pocket has a small piece of paper, and my fingers clutch it tightly. Chase's eyes are already heavily landing on me again, so I say, "What is there to talk about?"

My question hangs in the air between us. He rubs his hand over the back of his neck, but his eyes never leave mine. The weight of his stare has my nerves frayed, my pulse quickening beneath the surface. My fingers crumple the small paper, my tight fists hidden within the jacket pockets.

"I think you like me."

My cheeks flare, and I let my eyes track a car passing because it's easier than looking at him. "Well, I did sleep with you."

"No." He takes a step forward, forcing my attention back to him. "I think it's more than that."

He's going to corner me about *my* feelings? Half of me wants to run while the other half wants to march up to him and remind him that he was the one who made this fake. He was the one who didn't mean to ask me out in the first place. The result has me frozen in place, stuck between the two. My only defense is to raise an unimpressed brow. "You think it's more than that?"

He considers me as he takes another careful step in my direction. "A lot more."

I let out a huff and *beg* my cheeks not to give me away.

Even though I haven't said anything, Chase closes the space between us with one final step. My body feels more alive than it has in days. When it comes to Chase, my body doesn't care about self-preservation one bit. It's only my heart that stands tall with the caution tape around it.

"I want a lot more," he finally says, his voice quiet.

I blink, my hand loosening around the tiny paper. "No, you don't."

Chase forces a laugh. "How are you going to tell me what I don't want?"

Instead of answering his question, I blurt, "Your boss," and hope he understands what I mean, even though I can't make a coherent sentence right now.

He waves off my concern. "We don't have to worry about her."

My eyes widen. "She's going to ruin me."

He stares at me for a beat too long, like he's trying to figure something out. He needs to understand that it's not a matter of just not wanting to lose those clients. I can't afford to lose them.

"How much?"

"What?"

He keeps his eyes steady on me. "How much do you make from them each month?"

"A lot."

"How much?"

I let out a breath. "Close to a grand? Sometimes more."

He shrugs. "Cut my hair instead."

"No," I say with a snort of laughter. He can't be serious.

Chase doesn't crack. "Charge me whatever you want, and I'll pay it. There's no reason for you to be stuck under her thumb."

"Because being stuck under yours is so much better?"

The corner of his mouth twitches, and for the first time since getting here, he looks more like himself. "Yes, being stuck under me is better."

He knows exactly where my thoughts have gone on that one because his lips pull into a subtle smirk. I stare at him, my eyes narrowed as I try to figure him out. "When did things change?"

He tilts his head. "What do you mean?"

"When did you want this to be real?"

He stares at me, his expression open and vulnerable. "Right after I met you."

My eyebrows furrow. "Right after you met me, *when?*"

He swallows. "At the coffee shop."

That doesn't make sense. It wasn't until a week later that we got drinks, and a week after that when we went on our *fake* date. My emotions swirl beneath the surface, but I make sure to keep my expression neutral. He's lying. As much as I wish Chase were different from the other guys I've gone out with this year, he *has* to be lying . . .

His jacket suddenly feels too hot. The few people walking the streets fade away. Even the paper in my clenched fist threatens to burn my palm. I pull my hand out and unfold it, no longer caring if I look nosy. It might be a receipt. It might be a gum wrapper. I don't care. I need something to look at other than him. But what I pull from Chase's suit pocket isn't either of those things.

It's a woman's phone number.

forty-five

THE SMALL, crinkled paper looks like the top corner of a page that's been torn out of a notebook. The neat handwriting unmistakably belongs to a woman, and if that weren't enough to give it away, there's a small heart drawn under it.

Chase says something, but I barely hear him. I can't stop staring down at this small strip of paper that validates every doubt I've had. I wonder where they met. Was she blonde? Did she come up to him? Did he pursue her? Have they gone out together? Did they sleep together?

That last one feels like a punch in the gut.

My eyes burn, but there's no reason to cry. I knew this was the case. Every part of me knew getting involved with Chase was a bad idea. I knew I'd get hurt, I knew I'd regret it, and I knew it would mean more to me than it did to him.

"Candace." Chase's voice finally breaks through my anger-induced fog. Is it even anger I'm feeling? I might just be disappointed.

I look up and collect my bearings in a matter of seconds. The small paper crumples in my fist again. "I'm sorry you want more."

He gives me a questioning look. "You're sorry?"

I raise my chin, determined to look stronger than I feel. "Yeah. I'm sorry."

"This is what I mean," he says with an outstretched hand. "You'd rather we both be unhappy than admit you have feelings for me, and I don't get it."

I scoff and shrug off his jacket. Walking it back to him, I put his jacket in one hand and the woman's phone number in the other. "I'm sure you'll find someone else in no time."

Ignoring the surprised look written in the planes of his face, I wrap my arms around myself to fight the sudden chill and turn back toward my apartment, my friends, *my life*.

"Candace, wait!" he says, but my steps quicken. When he picks up his pace behind me, I let the lobby door shut in my wake. My fingers barely graze my apartment door handle when he grabs me by the wrist and spins me around, forcing me to face him. His hands move to either side of the wall like he's afraid I might slip away at the earliest chance. "Wait," he says again, more breathless this time.

My chest heaves as I try to hold myself together. "It's fine. We never had an agreement to be exclusively fake. You're free to ask out whoever you want. I just don't want to be a part of it."

"But I didn't—"

I cut him off with a dubious lift of my brow.

"Okay, I did, but—"

Trying to sneak out of the cage he's built, I mutter, "It doesn't matter."

Chase grabs one of my shoulders while he holds up the slip of paper with the other hand. "This is old." He flips up a folded corner and flattens it for me to see. "It's Layla's."

I honestly don't care who she is. It doesn't matter, but he's looking at me expectantly, so I say, "Who?"

He sighs. "Layla." When I don't say anything, he raises his eyebrows and adds, "The barista?"

Realization dawns on me, but I'm still confused. "The one with the boyfriend?"

Chase slowly lets go and runs a hand through his hair. "She doesn't exactly have a boyfriend."

He's watching me expectantly for some type of reaction, but all I feel is confused. "So . . ." Instead of guessing, I just shake my head. "I'm not following."

Chase's hand drags down his face. "I went back the next day, like I told you, to ask for her number. She doesn't have a boyfriend. She gave it to me, but . . ." His eyes lock on mine. "But then you and I talked, and I liked you. I was more interested to see where things would go with you, so I never used it." He pauses, and the way his eyes burn into mine makes it harder to breathe. "I liked you, Candace. Even then. But when I asked you out for drinks, you had already written me off. You were adamant about us being only friends, and I knew I fucked up. I knew you wouldn't agree to a date, but I thought you might agree to a fake one. I thought it might be the only way you'd give me a chance."

I try to take in all the information he's given me, but my mind can only process it one piece at a time. "So, you lied."

"No, everything I've ever told you—"

"About her having a boyfriend."

He winces. "Oh. Yes. I guess I did lie about that."

I frown. "Then why even ask for her number in the first place?"

"I thought I wanted it. You and I were texting, and even though you were fun to talk to, my mind was still made up from the day before. It wasn't until I had it in my hand that I realized I didn't care."

"And that's why she kept staring at you when we got coffee? Because you asked her out and never called?"

Chase grimaces. "Yeah. I don't think she's very happy with me."

"No," I say quietly as I try to recall my brief interaction with her. "I don't think she is either." Refocusing, I add, "But why give her a boyfriend? Why not just tell me?"

He wipes his hand over his mouth like he's considering how to answer. "I thought you'd brush me off for that, too. At least if I gave her a boyfriend, you'd know she was out of the picture. I didn't want you to wonder if I'd change my mind."

As much as I don't want to think of myself as being insecure, I probably would have wondered. Knowing a willing, gorgeous blonde was waiting in his back pocket would have changed the way I looked at things. "You like me," I say, my voice small.

The corner of Chase's mouth lifts. "I more than like you."

All I've wanted was for him to tell me he wants more, and now that he has, my brain can't keep up. He wanted this to be real. From the beginning. My heart swells until there's no room for me to keep my thoughts bottled, and I blurt, "I like you, too."

His smile stretches further. "I know."

"But she's going to ruin everything. You know she will." I don't need to specify who I'm talking about. There's only one person standing in the way of this now.

I know it's a risk. Relationships are never a guarantee, but there's no way Nicolette will let this go. She'll up her game with him. I'm sure her emails will get worse, and she'll force him to stay and work late more often than not. She'll call him while we're out just to pull his attention away. I can see all these conclusions so clearly in my mind, like a movie I've seen a million times. Because I *know* Nicolette, and if she thinks she's losing her hold on Chase, she's just going to dig her claws in deeper.

But Chase is unfazed. If anything, his smile steadily grows. "She got fired."

My mouth falls open. "What? Why?"

Scratching the back of his neck, he says, "Remember the man with the pregnant wife? At the Christmas party?"

I nod.

"Well, he sort of owns the firm. He works out of our bigger office in Tampa, so he's rarely at our firm here, but he overheard what happened at the party."

My eyes widen. "Everything you said to Nicolette?"

He takes in a breath and nods. "Everything." Dropping his hand from the back of his neck, he stares at me with beautiful, earnest eyes. "He looked into the emails Nicolette's been sending at work and thought they were enough to fire her. She's gone."

I clap a hand over my mouth. "She got fired on Christmas Eve?"

At first, I'm not even sure he can understand my muffled words, but he goes on to say, "Just before Christmas Eve. It happened Monday night. That's when I got the call, anyway."

It must have happened right after her last hair appointment with me. She came in on Monday since her usual Tuesday appointment fell on a holiday. My eyebrows pull together. "Wait. He called you? To tell you he fired Nicolette?"

Chase's mouth quirks, but not in the usual, confident way. If anything, he looks bashful. "Yeah. He, uh . . ." He shakes his head a little in disbelief. "He wants to give me her job."

I blink, and now it's hard for me to fight my own smile. "Are you serious? Chase, that's amazing!"

A nervous breath of laughter leaves his lips. "Yeah, I still haven't wrapped my head around it. It's a bigger promotion than the one I was going for, but it's not like I don't know how to do the work."

"You'll be incredible," I assure him, my smile warming as it stretches further across my face.

Nicolette got fired. She's no longer Chase's boss. She won't have any control over him. Because she won't be his boss. She won't be anything.

The realization dawns on me, and my eyes lock on Chase.

Nicolette is unemployed.

As if reading my thoughts, Chase says, "She might not keep her weekly appointments with you. She might for a little while and then drop off, or maybe she'll find a new job in no time and it will change nothing." He shrugs. "I don't know."

My eyes scan his as I try to imagine every scenario that can come from this.

"But, Candace, she got *fired*. It will be hard to turn everyone against you when she's clearly the one in the wrong."

He's right. God, I hope he's right. "And if she asks me about you?"

Chase's eyes are bright when they meet mine. "You don't even know my name."

My laugh comes out sounding more like a scoff, but I can't fight my smile. "I'm serious, Chase."

"So am I." He grins. "You have no idea who I am." He holds my chin between his fingers. "Never seen me a day in your life."

I suck in a breath. He's so close to me like this. With him holding my chin in place, I'm forced to look at him. *Really* look at him. The scent of spice and teakwood floods my senses, and I'm overwhelmed with how badly I want to kiss him.

Keeping his voice low, Chase says, "As far as Nicolette is concerned, we can be strangers. But between us, I want to know you better than anyone."

He's put me completely in a trance. All I can do is nod more than I need to and utter the word, "Okay."

Gently brushing his thumb over my bottom lip, Chase's

eyes dip to my mouth for a fraction of a second before he meets my stare again. "I'm going to kiss you now."

"Please do," I say and the words come out breathless.

Then his mouth is on mine. Warm and familiar. New and exciting. He's everything. Everything I've ever wanted feels packed into this kiss, and before I know it, my hands are in his hair. My tongue grazes his bottom lip, and Chase lifts me up against the wall to kiss me deeper. His long fingers curl into my hair, and my legs wrap around him. I'm completely lost in him. Lost in the way he still tastes like traces of mint and in the way his tongue perfectly teases mine. Lost in the feeling of having him pressed against me. I'm completely lost in the feeling of being wanted by him. *Truly* wanted.

Pulling back, Chase nips at my bottom lip. "You're the prettiest stranger I never met."

Laughter blooms in my chest. "You're ridiculous."

Chase grins as he sets me down and takes my hand in his, his thumb rubbing over the backs of my knuckles. "Let me take you on a date. A real one."

I let out a short laugh. "No."

His eyebrows shoot up. "No?" He points over his shoulder, his smirk growing. "Not even if I take you to see the Surfing Santas?"

A smile pulls at my lips, and I shake my head. "Please don't." I feel like I'm the one who should make it up to *him*. I'm the one who thought I had him pegged. And I'm the one who was wrong again. Pushing up on my toes I kiss him. "You don't have to make anything up to me with a date. You're here. That's more than enough."

"You're more than enough," he says, and then his mouth is on mine.

The door to the apartment opens, and Miles pokes his head out to find us pressed against the wall. Chase and I look at him, but Chase keeps my hands pinned against the wall like once this interruption is over, he plans on going back to what he was doing before.

Miles grins and points over his shoulder. "Uh, you do know she has an entire room you can use."

My cheeks flare, and my voice is breathless when I say, "We'll be right in."

"Merry Christmas, Miles," Chase says before settling his stare back on me.

Miles tilts his head playfully. "Merry Christmas, Daddy Chase."

Chase's mouth quirks, but he doesn't take his eyes off me, and Miles ducks back into the apartment. "Think he'll ever stop calling me that?"

"Probably not," I admit.

Chase lets out a low chuckle that I feel in my bones. "Good to know." He kisses me again, and warmth spreads from my head to my toes. "Merry Christmas, Candace." His words flutter against my lips.

"Merry Christmas."

He smiles against my lips before he kisses me again. His hands move to my hair, and mine grip the material of his shirt. Each press of his lips on mine feels like another reassurance. He's kissing me with more care and feeling than he ever has, and I'm just glad I get to kiss him again at all.

Pulling back, Chase smooths down my hair with a slight smile. "We should probably go in there before I mess you up."

I look at the apartment door and then back at him. "Yeah, we can save the messing up for later." I kiss him one more time, and he groans as I pull him to follow me.

The apartment looks exactly the same as it did before I stepped outside. Miles and Elvis are still drinking their cocktails on the couch. Soft holiday music plays throughout, and the smell of roasted chicken wafts throughout the entire apartment. The decorations are the same, my glass sits on the kitchen counter, even the snacks laid out don't look like they've been touched since I left a few minutes ago. But one thing is very different. Outside the windows that frame the back wall, there's... snow.

Chase and I both stand there, staring at the little tufts of white cascading from the sky. He's first to point at the window. "Is that—"

"Fake snow," Miles says with a laugh. "It's coming from the balcony above us. The machine is loud as a motherfucker, and it looks like it might be made with PVC pipe, but from here it's cool." He shimmies his shoulders. "Lenny is making me feel festive."

I blink before looking at the ceiling like it will somehow give me insight into the apartment above. "That's what he's been working on? A fake snow machine?"

"Seems like it," Miles says with a shrug.

"I love it," Elvis chimes in. "Florida never feels like Christmas."

"Yeah," Chase says. "I love it, too."

I look over at him, but he's not looking at the fake snow anymore. He's looking at me. I swallow.

The corner of his mouth quirks, and he takes my hand, pressing his lips to the back of my knuckles.

Smiling at Miles, I say, "I think I'm ready for another one of those drinks."

Miles cocks an eyebrow. "In the mood to celebrate?"

I look at Chase. This beautiful man inside and out who has managed to beat all my expectations. It's all been real. I wasn't his fallback plan. I wasn't his second pick. It wasn't fake. A slow smile pulls at my lips, and Chase mirrors my expression. Turning back to Miles, I grin. *This* feels like Christmas. "Yes. Let's celebrate."

epilogue
ONE YEAR LATER

"YOU WEREN'T KIDDING. This is . . . uh, this is impressive." Chase might as well have his face glued to the car window as we pull up to my parents' heavily decorated home.

A full Santa's sleigh with eight reindeer is supposed to be the focal point, but they almost get buried under everything else around them. There's blow-up polar bears and penguins, seven twinkling trees, and enough string lights to flip a circuit breaker.

"You have no idea what you're in for."

Chase looks over at me with wide eyes, and I'm sure my smile looks more like a grimace as I put the car in park. He's met my parents, but this is the first time he'll see their home, and he's definitely seeing it at its finest.

He points out the window. "Is that an actual candy cane forest?"

I crane my neck to look in the direction he's pointing. "Oh, yeah. It is."

He balks at me. "Your parents have a candy cane forest in their front yard."

I take in a breath and nod. "Yeah. They're kind of big fans of candy canes."

As if on cue, my mother comes running out of the house with both hands waving in the air like a lunatic. "Candy Cane!" Looking over her shoulder, she hollers for my father. "Bill! They're here!"

Chase looks from my mother back to me with possibly the biggest smile I've ever seen plastered on his face. "Oh. I'm so excited for this."

"Gotta love weird parents, right?"

He doesn't take his eyes off my mother with that same stupid grin on his face. "So much."

The woman is now frantically rubbing her hands on her apron and hurrying toward the car. She looks like a dark-haired Mrs. Claus equipped with a gingerbread skirt and all.

"I love her."

Looking over at him, I scoff. He still hasn't taken his eyes off her, but he reaches for the door handle.

"Chase!" I playfully scold with a laugh.

Quickly darting his eyes to me, he adds, "Not the same way I love you, Candy Cane." He smirks, and I know this is only the beginning of him using that nickname as a weapon against me.

"Despicable," I mutter, but he just laughs as he gets out of the car.

By the time we're both standing, my mother has reached us, and is practically bouncing on her toes, trying to decide who to hug first. She ends up going for me, her arms squeezing tightly around my neck. "How was the drive? Are you hungry?" She pulls back to examine me, her hands still firmly clasped on my shoulders. "Your aura is radiant." She looks over at Chase. "You're doing wonders for her."

He grins. "I am, aren't I?"

Narrowing my eyes at him, I shake my head.

If only the smug look that coats his features made him any less desirable. "Auras don't lie, Candace. Listen to your mother."

My mom beams at Chase before looking back at me, and literally booping me on the nose with her finger. "See, he's a good one."

This is going to be a long visit. Technically, we're only staying for a couple of days, but I already know how this will go. Especially when my mom releases me and turns to my boyfriend. "Chase," she says with open arms and a warm smile.

"Pat," he says, mirroring her gesture in return. The two hug, and I swear my mother breathes in the scent of him. Rolling my eyes, I walk around the car to gather my things.

"Candy Cane!" my father boasts from the front door. Ducking around the trunk, I smile and wave.

"Hey, Dad," I say as I reposition my bag on my shoulder. "Merry Christmas."

"Merry Christmas!" my mother exclaims like she had somehow forgotten. I'm not sure how that's possible since we're basically standing in the center of the North Pole, but at least the realization freed Chase from her grip.

He walks over to my father and holds out a hand for him to shake. "Bill, it's nice to see you again."

Glancing down at his hand, my father pulls Chase into a hug. "We hug in this family," he says gruffly as he pats Chase on the back. He has to be almost a foot shorter than my boyfriend, and the sight pulls a laugh from me.

Chase doesn't even hesitate. He just embraces my father like he was expecting it, and a fresh wave of appreciation for him washes over me.

"I can't believe Miles didn't come with you. He could have brought his boyfriend," Mom says in a sulky voice as she gazes longingly at the car, like Miles might jump out and surprise her.

"He sends his love." Miles is spending Christmas with Elvis and his family. Elvis came out to them a few months ago, but this is their first holiday around his family as a couple. Well, that and neither of them were willing to trust someone to watch their new kitten. I have to admit, Oscar is cute. I'm still glad Miles waited to share an apartment with Elvis before getting a cat, but he's really fucking cute.

"Do you think he needs any Christmas decorations?" my father asks with a thumb pointed over his shoulder. "I have some in the shed I didn't have room for this year." Looking between Chase and me, he adds, "How about you two? Need any decorations for that fancy apartment?"

When my lease ended with Miles, it just made sense to move in with Chase. I was spending most nights at his place anyway, and Elvis was spending most nights at ours.

I can practically see Chase start to sweat at the thought of bringing a box of discarded decorations into his apartment. "We've got it covered," I assure my dad. "The place is looking very festive. You'd be proud."

Compared to the state of his apartment last year, this year *is* festive. I'll never be on the same level as my parents, but we did put up a tree and hang stockings. I try to only get mild enjoyment out of Chase reaching for the vacuum three times a day to get rid of any pine needles that have fallen, but it brings a smile to my lips every time.

"I'm sure we would be," my father says with a grin. Heading toward the house, he waves for us to follow. "Come in. Come in. We've got more food than we know what to do with."

Chase takes our bags and puts his arm around my shoulder, giving me a squeeze as he kisses the side of my head. "This is my favorite Christmas."

Looking up at him, a smile warms my lips. "You rank your Christmases?"

"Of course I do."

"What was your favorite Christmas before this one?"

Chase and I walk a few paces behind my parents, our steps slow as we take in every detail of the front yard. "Oh, that's easy. When I was six, my parents got me a Darth Vader bike with a matching helmet. I was the coolest kid on the street."

My brow lifts. "Darth Vader?"

Chase nods. "The one and only. I don't think I had even seen the movies at that point. I just knew he was cool, and having that black and red bike made me cool, too." With a tilt of his head, he adds, "Last year almost made the cut, but you're scary when you're mad."

My mind wanders to last year, and how determined I was to keep him away. It feels like so long ago now. When I think of last Christmas, all I think of is fake snow and a long night of laughter with carefully curated cocktails. I give him a sideways glance. "I'm scary?"

"Yup," he says curtly. He wiggles his fingers over my head. "That's when you get all prickly." I laugh with a shake of my head and go to pull away from him, but he only squeezes me tighter.

The day goes by in a blur of baked goods and glasses of wine. My parents have been glowing all day with the joy of having us here, and it makes me think we should have visited sooner. It's not like they're *that* far. Life has just felt hectic lately. I had to work longer hours than I was used to because I've been determined to build up a new group of clients I actually like, and Chase has been thriving with his new promotion.

We both did it. We got to a point where we didn't care if Nicolette knew about us, and when she eventually stopped scheduling her weekly appointments with me, I didn't miss her.

A few of her friends still come to see me every now and then. I haven't asked them about Nicolette or how she's doing. I feel like we have an unspoken agreement not to talk about her.

My old bedroom has a new queen-sized bed with matching oak nightstands on either side, but the walls are still the same shade of lavender from when I lived here.

Chase walks around the room with a slight frown pulling at his lips. "I was really hoping your room would still have all your stuff in it."

I take a seat on the bed as I watch him with amusement. "Why?"

"So, I could snoop," he answers without shame. Walking over to the dresser, he opens the drawer, the hollow sound of the wood sliding against the track filling my ears. "Damn," he mutters. "Even the drawers are empty."

With a laugh, I point to the closet. "If it makes you feel any better, I'm pretty sure all my stuff is in the closet. Furbies and all."

Chase's eyes widen. "*Furbies?*"

"Yeah, I used to love them."

He points over his shoulder with his thumb. "And they're in that closet? Right now? What is this, a fucking house of horrors, Candace?"

"Would you stop being so dramatic? They're like Tamagotchis you can cuddle."

He shakes his head. "They're what nightmares are made of." Walking over to the bed, he lies flat on his stomach, his head in my lap.

Reaching out, I run my hands through his hair, and he

relaxes the way he always does. "You don't want to snoop anymore?"

"I don't even know if I want to sleep here, now that I know I'm being watched," he grumbles, keeping his eyes closed.

"You are such a baby," I say with a laugh. "The Furbies are not watching you."

He cracks one eye open to peer up at me. "You don't know that."

I roll my eyes. "I do, but if you're that worried about it, there's another room down the hall. I'm honestly surprised my parents didn't make you sleep there, anyway. They used to always have this rule about only sharing a bed when you're married."

He lifts his head. "I find that . . . surprising."

"Yeah," I agree with a nod. "That was before their hippy phase. They've loosened up. Either that, or they've given up on me ever settling down."

His eyebrows furrow. "You're settled down with me."

"You know what I mean."

Chase props up on his elbows, his arms on either side of my crossed legs. The gentle graze of his thumbs against my leggings sends a rush of warmth through me. "You mean making you my wife?"

Those words stop the air in my lungs. My heart pounds in my chest, but there's something so comforting about that thought. Swallowing, I nod.

Chase studies me, his head tilting slightly. "Would *you* like it if I made you my wife?"

My mouth has suddenly gone dry. We've never talked about this. This has never even come up. He told me he loved me as soon as we started dating, but there's been no talk of the future like this. "I wouldn't be opposed," I say, my voice barely above a whisper.

He grins before placing his head on my lap again. "Good.

We both know you don't have the best track record when it comes to this thing."

I playfully swat at him. "I only turned down one proposal!"

He dramatically winces and puts his hand on his head where I barely tapped him. "Were there more?"

"No!" I say with a laugh.

Sitting up, Chase makes a show of rubbing his head. "Then the way I see it, you've turned down one hundred percent of the proposals you've gotten."

I roll my eyes. "Oh my god. You're ridiculous."

The corner of his lips kicks up into a smirk, and he kisses me. It has the same dizzying effect it's had from day one. His mouth slowly moves over mine, and he murmurs against my lips. "When I ask you, please don't say no."

Not *if*.

When.

My heart stutters in my chest. Has he thought about this? Clearly, he has. The thought thrills me more than I expect, and the idea of Chase thinking and planning for our future warms my heart with such an unsuspecting force, I've nearly forgotten how to speak. All I can manage to say is a breathless, "Okay."

Chase smiles before kissing me again. "Thanks, beautiful." And when he pushes me back onto the bed and kisses me more, I'm overwhelmed by how much I love this man.

also by heather garvin

Just Don't Call Me Yours
I Just Want To Be Yours
Make Your Move
Crossing The Line
Take What You Can
Give Nothing Back

acknowledgments

Candace and Chase's story was such a fun one to write, and thanks to a few amazing people it just kept getting better and better.

Whether it was squealing over Chase, giggling because of Miles, or criticizing the plot on a deeper level, I needed to hear it all. I'm so grateful to have honest and caring people in my corner who want my stories to shine as much as I do.

Dani Keen, Tisa Matthews, Sarah Hill, Dawn Anderson, Kort Combe, and W.H Lockwood are all incredible authors who offered their thoughts on this story. As authors, it's so hard to find the time to look over someone's work while you're trying to perfect your own. I know how much of a commitment it is to provide feedback on another author's story, and I can't thank you enough.

Another massive thank you to Gabby Spiller, Brooke Reno, Corey Wys, and Courtney Grifo, these avid readers gave incredible insight, and I loved seeing your reactions to some of my favorite scenes unfold! Thank you so much for taking he time to read this book before its polished version and help me brainstorm ways to make it better. I appreciate you so much!

If you read the acknowledgments in my *Just Yours* series, you know I could scream how much I love my editor Kristina Haahr from the rooftops. Her attention to detail and the careful consideration she gives the plot and characters are such valuable assets when it comes to publishing a book. Thank you, Kristina, for going above and beyond for every book I place in your hands. I absolutely love working with you!

As always, thank you to all of these incredible people and thank you to readers like you, who make writing these stories so much fun in the first place. I can't thank you enough.

about the author

Heather Garvin works as a nationally certified sign language interpreter by day and writes a variety of romances in her spare time.

Aside from working and writing, she's also a wife, mom, and a fur mama to two dogs, two cats, and Tuskan: the horse who inspired her publishing company, Tuskan Publishing LLC.

There's nothing Heather loves more than hearing from readers. Connect with her @heathergarvinbooks

www.ingramcontent.com/pod-product-compliance
Lightning Source LLC
LaVergne TN
LVHW091718070526
838199LV00050B/2454